GENESIS FLOOD

GENESIS FLOOD

Shelley Cox

The Book Guild Ltd

First published in Great Britain in 2023 by
The Book Guild Ltd
Unit E2 Airfield Business Park,
Harrison Road, Market Harborough,
Leicestershire. LE16 7UL
Tel: 0116 2792299
www.bookguild.co.uk
Email: info@bookguild.co.uk
Twitter: @bookguild

Typeset in 11pt Minion Pro

Printed on FSC accredited paper
Printed and bound in Great Britain by 4edge Limited

ISBN 978 1915603 951

British Library Cataloguing in Publication Data.
A catalogue record for this book is available from the British Library.

This book is dedicated to my beautiful Mum, Dot,
who we all miss more and more with each passing day.
Always and forever our sunshine.

PROLOGUE

Sri Lanka – twenty years ago

The two young women, nameless, faceless and inconsequential in the presence of disaster, collide in the powerful torrent of water. No more than moments before they had each been in the same sun-soaked street – one shopping for souvenirs, one enjoying breakfast alone at a pavement café – cheerfully oblivious to each other and the cataclysmic event that was about to unfold. Now, confusingly, they find themselves flung painfully together, transported to an unfamiliar and dangerous territory; strangers forced to meet under the shadow of almost certain death.

The sunny street, and all that belonged in it, has been crushed and recycled into a treacherous conveyor belt of rubbish by the brutal invasion of the wave. Large slabs of concrete and splintered wood, whole cars and buses, tables, refrigerators and TVs, decades-old trees ripped out at the roots like weeds, all jostle for space alongside smaller trinkets, shoes and clothes, bits of metal and broken glass. The noise is primal, a cacophony of screams and shouting above the animalistic roaring of the water, with percussion-like cracks and thuds as trees and structures are uprooted and collide.

The young women are magnets to the broken and twisted everyday objects that have become lethal missiles in their new environment. In clinging to each other they have created a small "school" in the way fish do to avoid predators. Their subconscious has told them that there is safety in numbers, however small the number, or maybe it is just their human instinct to not want to die alone.

As the slippery water greases the women's grip on each other, and the force of the undulating swell plays its treacherous game of tug of war, one woman not so much as floats away as is ripped and tossed and torn by the tongue of the water and jaws of the debris collected in its cavernous mouth, before it swallows her beneath the surface and she is gone.

The other woman finds herself swept into a small space between two battered adjacent buildings, and, somehow, she finds the strength to haul herself, and the purple velvet bag she has incomprehensibly managed to keep hold of, onto the tin roof of the tallest of the two buildings.

The water continues to rise insidiously, its muscular weight lifting objects in its path effortlessly, seemingly determined to pursue her in the unrelenting way a killer does in a slasher movie. As it reaches the roof of the building beside her, it becomes a can opener, peeling off the tin roof to reveal bodies bobbing face down in the water, as if they are merely snorkelling, rather than having become bit parts in a real-life horror movie. Whether it is the sight of those bodies or simply the amount of salt water that she has ingested during her struggle to survive, she is violently sick before everything goes black.

PART I

"Is it possible to disappear, never to be heard from again?"

CHAPTER 1

UK – twenty years ago – one week before the tsunami

Jeannie

My stepfather first raped me when I was sixteen years old.

I had enjoyed a rare carefree day out with my mother. My stepfather was away for a few days on business, the chains of restraint were off and, for a short, blissful while, I had my old mum back. We shopped and chatted and laughed and for the briefest time I experienced what life could have been like had he not come into it.

Mum had bought me a new outfit – one that "celebrated my advancement into adulthood", as she had rather melodramatically put it. It was a dusky-pink off-the-shoulder blouse with a low-rise denim mini skirt, romantically sexy, the kind of trendy outfit young pop stars could be seen wearing in magazines, having been "papped" on a shopping trip.

I loved that outfit, not just because it was cool and grown-up and had made me feel for the first time that I fitted in but because there was no part of *him* involved in it. I felt courageous, almost powerful: the act of trying it on was rebellious, the purchase subversive. My mother and I had formed a secret coalition, had our own agenda, and it gave me hope.

3

When we returned home later that afternoon, my mother surprised me again by telling me to get showered and changed into my new clothes. We were going out for pizza, she said, and I was buzzing with the anticipation of wearing my new outfit in public. She even allowed me to apply a slick of her pale pink lipstick to my lips, and use some of her mascara, which felt strange and heavy on my already long lashes. The effort of keeping my newly encumbered eyelashes open managed to give my face a look of mild astonishment, as if I couldn't quite believe what was happening, which to be honest I couldn't, but I remember feeling euphoric, as if I had finally woken from a bad dream, and certain that I could take on the whole world if I had to.

This simple act of getting dressed up and going out without him was a bold move. We had never done anything like it before; it was audacious and not without risk but, as the saying goes, it is easy to be brave from a safe distance. I guess it is a bit like pointing out a guilty man in a line-up: he is behind one-way glass, he can't see you pointing, so you gain a certain sense of security in calling him out. Of course, courage can only exist where there is something to fear. We knew that the object of our fear was at a safe distance on his business trip, and as pizza places were "for the lower class", as he put it, and not somewhere he or his acquaintances would ever be seen, the chances of being caught out were negligible. And so, in a rare act of defiance, my mother decided it was a chance worth taking.

To increase our chances of not being recognised, we took a taxi to a town ten miles away. I couldn't stop chatting excitedly the whole way there and, as my chatter did not really require any particular response, my mother smiled and nodded at me indulgently throughout the journey. Walking into that pizza place was like walking into a secret world that bombarded my senses. My eyes feasted on disparate groups that were sitting around their tables, each deep in their own conversations and oblivious to the people around them. Peaks and troughs of laughter wafted around the restaurant along with the smell of freshly baked dough and garlic that made my mouth water in anticipation. My mother's shoes made a clipping sound as we walked across the terracotta tiles to our table and I could hear snippets of conversations as I passed: a waitress confirming pepperoni but no olives; a family group singing happy birthday to an embarrassed teenager; three teenage girls whispering a little too loudly about what happened last night. It was a fleeting peek into the lives of others and I was fascinated and excited to be part of it all.

I remember taking ages to decide on which pizza to have. A pizza was such a rare treat for me that I was desperate to make sure I made the perfect choice, and eventually I decided on the supreme with a stuffed crust. My mother ordered a classic margherita, and as we ate she teased me that I had been noticed by a group of teenage boys at an adjacent table. I pretended that I had no idea what she was talking about, but the truth was I had already seen them whispering conspiratorially to each other as they looked and nodded my way, and my gut had flip-flopped as I caught the eye of one of them in particular before I quickly looked away. When I looked up again, a couple of girls had arrived and sat down with the boys, commanding the full attention of all but that one boy, whose gaze continued to wander to me from time to time. Eventually they got up to leave together, animatedly discussing what they were going to do next, and as I watched them leave the boy smiled shyly at me, and I wished with all my heart I could have gone with them.

After my mother and I had eaten, and I had noisily sucked the last of the Coke through my straw, my mother reached out her hand to brush back a loose strand of my hair. She sighed in a melancholy way as she did this, telling me it was time we went home, and I felt like Cinderella at the stroke of midnight, running away from momentary happiness back to misery. I fantasised about leaving a shoe behind that the boy from earlier could find, and imagined him searching house after house for me, until he finally found me and saved me. But I knew that even in my own fairy tale I would never have a happy ending.

It was past eleven o'clock when we finally made our way back home. I had never been out so late before and, as we drove home, I marvelled at the unfamiliar and twinkly, post-dusk world and the nocturnal people that inhabited it. When the taxi finally pulled up outside our house, the first thing I remember noticing was how the lights inside illuminated the front windows like giant, unblinking eyes. Then I noticed my mother's face, her fading smile and trembling hands as she handed some notes to the driver, and it suddenly hit me, I instantly understood the change in her demeanour: we had switched off all the lights in the house when we had left earlier that evening.

As my mother shakily put her key in the lock to open the front door, I remember feeling sick. A hard knot in the pit of my stomach had formed, squeezing out the pizza I had eaten earlier, the acid making my mouth water in a different kind of anticipation The function of the brain in relationship to fear is to record the minutiae of the moment and store it in your long-term memory – nature's way of helping you to recognise potential warning signs of impending danger – and, from that moment on, even the smell of pizza would be enough to make me feel sick.

My stepfather was waiting for us at the kitchen table, drumming his fingers in a slow, measured beat on the polished glass top. The summer air was warm and sticky, despite the lateness of the hour, but the beads of sweat on my forehead had nothing to do with the heat. He locked eyes first with my mother, holding her gaze for a few menacing seconds, before turning his gaze to me. He never spoke; instead, he allowed the soldier of silence to load and aim his gun on us. This was a strategy that had caused me to wet myself with anxiety in the past, but at that moment I still had a few drops of courage left in my veins, just enough to hold my bladder composure at least.

The slow drumming of his fingers continued, the sound of his manicured nails clipping the glass table top and echoing with intent around the large, immaculate kitchen. Finger-drumming had always been his mood-metronome, measuring the timing and tempo of his emotions. Classical music lessons had taught me to recognise and name the tempos. Allegro, the fast drumming used when he is impatient, usually when he is waiting for an answer to a damning question: "Do you think bad behaviour should be left unpunished?" Tap-tap-tap-tap-tap-tap.

But the tempo I had learned to fear the most was the one echoing around that kitchen as we stood there: slow and measured, somewhere between grave and lento, it was the drumming of a slow-burning rage.

Eventually his fingers fell still and a perfectly composed silence descended. It reminded me of the silent pause in Haydn's *The Creation*. Right after the chorus sings "let there be light" you are left waiting, anticipating the explosion that the light will bring, except in this case I wasn't waiting for light; I was waiting for something dark and fearsome to explode. From where I was standing, I could see the glint of kitchen knives behind him, evenly spaced on their magnetic holder, standing to attention like a mini military force waiting for a command, and I recall wondering if this would be the day that he became angry enough to use one of them. Only hours later, I would find myself wishing that he had.

After the silence, he spoke.

"So, this is what happens when my back is turned?"

His voice was surprisingly calm, a soothing re-entry to noise, and not the immediate explosion I had been expecting. He has a beautiful voice, deep and resonant with the clipped vowels of someone who has been privately educated in a prestigious school. It is a voice that hypnotises you, soothes you, lulls you easily into a false sense of security before turning into a blunt force instrument. It is a voice perfectly suited to a barrister.

"You dress like *whores* and put yourselves on public display. *Humiliate* me."

There was more force to his tone this time, his voice deeper and loaded with contempt. My mother and I both knew that we were in serious trouble. Every day we walked a tightrope with my stepfather – each step carefully placed so as not to lose our balance and fall from his grace. We were like birds, sensitive to even the most imperceptible changes in atmospheric pressure, and had learned how to adjust our behaviour to avoid a storm. But this night was different: we had defied him. Even worse, we had made a deliberate attempt to deceive him, thinking that he would never find out. In his mind, we had made a fool out of him and that had been a monumental mistake.

"Did you stop to think *for one moment* of the damage you could do to *my reputation*?"

His fingers were drumming again, allegro, impatient for an answer that we knew would not satisfy him. When we failed to reply, he continued.

"What the *fuck* did you think you were playing at? Did you think I wouldn't find out? You *fucking bitches*."

He stood as he spat out the last few words, slamming his fist down onto the table so hard I was sure the glass table would shatter and I shut my eyes to avoid any potential shards of glass. The physical outburst seemed to slow him down and he breathed deeply for a few seconds, his nostrils flaring slightly as he tried to regain some composure. I knew, though, that he would not calm down, that the fire was already steadily burning, and each breath he took was an oxidiser. Oxygen feeds a fire – that is one of the first things you learn in chemistry, and in that moment I could clearly hear the voice of Mr Wren, my old chemistry teacher, addressing the class: "… adding oxygen to a fire can cause a violent reaction…"

How I prayed right then that my stepfather would somehow just stop breathing, stop feeding the fire, but I knew it was a futile prayer.

As I stood stock still, terrified of what was to come next, I became aware of a faint hum, gradually getting louder and louder, as a fly entered the room. I watched it out of the corner of my eye, zig-zagging back and forth, its buzzing becoming more and more frantic as it desperately searched for a way out. Beyond the kitchen window, garden lights were illuminating a backdrop of trees, and it headed for this, launching itself against the window again and again with a thud that seemed disproportionately loud for its size. It didn't seem to realise that, no matter how hard it flew at that window, it wasn't going to make it to those trees, and I felt a sorrow in my heart for it.

After a few beats, my mother opened her mouth to speak, although I had no idea what she thought she could possibly say that wouldn't make things worse, but she couldn't make a comprehensible sound anyway, her mind too frozen with fear to remember how to construct sentences.

"Shut your mouth, Charlotte, you look like a guppy. You smell like one, too. You are nothing but a filthy little slut, with your slutty little apprentice in tow." His tone was derisory, disgusted.

He turned his attention to me, then, but only with his voice; his eyes remained ominously on my mother as he addressed me:

"Get upstairs, Jeannie. Remove those trashy clothes and scrub your face. I shall deal with you once I have dealt with your mother."

I somehow managed to walk to my room, despite my legs feeling like the bones had been removed from the inside. I didn't turn the light on - for some reason I felt safer in the dark, as if the darkness could swallow me up and hide me, protect me, from what was to come. I wasn't sure what my punishment, my lesson, was going to be and this served to heighten my fear.

He rarely hit me, afraid of the tales the bruises might tell at school. Instead, he usually punished me vicariously through my mother, making me stand and watch as he beat her, sometimes with a belt, sometimes with a tennis ball wrapped inside a tea towel, but never, ever with his bare hands. In his warped mind, it wasn't him doing the beating, it was me. *I* was the belt, the tennis ball, the reason. Before each blow was struck, he would make me apologise to my mother for the transgression that had led to it. My transgression was usually something ordinary that he arbitrarily interpreted as defiance, insubordination, laziness, whatever, but in reality it was just bloodletting for his own frustrations.

After a beating, he would tell my mother he was sorry that he had been forced into doing it, but she must understand that she only had herself to blame for raising such an impertinent, ungrateful and disrespectful child. My mother never dared to contradict him; instead, she would apologise, ask for forgiveness.

I learned early on that if I refused to co-operate, refused to watch or to apologise, my mother's ordeal would continue for longer, and afterwards I would also be punished, albeit in ways that did not involve bruises. When I was eleven, he made me spend the night in the dark basement, tied to a chair, with a canvas sack over my head, and ear defenders on so that the terrors that lurked in my imagination had full control of my mind. But the worst punishment of all was when he made me watch as he killed my puppy in a way that would haunt my nightmares forever, and left me in no doubt that he was capable of killing my mother if I pushed him too far.

This night, though, felt different. My mother and I were both guilty of the same wrongdoing, so I did not need to watch or apologise for any beating that she took, as it was her punishment alone to endure. As I stepped out of my new outfit, I stepped out of any residual courage that I had left. I ran the sink in my en suite and started to wash my face clean of the make-up that had made me feel invincible only hours earlier. The sound of the running water was just about loud enough to muffle, but not drown, the cries and thuds that came from downstairs, and, as I wiped off the remaining mascara that my tears had not already removed, my hands shook uncontrollably, the shaking moving violently from my hands to the rest of my body when I heard the slow and steady footsteps of my stepfather coming to deal with me.

My lesson that night was to show me exactly what men like to do to whores who dress the way I had been dressed. I heard my mum running the taps in her room, no doubt to wash the blood from her face, and I wondered if the sound of the water was just loud enough to muffle, but not drown, the sick noises that were coming from my room.

At breakfast the next morning, nobody spoke. The only sounds were the rustle of the newspaper that my stepfather was reading whilst he drank his espresso in silence, and the swish and plop of my mother washing the same mug and tea plate over and over again in the kitchen sink. My mother wore her hair loose about her face, and a long-sleeved blouse despite the heat, in an inadequate attempt at hiding the purple-blue marks that mottled her pale skin. It looked bad, worse than I had seen it look before, but it was an unspoken rule that she would hide away in the house until the bruises had faded. As she repeated the motion of washing the same two pieces of crockery over and over, I thought about a hard-boiled sweet and how it slowly dissolves in the mouth if it is repeatedly sucked, and I imagined the same thing happening to that mug and plate; the same thing happening to my mother and me.

At exactly 8am, the sound of a chair scraping against the Italian floor tiles broke the silence as my stepfather rose to leave for the day. Just a normal day, except for me it was far from normal – nothing would ever be the same again.

As he walked slowly towards the front door, the smell of his leather briefcase and expensive aftershave wafting through the warm air of the kitchen, he hesitated. His head tilted marginally to the left, as if he could sense that I was watching him, and he said, "It was your own fault, Jeannie. Things like that don't happen to good people, do you understand? I had to teach you a lesson. What kind of a father would I be if I didn't teach you a lesson?"

When the door clicked shut behind him, I watched my mother slide to the floor, a guttural moan escaping her lips, the tea plate shattering beside her into a thousand tiny fragments.

My mother never mentioned what happened to me that night, nor any of the nights that were to follow. A new and insidious darkness had been awakened in my stepfather and my mother's way of dealing with it was to withdraw from reality, pretend it wasn't happening.

Of course, I knew what was happening was wrong, what he was doing was wrong, but my mother's reticence confused me and I began to wonder if maybe, in some unaccountable way, I did deserve what was happening to me. Over the weeks and months that followed, I learned to stay out of his way as much as possible. When it wasn't possible, I found a way to detach, disassociate from it when it happened. In my altered reality, I considered it to be a sacrifice to protect my mother, whose beatings had lessened as a result. I had stopped being the innocent child that needed protecting; I had become the protector.

Just before I turned seventeen, something in me snapped and I tried to fight back, tried to threaten him with the police. I watched him stiffen, momentarily caught off guard by my sudden brazenness. He wasn't used to being challenged and his eyes narrowed as his brain processed my threat. For a moment I thought I had him, until I saw his uncertainty turn to amusement and a slow, sardonic smile spread across his face as he shook his head and sighed at me, adopting a mock avuncular manner.

"Jeannie, Jeannie, Jeannie."

His tone had been school-nurse comforting in a "there-there" kind of way, his voice so at odds with the monster inside of him that it was discombobulating.

"You really are a silly girl sometimes. Do you honestly think anyone would believe you? I am a member of the Queen's Counsel."

He waited for that fact to settle before he continued:

"I poke holes in the statements of eminent experts. I make *intelligent* people look like prevaricators and fools. What makes you think I couldn't discredit *you*? A silly hormonal teenager with an unrequited crush on her stepfather, seeking revenge for being rejected?"

He grabbed my face with his hand, gently squeezing my cheeks with just enough force to make me raise my head so that I was looking directly into his eyes, and could smell the fading mintiness of his breath.

"You would be seen as a pernicious liar at best, Jeannie; mentally ill at worst."

He let my face go, and turned away from me as he concentrated on buttoning his shirt.

"Of course, my colleagues have been aware for some time that I have been concerned about your behaviour around me being inappropriate, and that I am worried about your mental state. I have influential friends in the psychiatric field and I am sure I could find you the best possible psychiatric care facilities should the need arise. No expense spared, naturally."

My balloon was popped. I was floored. I realised then how trapped I really was. He had already thought about what would happen if I spoke out and had prepared for it. It really would be my word against his and he was the master of manipulation. I was no match and I started to cry.

"You know, Jeannie, that you only have yourself to blame for all of this. You do it to yourself, force me to teach you such lessons. You can stop it any time you want by being a better person. All I want is what is best for you, for you to be the best you can be. Am I really so wrong to want that?"

He gently brushed the tears from beneath my lashes with a tenderness that was out of place in the context of what was happening. Then he took my hand and placed it over his heart.

"You disappoint me, Jeannie, hurt my feelings. I have given you everything – your own father abandoned you; I am the only person that can put up with your errant ways. I love you like no one else ever will. Think on that and come down when you are ready to apologise. I will have a word with your mother: she is clearly not having a positive influence on you."

And so my mother suffered once again for my actions, and I was wracked with the same old guilt and fear and hatred.

In my naivety I believed what he was saying – everyone respected and admired him. Who would believe me over him, a powerful man of the law? From the outside, he is a perfect husband and father. If his good looks alone are not enough to win you over, his effusive charm almost certainly will. Everyone loves him – even I did at the beginning, before the serpent emerged from his hiding place – and it is easy to see why my mother had fallen for him.

There is a presence about Ben. When he walks into a room, he commands attention and adulation. He is textbook handsome – just over six feet tall, evenly set features with a classic, square jawline. By nature, we have a subconscious bias towards attractive people, tending to trust them more at first sight than their less attractive counterparts. It is as if better facial features equal better principles and morals, which is why the media love to use unappealing mugshots of an accused person – the uglier the crime, the uglier the photograph they dig up. We just don't like to believe that a beautiful person can be anything other than beautiful on the inside, and this allows evil to roam freely amongst us unseen.

His eyes are particularly beautiful and dangerous. Hypnotic hazel eyes that appear to change colour from copper to green, dancing with the light in the room, and he knows that they are a source of tremendous power. Once you lock eyes with him for the first time, you don't want to let go, mesmerised by the kaleidoscope of shifting colour. Like silence, eyes can be a perfidious psychological tool. Prolonged eye contact creates a bond, it releases oxytocin, a "love" hormone. It is the same hormone that is released during breastfeeding, a time when a mother tends to stare into her baby's eyes, and my stepfather uses this technique to stupefy his targets. He is attentive, maintains eye contact, nods and smiles in agreement at what is being said, never interrupts. He makes you feel like you are important, that what you have to say matters. You feel that somehow you have shared an intimate moment, that you are *special*. You have slept with the incubus and you don't have a clue.

From that moment on, there is no reason to doubt anything he says.

He has used this technique to effectively build a rampart around me, preventing a breach of the truth. My teachers all fell for him – especially the ludicrously young female teachers, with whom he would flirt, calling them "miss" and making them giggle and blush. He easily explained away my poor social skills and withdrawn behaviour as being the result of trauma caused by being abandoned by my real father. The truth was I had never known my real father – I never really thought about him, and certainly didn't feel traumatised or abandoned by him. My lack of social skills, the reason I was withdrawn, was because I wasn't allowed to have friends, I was forced to witness such brutal behaviour towards my mother, and lived in a perpetual state of fear. My teachers thought I was lucky to have such a caring and dutiful stepfather.

I will never forget the first time I saw the real him emerge. I can still feel the horror I felt as a young child, as I watched him push my mother up against a wall and choke her to the point she nearly passed out. His face had gone a deep red with the effort of choking her, and frothy spittle had formed at the sides of his mouth that looked like the "devil spit" you find on blackberries in October. As a terrified six-year-old, I became convinced he must be the one that spits on the blackberries, he must be the devil, and I probably still would believe that if it wasn't for the fact that I no longer believe in God, so by default cannot believe in the devil.

When the time came to leave school and go to college, I could sense a nervousness in my stepfather. He seemed to be on a state of high alert, realising that college meant the first steps towards independence and a potential loss of control over me. He made sure that he gained the trust of my tutor, constantly checking on my progress and seemingly keeping me on track. My tutor and lecturers confused my solitude with diligence, and my stepfather hinted to them that I was on the autistic spectrum, making me a high achiever with problems interacting socially, which was not true, but the fact that I was gaining straight A grades and was struggling to make friends seemed to reinforce that suggestion, and they didn't consider the possibility that there could be anything wrong. If they had known about the study regime and "discipline" that had been imposed on me at home, they would have been shocked. But it seems that safeguarding only protects those in obvious categories. My family were rich; I was privileged. I wasn't rude or sullen or going off the rails on drink and drugs, hell-bent on sabotaging my future. I kept my head down, never spoke to anyone unless I had to, ate my lunch alone, never missed an assignment and was never late. It wasn't normal, yet nobody thought to ask me if I was OK.

Two years have passed since my first day at college, and I have somehow made it to the end. I turned eighteen a few weeks ago, and tomorrow I am off on a so-called gap year at a hospital in Sri Lanka. It is the same one that his friend's son attended a couple of years ago, which is the only reason I was allowed this rare window of freedom. He has been boasting about me attending med school for some time, and, when his friend asked what gap year I had chosen, he couldn't come up with a believable reason as to why I wasn't doing one, so he was effectively backed into a corner.

I have known I am going to be a doctor since I was eleven years old, because he told me that is what I am going to be. His first choice for me would have been law, but he reasoned that I wasn't clever enough for law, my mind wasn't sharp enough. Becoming a doctor was within my reach, he said, and although it was a poor second it was an acceptable career for me, one that wouldn't embarrass or demean him. When I was fourteen, I told him that I really wanted to be a vet. He became incensed – did I not trust him to know what was best for me, he had bellowed. What is the point of a vet, he said, what kind of person thinks it is more important to treat a fucking *hamster* than treat a human? That was the day he threw my beloved puppy, my only friend in the world, against the wall of the study so hard that when he landed on the wooden floor he was twitching, blood seeping out of his ears and creeping through his soft fur, turning it to rust. He looked me in the eye with defiant sarcasm as he said that if I thought I was good enough to be a vet, now was the time to prove it. Then he told me to think twice before I dared open my mouth to contradict him again. I never did.

For some reason, knowing that I am leaving tomorrow has made me feel different. I can feel the strength growing inside me, twisting its way around the fear and shame that has been settled there and squeezing it out of me. It is making me see things more clearly, making it easier to cope with what is happening to me right now.

I knew that he would "visit" me in my room tonight. He knows he is losing some of his control, and raping me is his way of showing dominance, like a dog humping a leg. But tonight he is being particularly violent even for him, because tonight he has something more to prove. Today he lost an important case to a relatively newly qualified barrister, one who happens to be a woman. Even worse, she is a lesbian with an aversion to his charms and he feels mocked, emasculated. So, inevitably, I have found myself staring at my bedroom ceiling with him grunting and panting as he thrusts himself into me. His hand is pressing hard on my throat and I am struggling to breathe, but this is fuel to his twisted fantasy. He is calling me a fucking lesbian whore, telling me that this is what a real man feels like, until, to my relief, his thrusting accelerates and I know it won't be long now until it is over. A final thrust against my hipbones and he makes his strange coming sound, a pathetic groan, and he becomes still as his vile semen pulsates into me. Eventually he slumps, his full weight bearing down onto my body; his chest is slick with sweat against mine and I can feel his wretched heartbeat slowing against my breasts. I resist the urge to throw up, can feel the bile rising from the depths of my stomach, burning into my oesophagus, until he finally pulls out of me. He sits on the edge of my bed – the one I have been sleeping in since I was five years old – and wipes himself before pulling on his trousers in silence. He stands and turns towards the door without making eye contact with me, and I am left wondering once again if his failure to meet my gaze is due to an unacknowledged shame or whether it is arrogance, hubris. As he walks towards the door, he hesitates for a second, eyes still trained ahead.

"Make sure you come home, Jeannie. It will kill your mother if you don't."

This isn't an innocent idiom. It is a threat, and I know what he is alluding to. All I can think of is my poor dead puppy and my mother being left behind to fend for herself. All of the strength that I have fooled myself into believing I was growing suddenly withers and dies along with any hope I had harboured.

As he closes my bedroom door, I run to the bathroom and empty the contents of my stomach into the toilet. After I have finished retching, I stay hunched over the bowl for a few moments to recover, when I feel a spasm in my stomach and wonder whether it is caused by the stress of knowing that I will never be able to leave for good or whether it has anything to do with the period I have missed.

I close my eyes and wonder if it is possible to simply disappear, never to be heard from again.

CHAPTER 2

Benedict

Charlotte was frantic when we heard news of the tsunami and the places that it had struck. She was on the phone to the British embassy, being kept on hold in a queue for hours whilst she waited for a human voice to speak to.

After more than eight hours of holding on, a person finally came on the line and I heard her intermittently give bits of information about Jeannie as she answered their set questions: name, date of birth, height, hair and skin colour, where she was staying, when had we last heard from her, do we have any idea exactly where she might have been when the tsunami hit? At one point, Charlotte sobbed as she was asked to describe any distinguishing tattoos or features, knowing that they were only asking this in case they needed to identify her body at some point, and I listened as she was forced to remember and describe Jeannie's birthmarks. I noticed that she had forgotten to mention the birthmark on the inside of Jeannie's left thigh, and as I thought about it a familiar excitement rose within me. At the end of the call, Charlotte wrote down a phone number that she had been given to call if we were to hear from

Jeannie, so that they could cross her off the growing list of those missing.

That was yesterday, we have still heard nothing, and today I am sitting in the lounge watching Charlotte kneeling in front of the television. Her arm is extended out towards the TV screen, the remote control in her hand jabbing back and forth every minute or so, like the fire and recall of a gun, as she flips urgently between news channels. She is not listening to the news coverage, though, she is just desperately scanning the images of chaos and destruction, of shocked tourists wandering amongst the devastation, hoping for a sighting, a glimpse, of Jeannie. She is almost catatonic, barely blinking except to release the tears that brim and flow over her lower eyelids, like little tsunamis of their own.

She refuses to talk or acknowledge my presence. If I try to touch her, she pushes me away without even looking at me. I find it fascinating that it has taken a potential tragedy for her to grow some courage, some spunk. She didn't have the courage to stand up to me when Jeannie was here and needed a mother, yet, now she may be dead, she has suddenly found the strength to push me away! I almost find some respect for her, nestled in amongst the usual contempt that I feel for her weakness. I wonder how far she would be prepared to go to fight me off right now and I imagine her eyes, shining with defiance and grief, challenging mine; maybe she would even have the strength to attempt to slap me. In my mind's eye I grab her wrist as she tries to do this, and it makes me want her in a way I haven't wanted her for a long time.

I don't try to offer Charlotte any words of comfort; that would be pointless. I also believe that the number that the Home Office gave her to call is pointless, because I am certain Jeannie won't be contacting us. Not because she is dead but because I believe she is alive and has no intention of calling us to let us know. I don't know why I think this, it is just a feeling settling in my gut, and this kind of feeling usually turns out to be right. Before she left, I could sense something slowly changing in Jeannie; it was becoming more difficult to keep the lid on the box with her. No doubt she will think she is being clever, that she has fooled me, that she has got away. Of course, it is possible that I might be wrong, that she could be lying dead somewhere, but if I'm *not* wrong and she *is* alive, I will track her down and find her; and, when I do, I will make sure that bitch wishes she *was* dead.

CHAPTER 3

Becoming Dawn

I am sitting on the plane as it taxis into position. My heart is thumping in my chest so hard I swear it can be heard above the noise of the engines. I feel as transparent and vulnerable as a prawn, as if everyone on the plane can see right through me, that they know what I am planning. I shift a little and can feel my purple bag under the seat where I have been instructed to place it by one of the cabin crew, the velvet material is caressing the Achilles tendon of my left leg. As the engines rumble and roar, I glance at the stranger sitting next to me and they glance back, smiling reassuringly at me, sensing my nervousness. They think I am nervous of flying, of dying from dropping from the sky like a lead ingot, but they are wrong. There are worse things than dying in a plane crash. I should know.

I look down at the passport in my hands, hands that won't stop trembling. The cover is stiff and curling from water damage, and I have an uninvited flashback of muddy water, screams and fear. Of dead faces with misty eyes searching the heavens for an answer as they float unceremoniously by. Slowly I open the passport and run my finger over the smudged and wrinkled photograph. I know it is a typical passport photo, banal and unsmiling, and I wonder about the people who process the passport applications, whether they look at the photos and have some kind of sixth sense about the lives of the people behind the image. When they received my photo, did they see the unhappiness? Did they see the lack of hope, the abject despair in my eyes? Or were they oblivious to the 2D cry for help staring out at them, focussing instead on searching for eyes that looked duplicitous, dishonest?

My eyes move from the photo to the name that is now rolling over the undulating ridges in the pages, reminding me of the waves that helped create them. Art imitating life. Jeannie Eleanor Sutcliffe. It looks longer, I think, on that damaged passport than it does on my plane ticket, as if it is already shrinking. By the time I reach England and walk out of Heathrow Airport it will have almost disappeared completely as I ditch the name Jeannie and begin the process of becoming someone else, of reinventing myself.

We are in the air now. Somehow my thoughts have made me miss take-off and I am jolted back to the present with a "ding" and the announcement that we can remove our seatbelts. There is a collective jostling of passengers unbuckling and settling themselves in for their long flight. Bags being taken down from overhead lockers, seats being reclined to the annoyance of those sitting behind, requests being made of the aircrew. I am sitting in a window seat; it is 6pm and I am tired so I decide I will close the shade. I intend to sleep for as much of this flight as is possible, but have already been elbowed twice by the stranger sitting next to me so I am not holding out much hope of a restful journey. As I turn my head to reach the window shade, I am met with a beautiful Asian sunset, purples and yellows, the colour of bruises, and I am suddenly overwhelmed with emotion. The sun is setting, closing the day down in readiness for a new one to begin tomorrow, and, as a tear winds its way down my cheek, I think of all the hope that I am pinning on the new dawn.

A new dawn. A new day. A new me. Something registers in my brain and I realise that I have found my new name: Dawn. I close my eyes and welcome the blackness it brings.

I am in the raging torrent of water, holding on as tightly as I can to the stranger that has slammed into me. We are like the arms of two jumpers caught together in a washing machine, tumbling around and around, jostling with everything else in the drum. Instinctively I am holding my breath, trying desperately to protect my lungs from the invasion of water, gulping in a mouthful of air each time my head is thrust up to the surface for a split second. The deafening roar of the water, the screams, the loud bangs and cracks at the surface are dulled each time I am forcibly submerged again, but these noises are somehow even more terrifying under water, directly vibrating behind my ears, filling my skull until my head feels like it will burst.

Suddenly we stop tumbling, I can breathe again and I realise I am snagged on a piece of metal that is jutting out from the side of a pulverised building. I am close to the building, and to my right a large chunk of tree is holding back some of the force of the water, creating a sort of mini cove and shielding me from the full assault of the torrent.

The stranger and I are still somehow clinging on to each other, but she is at the violent edge of the water, not as protected as I am, and is being pushed and pulled at like a bully in a playground. Suddenly a large object – a chair, I think – rushes at her and slams into her like a rugby player, catching the side of her head, forcibly knocking it backwards. As her head rebounds, our eyes meet and I can see a trickle of blood oozing from a wound to her left temple. Everything seems to slow down as we stare at each other, and I get the weirdest feeling that I am staring not at a stranger but at myself. We are two

people with one decision: hang on, or give up. As if she is
reading my thoughts, she smiles at me, untroubled. In her
eyes I see resignation, acceptance, maybe even peace. At
the next pull of the water, she is swept away from me – not
ripped from my grasp, as she has offered no resistance; she
has simply let go. She wanted freedom and she found it in
death. I never tried to stop her. I understood.

I waken to the sound of the cabin crew working their way down
the aisle with their trolleys, asking passengers over and over at
each row if they would like chicken or vegetable. My stomach
gurgles involuntarily and I realise I am starving – I slept through
the earlier serving of food and can barely remember the last
time I ate a proper meal. I decide to take the vegetable option
and, when asked if I would like wine with my meal, I decline,
subconsciously placing a protective hand on my stomach. This
tiny foetus is the reason I found the strength to hold on, the
reason I never gave up, and I intend to do everything I can to
keep it safe.

The meal was predictably bland, but it appeased my
grumbling belly. Absently, I wonder what a rumbling tum sounds
like to a baby in the womb, whether it is as loud as thunder to its
delicate, still-forming ears. Then I imagine the rumbling might
actually be the baby itself, beating on a drum to let me know it
needs a feed, and that thought makes me smile – the first real
smile on my face in a long time. I am already feeling bonded to
the tiny squatter that has set up camp inside me, it already has a
personality; it is feisty, brave.

I have given it some thought as to what sex it might be,
and what I might prefer. At first, I thought I wanted it to be
a boy – not because I prefer one sex to the other but because
I felt – feel – that life just seems easier if you are male. But
then I thought, if I had a little girl, I could teach her to be
independent, to be equal and strong and not take any of the

shit that I have had to take in life. But I haven't really dwelled on this. I know the decision is not mine to make, and whatever I am delivered I will love it unequivocally. Until then, I have given it a nickname: *Shrimp*, after the pink foam sweets that remind me of tiny little foetuses.

Before the cabin crew make their way back around to collect the trays and remnants of our meals, the woman sitting next to me gets up to make her way to the toilet, and I notice that she has left a small carton of orange juice, cheese and crackers and a bread roll from her meal. Furtively I take these, and put them into my bag – at this point I have no idea when I may be likely to eat again, and these may just help to keep me going. The woman returns and I can see a quizzical look on her face as she registers that something is missing, but shrugs it off as she is politely asked for her tray by the air steward.

The rest of the flight is uneventful, except for a short period of turbulence that makes me feel nauseous and makes me hope that I won't be one of those people who suffer badly from morning sickness throughout their pregnancy. Eventually the plane begins its descent, and my ears react to the dip in altitude with the unpleasant sensation of hearing under water. For a second, I feel panic rise in me as the memory of actually being under water, of slowly drowning, is spontaneously triggered, and I grapple to dissociate that memory from this reality. It isn't until my ears finally pop that I start to feel calmer.

At about 10,000 feet, the pilot instructs the cabin crew to make their way to their designated seats to buckle in for the descent, and shortly afterwards I can feel the curve of the plane as the pilot guides it into the wind to help slow it down. As it begins its initial approach to the runway, the alarming sounds of wing flaps being deployed, and landing gear being lowered, keep any conversation in the aircraft to a minimum as prayers are silently offered by religious passengers, and secretly offered by some of the atheists and agnostics on board, including me.

Eventually the plane lands with a jarring thud, and bounces – way too fast, it feels – down the runway. The spoilers on the wings have been opened, and the noise of the engine seems to rev as the pilot deploys "reverse thrust", slowing the plane down quickly, much to my relief. Soon the plane is travelling at a sedate pace to the place where all the passengers are eventually permitted to disembark, instantly breaking the stillness that had settled over the cabin during the landing. I decide to remain in my seat and wait until everyone else has started to make their way towards the exit, before collecting my bag from under the seat and tagging on to the end of the queue of people shuffling their way out.

I continue to follow the herd of passengers like sheep making their way to arrivals. Despite sleeping for much of the flight, I am exhausted and it takes longer than I expect to reach passport control. By the time I reach the long queue for passengers from the UK, I feel nervous and tearful, my throat aching with the effort of trying to hold back my emotions.

It has been a few weeks since the tsunami and most people affected by it have already travelled home, but there are some survivors, like myself, still passing through the airport and there are delays and confusion as staff try to help those whose passports and documentation were lost or destroyed. As I watch several dramas unfold, I hug close to me the purple bag that holds the precious cargo of a passport, grateful for that at least.

Eventually it is my time to be called forward and I hand over the passport, as battered and beaten as I feel. My eyes are red and puffy; I don't resemble the warped and water-damaged image it carries, but after a brief conversation confirming what has happened to me it seems I am deemed recognisable enough to be waved through. With an unusual compassion for passport control staff, whose faces are normally stern and unreadable, the officer nods and smiles at me. "Good luck, Jeannie, you are safe now," he says.

Those words jar me, for I am not sure I know how safe feels, and whether I will ever recognise it again. I am also struck by the fact that he called me Jeannie. The last person ever to say that name again, as today is the day that I will walk out of the airport, into the bright winter sun, as Dawn.

"Well, Shrimp," I say to my squatter, as the automatic doors open onto UK soil, "What the hell do we do now?"

CHAPTER 4

Dawn

I decide to make my way to the bus station which I have been told is somewhere between Terminals 2 and 3. When I get there, I still have no idea what I am going to do, where I am going to go. I am scared beyond words, the fear magnified by the fact that there is another life inside me to worry about; it is not just me anymore.

Despite the bright sunshine, it is cold, and I am not really dressed for British winter weather. Before I left Sri Lanka Colombo Airport, I managed to secure some clothing for my journey thanks to International Aid volunteer workers. The volunteers responsible for handing out clothing were not interested in taking my details – there were other volunteers whose job it was to do that, and I had avoided them. I gratefully accepted a pair of jeans that are a size too big for me, but acceptable with a belt, and an orange woollen jumper that has seen better days and smells faintly musty. On my feet I am wearing flip-flops; my hands and feet are so cold I can barely feel them and part of me wishes that I couldn't feel the rest of me either, that the fear could be numbed along with my fingers and toes. Even so, I refuse to feel sorry for myself. I know how lucky I am just to be here.

I worry about my baby, though, whether it is possible for the cold to work its way from the outside through to the growing space inside of me. I imagine the amniotic fluid slowly getting cooler in the same way bathwater does, until eventually Shrimp is floating in cold water, shivering, and I am powerless to do anything about it. I try to shake this notion from my head, telling myself not to be silly, and am helped back into the here and now when a person knocks into me as they rudely push past.

The bus station is busy, crawling with people starting, ending or continuing their journeys. Some seem to know exactly what they are doing, others look confused, but, still, I can't imagine any of them are in the state of flux that I am in right now. It is noisy, too – the throaty sounds of engines idling or starting up, the squeak and scrape of suitcases along concrete paths, the chatter of people debating which stand they should be queuing at. Above me is the ubiquitous sound of planes taking off or coming in to land. Life goes on, predictable for some, exciting for others, but I am not one of them.

I am not used to being on my own, and certainly not used to having to make decisions for myself. For one minute I almost consider going home – better the devil you know than the devil you don't – but then something stirs in my tummy; it is Shrimp reminding me why I am doing this, why I can never go back. As I place my hand over the barely-there bump, concealed beneath the scratchy wool of the jumper, a bus pulls into a bay near to where I am standing. The driver rises from his seat and leans above him to change the destination roll-sign. I watch the names of various destinations roll by, as seemingly confused about where to stop as I am, and I make the decision that I will head for whatever destination that the sign finally rests on. Shortly after, I am in the ticket office purchasing a ticket to Victoria Coach Station.

I had exchanged my water-damaged money back to sterling at one of the currency exchange booths inside the airport, but it worried me that I had such limited cash. Thankfully a ticket to Victoria Station wasn't too expensive, but I know that what I have left might only pay for a hotel room for a couple of nights if I am lucky; after that I am pretty much destitute. There is no way I will survive sleeping rough on the streets in this weather, but I try to put this out of my mind for now.

The bus finally arrives at Victoria Coach Station and I disembark into what feels like a large warehouse. In the absence of knowing what else to do, I follow a couple of people as they make their way out of the arrivals station and onto a busy street. I continue to follow them as they cross the road onto another with a sign that informs me that I am on Buckingham Palace Road. We carry on for a bit and before long I am walking through what looks like a shopping complex, and I wonder where these people are headed and what I should do if they enter into one of the shops. Thankfully they don't enter any shops, and eventually they lead me inside Victoria Railway Station, where I stop walking and let them disappear into the throng.

I feel like a child on my first day of school, surrounded by the unfamiliar. The station feels enormous, chaotic. The ceiling of the building is domed with panels of glass, letting in a dimming winter light that is shining down on commuters and tourists. All around me there are signs, but they are only serving to confuse rather than help me right now. People are rushing in all directions, some are running to catch trains whose engines are rumbling and eager, and some are queuing at food outlets and customer service desks looking impatiently or nervously at their watches. There are unintelligible tannoy announcements and a confusing mix of different accents and languages competing with each other in the acoustics of the building. If I was scared before, I am paralysed with fear now. I don't know London at all, and have absolutely no idea of where I might go from here. I suddenly feel like I am going to be sick and I need some air, so I make my way to the nearest exit out of the station and back onto a bustling, jostling street.

As I stand on the street, alone and terrified, like a fox surrounded by hounds, I hear a voice immediately behind me, above the rest of the extraneous noise; it is loud and commanding.

"*Big Issue, Big Issue!*" the voice shouts and I turn towards it.

A large hulk of a man in a fading black duffle coat and wool beanie is standing by the entrance to the station, holding up a copy of the paper he is selling, smiling and nodding cordially at people as they pass him. A few people smile back, some even stop to buy the paper, but most pass with their head down, or eyes trained straight ahead, in a deliberate act of avoiding any eye contact with him. A couple of people glare at him, shaking their heads as if he is scum and I notice that he smiles even harder at those people, nodding and bidding them a good day. His tone feels genuine to me rather than sarcastic when he does this, and it reminds me of something I once read or heard – I can't quite remember where, or exactly how it goes, but it is something like "Smile the hardest at those who frown, as they are the ones who need it the most."

Even though he is a complete stranger, I sense he is a nice man, a decent man. After a while the man notices me watching him and turns his attention on me and, for a brief moment, I think I see pity in his eyes. His eyes are crystal-blue, so pale and clear it feels to me like they are capable of seeing everything with a supernatural clarity and I swear he can see straight into my soul, to the core of who I am. After a second, he speaks to me.

"You look like you have a story to tell, lass," he says.

His accent is from somewhere up north, not particularly strong, and I am not great at identifying accents, so I am not sure of its origins: Leeds, maybe, or Newcastle. Wherever he hails from, his voice is as warm and rough as the coat he is wearing and I imagine him to be the type of man that swallows you up in a bear hug to show his love for you. It makes me wonder what *his* story is, why he is here on this street selling the *Big Issue*. His head is tilted a little to one side as he contemplates me, as if my story is inked on my skin and he is reading it. After a moment he says, "Nah. That's not quite right. You're still walking through your story, lass; you haven't reached the ending yet. Am I right?"

I just smile feebly at him, fighting the urge to tell him everything right there and then, just to feel that I am not alone in this.

"How much for the *Big Issue*?" I ask instead.

I know this is a magazine to help the homeless, and I am hoping there might be some information in there to help me right now, so could be worth spending some of my precious cash on. The man looks at the flip-flops on my feet and the waxy tips of my freezing fingers, the dark circles under my eyes, and he proceeds to roll one of his magazines up and walks towards me, doffing me lightly on the head with it in a playful gesture, before handing it to me. "On the house, love," he says. "It looks like you could do with the money more than me."

My eyes well up as I thank him. "You are right," I say. "About my story not having an ending yet."

"Whatever your persuasion or story, you are not unusual in London, lass. People look through you, not at you; it is the perfect place to hide," he says, winking. "If that's what you need to do."

I am startled and want to ask him how he knows I need to hide, but at that moment a man in a smart suit approaches him with a broad smile, and his attention is directed elsewhere.

"Hello, Mack, thought you could do with this," the man in the suit says, as he hands over a steaming polystyrene cup. They engage in some banter and then the man passes over some change in exchange for a copy of the *Big Issue* before walking off to catch his train. The man in the suit doesn't even look at me as I stand there, and I realise I really am invisible, which kind of proves the theory of London being the perfect place to hide.

I glance over to Mack, the *Big Issue* seller, not wanting to leave his presence – he makes me feel secure for some reason –

but he is busy with another customer. He notices me as I start to walk away, though, and calls out to me. "Hey! Jackanory!" he shouts. "What's your name?"

"Dawn!" I shout back, without hesitation, and it surprises me how easily I have adopted my new name.

"Page 5!" he calls out, pointing at a copy of the *Big Issue* in his hand. "Hostels. Don't forget, Dawn, you hold the pen that writes the ending. To your story, that is. Good luck, lass."

I wave my thanks at him, but I'm not even sure he has seen me do it as another customer has stepped in front of him holding out some money. As I hurry away, I wonder how he knows I have nowhere to stay and before long tears start to trickle down my face, leaving frosty tracks on the cold skin of my cheeks.

Although I am hurrying away, I realise yet again that I have no idea where I am hurrying to. This feels like one of those bad dreams where you are lost and frantic, everything around you an unfamiliar blur. My heart is pounding so fast I swear it is about to burst out of my chest, and my breathing begins to match my heart rate as I take short and ragged breaths. I feel like I am going to die but know that it is just a panic attack. I have had them before. I realise that I need to slow down, give myself time to really think, and, more importantly right now, I need to warm up.

I am shivering uncontrollably, partly from anxiety and partly from the cold. I think of the steaming polystyrene cup that the man in the suit gave Mack, and look around for somewhere that I can sit and have a hot drink. There are plenty of places to choose from, but I feel overwhelmed by the choice and incapable of making a decision despite my need. Once more I am jolted into reality by a person jostling into me, and a decision is inadvertently made as I am propelled in the direction of a small independent coffee shop.

I go inside and sit down; my fingers almost immediately react to the warm air of the café by tingling and throbbing painfully as the blood flow returns to them. I pick up a menu and my heart sinks at the prices, which seem preposterously expensive, but I am here now and cannot face trying to find somewhere cheaper. I order a hot chocolate – I remember when I was little my mother would give me hot chocolate, with little pink and white marshmallows floating on top, to warm me up on a cold day, and it feels comforting to order one, like being wrapped up in a warm memory. I decide not to order food as I still have the food that I took from the plane in my bag, which I can eat later, saving myself some of my precious money.

While I am waiting for my drink to arrive, I unroll the *Big Issue* and to my surprise a pair of little black woollen gloves fall out, the sort that look far too small but expand to the size of your hands. Mack must have put them there for me and I am overwhelmed by this act of kindness from a stranger. Before I have time to look at the *Big Issue*, my drink arrives and I wrap my hands around the body of the mug, allowing the heat to seep into my fingers. I stay like that for a short while before taking a sip of the silky chocolate milk, closing my eyes to help me concentrate on the feeling of warmth sliding down my throat and into my stomach. "There you go, Shrimp," I whisper to my baby, "your first hot chocolate!"

As the warmth of the drink takes hold, I turn my attention back to the *Big Issue*. Remembering what Mack had shouted out to me, I turn to page 5, where I find adverts for accommodation, hostels and cheap hotels. I know that I should be looking at hostels – they are the cheapest and most sensible option – but I also know that there will be shared facilities and over-friendly people with questions that I don't want to answer. I need peace and quiet, to rest and to think, so decide I will look for a cheap hotel. I should just about be able to afford it.

Now that my hands have come back to life, my attention is turned to my feet, and in particular the nails of my toes, which feel like they are being stabbed over and over with tiny frozen daggers. I realise that I need to buy some warm shoes, and maybe a coat, before frostbite or hypothermia, or both, sets in. This thought raises my anxiety levels as I now wonder whether I will be left with enough money to afford even a cheap room for the night.

I finish my drink, and after I have paid I pull my newly acquired gloves on to my now-warm hands and leave the café. Before long I stumble across a small charity shop in a side street, where I manage to buy a cheap, faded khaki coat and a pair of boots that are slightly too big but fit well enough when teamed with a pair of thick socks. I keep them all on as I go to pay for them and I must look a sorry sight, as the woman serving me throws in a woolly hat for free – she never says anything, just winks at me, my second wink of the day. I thank the lady, reach into my purple bag and hand over some of my dwindling cash before asking her for some directions. A couple of the cheapest hotels are located on the same street, according to the *Big Issue*, and so this is where I am headed, with just one more stop necessary on the way.

In the end I decide on the Sunrise Hotel, which is a cross between a guest house and a small hotel. The street it sits on is grubby and litter-lined, but the façade of the hotel seems pleasant enough, and I have just enough money left over to stay there for one night, so I make my way into the building, stepping into an old entrance hall that has been converted into a small, dark reception area. Despite several "No Smoking" signs, the air is heavy with old, stale smoke, as if no clean, fresh air has passed through this area since those signs were screwed to the wall. I feel a stab of concern as to whether these invisible, ageing toxins are still capable of being harmful to my baby, and I try not to breathe in too deeply.

After paying up front for my room, I am given a key. The key is on a piece of white string with a brown cardboard tag attached – the tag has "Room 6" handwritten on it in blue ink. Room 6 is an attic room and, as there is no elevator in the building, I walk the creaking staircase, its threadbare runner reminding me of a poor comb-over on a balding man. Eventually I reach Room 6 and place my key into the lock. At first, I think I must have the wrong key, or the wrong room, as I can't seem to make the key fit into its hole, but after jiggling it around a bit it finally clicks into place and I turn it and open the door.

The room smells of cheap cleaning fluids mingled with musty damp. There is a large, mottled-black mould stain starting on the ceiling and stretching down to behind the headboard, like the shape of an unknown country on a map. The thin blue carpet in the room has scarred patches of varying shades of brown, where God-knows-what has been spilled on and stained it over the years. It is tidy, but is one of those rooms that, no matter how well it is cleaned, will always manage to look grubby.

The room is one of only a few in the hotel that has its own bathroom, and the first thing I want to do is have a bath, to help warm the core of me. I notice that the bar of soap on the side of the bath has been used already, and the small complimentary bottle of shampoo has been opened and is half empty. There is a long dark hair curling around the curve of the chipped enamel bath, which to be fair looks clean other than that stray hair left behind by a cleaning cloth, and I can see only one hand towel and one bath towel, which looks like it may not be quite big enough to wrap around me. Although this should all feel depressing, it is not; the thought of a hot bath is paradise right now.

Before running my bath, I pick up the velvet bag and reach in to take out the hair dye and scissors that I bought on my final stop before the hotel. *Maximum Blonde* is the colour on the box and I sit on the side of the bed as I read the instructions on how to change the colour of my hair. *Am I reinventing myself or hiding?* I wonder. I don't even know if they are the same thing or different. I've seen many news reports of people missing, presumed dead after the devastating tsunami, and I am hoping with every fibre of my being that this is what he thinks has happened to me. It is essential that he thinks I'm dead because, if he doesn't, I know he will stop at nothing to find me.

CHAPTER 5

Dawn

It is nearly 9am and I have just checked out of the Sunrise Hotel. The receptionist barely looked at me as I handed the key over, and I was disappointed as I wanted to judge her reaction to my changed appearance. As I walk along the street, I decide that cutting my hair so short last night was a mistake: the cold air is biting into my newly bare neck and I really wish that the khaki coat had come with a hood. At least my head is warm, thanks to the free woolly hat that is covering my new haircut, just an inch of bright blonde peeping out from the bottom, like feet poking out of a blanket.

Despite the violent sounds of shouting and banging coming from other rooms in the hotel, I managed to fall into a deep sleep last night, and in theory I should have awoken feeling refreshed, but this is not the case. I feel exhausted and hungry and am finding it difficult to concentrate. The only food I consumed yesterday was the food I had taken from the plane – a small packet of cheese and crackers and a bread roll – which I know is not enough for me, let alone for me *and* Shrimp. At least the fear and anxiety of yesterday, although not gone, has lessened its grip on me today, which I think is mainly due to the fact that I now have a plan. Sort of.

Last night I had decided to read the *Big Issue* in bed, as reading always helps send me to sleep, and as I went to pick it up I clumsily dropped it and it landed splayed open onto pages 11–12. Page 11 happened to be a job vacancy page, and one vacancy in particular jumped out at me:

> *Live-in housekeeper/carer required. Experience preferred but training will be provided for suitable candidate. Send CV to Ms Marjorie Kent...*

The address given in the ad was in Pimlico, west London. There was a coffee-stained tourist map on the old dressing table in my room, and a quick look showed me that Pimlico was within easy walking distance of the hotel. This felt like a good sign, fate maybe. I didn't have a CV to send, and had neither the time, means nor relevant experience to produce a decent one, so decided that in the morning I would walk to that address, knock on the door and ask for Marjorie Kent in the hope that meeting her face to face would count for something. And so here I am now, making my way to Pimlico, to persuade a stranger to give me a job.

I am feeling nauseous and a little faint, and I am not entirely sure if it is due to nervousness, hunger or morning sickness, but I am determined to hold it all together until I speak to Marjorie Kent. I cannot afford to stuff this up, I'm pretty sure that this is my one and only chance.

Before long I find myself on a street, lined with a terrace of immaculate, yellow-brick, four-storey townhouses. Vertical iron railings run along the front of the terrace at street level, like little sentinel soldiers guarding the entrances with their spiked muskets. Each house in the terrace is identical: rows of symmetrical windows, each encased in white painted cast stone surrounds, with individual iron balconies embracing the two first-floor windows of each residence. There are a few concrete steps leading to each of the front doors, and you can just see the tip of basement windows peeping above ground level through the railings. The only thing that sets them apart from each other is the house number, and colour of the front door. Yellow, red and green catch my eye in particular as it makes me think of traffic lights. Red: stop. Yellow: caution. Green: go. There are also black and grey and blue, but I can't help hoping the one I am looking for will be green for "go", as this will feel like a good omen.

I wander up and down, scanning the house numbers – all of which are on the right-hand side of the doors as I look at them – and I eventually spot number 118, the house where Marjorie Kent lives. It is not green; it is yellow. Does this mean I should proceed with caution? I decide that yellow also symbolises hope and new beginnings, so this could still be a good omen. As I stand there, contemplating symbolism, the door to the house next door opens and a man – in his early thirties, I am guessing – emerges. He is wearing an expensive wool coat and striped woollen scarf, and as he descends the concrete steps to the pavement he looks at me with intrigue. For a moment I think he is going to say something to me, but he seems to think better of it and turns away from me, walking down the street with an air of purpose.

The look he gave me was transient, but it has suddenly made me feel self-conscious of the way I look, and I am now full of self-doubt. I must be stupid to think anyone would take me seriously looking the way I do, but I resolve to at least try; it is all I have left. I start to ascend the steps to number 118, but as I reach the halfway point I change my mind, I can't do it. The plug has been pulled on any confidence and hope that I had, and it is now draining from me faster than bathwater. I suddenly feel clammy and weak, there is a strange ringing in my ears and my vision is blurring; I know I am about to faint. As I turn around to leave, I stumble and grab the stair rail, but my legs no longer have the strength to carry my weight and I slide down the steps onto the cold concrete of the pavement before passing out.

***

"It's OK, darling. Jeannie, is it?" the woman says and I am confused for a moment as I take in my surroundings. I am in a beautiful room, a thin shaft of light beaming in through a small crack in some heavy-set lined curtains that are drawn across the window. Then I remember.

"Dawn," I croak. "My name is Dawn."

"Oh," says the woman. "I wasn't sure. The passport says Jeannie but I did wonder – it's rather damaged but I can see your hair is different and I wasn't sure." I could sense trepidation in her voice, and I could understand why.

"I've changed my name," I tell her quickly by way of an explanation, then fear struck. "You haven't told anyone I'm here, have you?" I think about the emergency contact information on the passport and I feel like I might faint again, I don't want my cover blown already.

"No, no darling. Not yet. You've only been out for a few minutes. Is there someone I should call for you?"

"No!" I say, a bit too forcefully to be polite and I immediately regret it; she is only trying to help. Then I burst into tears. I cry because there is no one to call; I cry because running away is futile – I have no money, no support, no feasible plan, no hope; I cry because I realise that he will forever own me; but I cry the most for my baby, who deserves better than a weak, pathetic excuse of a mother incapable of protecting it.

"Oh my, darling," the woman says as she scoops me into an unexpected hug, the movement giving rise to a waft of pleasant floral tones from her perfume. "What could possibly be so bad?"

If only she knew.

The woman is Marjorie Kent, and after I finally calm down she insists that I stay for some food.

"Look at you, you are so pale and thin it is no wonder you fainted," she says. "I am pretty sure that baby inside you needs some nourishment too."

I look at her, wide-eyed and open mouthed in amazement – I am too early in my pregnancy for it to be obvious to an onlooker, and I have absolutely no idea how she knows.

"Lucky guess," she says with an enigmatic smile when she sees the look of surprise on my face. "I used to faint during my pregnancy."

Marjorie is well-spoken, some might say posh, and is younger than I thought she would be. I had imagined a frail old lady who needed looking after, but she is fit and strong – she somehow managed to get me into the house on her own. She has thick dark blonde hair, the merest hint of grey at her temples and in her parting, and faint lines that fan out from her eyes like starbursts when she smiles. She is a little old-fashioned; her thick hair is long and wavy, wispy at the ends, and is all one length with no particular style. I get the feeling it has probably been that way since she was a young teenager.

She wears a pair of blue-rimmed glasses propped on top of her head, and there is minimal make-up on her face, just a hint of colour on her lips and some mascara. Her clothes are colourful but safe in a mumsy way, and do their best to disguise what I can tell is probably a good figure underneath. It is hard to pinpoint her age: she could be anywhere between forty and sixty. Either her clothes and hair could be making her look old for her age or good genes could be making her look younger. She reminds me of an old art teacher I once had at secondary school.

I am sitting on a stool at a large granite kitchen island, whilst Marjorie is stirring some soup in a saucepan. The smell is making me salivate and, if I could, I would eat it straight from the pan right now rather than wait for it to warm up enough to be put into a bowl. My stomach is growling, or at least I think it is my stomach and not Shrimp protesting from within. As she cuts large slices from a loaf of fresh bread, Marjorie asks me a question.

"I'm curious, Dawn. What brought you to my door?"

It is a reasonable question to ask, but I feel foolish and ashamed. How can I tell her that I was going to ask her to give me a job, knowing that it wasn't practical, that I am pregnant? Despite this, I feel I owe this kind woman the truth.

"I saw your vacancy in the *Big Issue*," I say, "and I had been hoping you might consider me for the position. I'm sorry, I realise how stupid this sounds now, now that you know I am pregnant."

At this, Marjorie puts down the breadknife and turns to face me.

"Oh," she says in a quiet voice, "there is no position anymore. My mother died." A silence descends before she continues. "I forgot to pull the advert. How silly of me."

So, it was her mother that required the care. That makes sense. "I'm sorry," I say, "about your mother." My thoughts shift to my own mother, and I find myself wondering what kind of mother Marjorie's had been, what kind of mother I will turn out to be.

"No need," Marjorie countered. "She had been ill for a long time. I cared for her full time – she steadfastly refused help from elsewhere – but during the last few years she had been suffering from dementia and was becoming increasingly difficult for me to handle on my own, which is why I decided to advertise for some help. She didn't really know who I was any more anyway, so I didn't feel guilty about betraying her wishes. As it happens, she died before I could appoint anyone – I'm sure she knew what I was planning, and this was her way of making sure she remained in control until the end, the old goat! I hadn't given the job advert a second thought until now – I must contact the magazine to have it withdrawn."

She ladles the soup into large china soup plates and carries them to the island, going back to collect plates of bread and butter. We sit and eat in silence for a bit and in my peripheral vision I am aware of Marjorie furtively watching me as I eat greedily. Before I have quite finished my soup, Marjorie gets up and refills my bowl, and I don't try to stop her – she was right; Shrimp needs the nourishment. Whilst I am eating my second bowl of soup, Marjorie busies herself at the butler sink washing up the soup pan and her own bowl. She is doing this despite the fact that there is a dishwasher in the kitchen, and I sense that she is giving me some space to eat without feeling awkward, and I appreciate her for that.

As I start to scrape the last of the soup from my bowl, I am feeling warm and satiated – almost human again – before a sadness descends upon me, knowing that with each scrape of the spoon I am closer to having to leave. As if Marjorie can read my thoughts, she drains the sink, removes her rubber gloves and walks to the island to sit next to me. She places one elbow on the countertop and lets her head rest in the palm of her hand as she looks at me.

"Where will you go from here, Dawn?" she asks, and I hesitate to respond because I don't want to accept the inevitability of the answer that I know deep down I have to give. I consider lying – to myself as much as to Marjorie – by telling her that I have somewhere to go, but it doesn't feel right to lie to such a decent person. I consider telling her an abridged version of the truth, that I don't have anywhere *safe* to go, but I don't want to be a burden on her conscience, either. In the end, I realise that nothing I say will alter the fact that there is only one thing I can do, so I may just as well accept it.

"Home," I whisper. "I have to go home."

Marjorie studies my face for a second. She is frowning as she looks at me, and two creases have appeared between her eyebrows. Her stare feels a bit like a laparoscope, as if she is delving into my thoughts with a camera, viewing the damaged images in my head.

"*Have to* is not the same as *want to*, Dawn," she says, and I begin to believe she really can view my thoughts. "The question is: do you *want* to go home?"

And now I find myself weeping as I sit and tell Marjorie the truth. I talk for hours, and Marjorie never says a word throughout; she just listens and nods and squeezes my hand from time to time, until I am finished. She now knows everything there is to know – I have left nothing out – and I realise how emotionally naked and vulnerable I am in the hands of a virtual stranger. After a second's silence, Marjorie speaks.

"Oh, darling, you brave, brave girl," she says, "you are safe now, I can promise you that." This is the second time a stranger has told me I am safe now – first the man at passport control, and now Marjorie – but this is the first time that I have dared to hope that it might be true.

The natural light in the room is draining fast, and before long it is dark outside. I stare out of the window into what feels like the abyss, the wraith that is my reflection staring back at me. It terrifies me, what awaits me out there.

"You must stay here tonight." Marjorie breaks into my thoughts. "Tomorrow we will figure out what we are going to do." I realise she has used the word "we" and not "you", and it makes me feel as light as a feather. Before I can say anything, she starts to walk off. "Follow me," she says with the authoritative air of a primary school teacher, and I happily do as I am told.

She leads me back to the bedroom that I woke up in earlier in the day, and walks to a tall chest of drawers, where she pulls out a nightshirt. "It will be a little big, but will do the trick for tonight."

She points to a door leading off the bedroom. "Bathroom is in there, you can take a bath or shower, whichever you prefer. Leave your clothes on the floor outside the bedroom door and I will wash and dry them for you ready for tomorrow."

"You don't need to do that," I protest. "You have done enough for me already."

"It is no bother, darling. I never thought I would say this but, to be honest, I miss having someone to look after." I don't protest anymore; it feels good having someone look after me, even if it is only for a short while.

With Marjorie gone, I take a long, hot bath, helping myself to some luxurious bubble bath, before putting on the nightshirt and crawling into the sumptuous double bed. The sheets are soft and cool against the heat of my bath-warm skin. They have a freshly laundered smell that transports me back to my early childhood, when my mother would lift the bedsheet right up under my chin and tuck me in so tightly that I could barely move my arms – it was like being swaddled. I wish with all my heart that she was here to do that for me now, even though I know that it is impossible.

As I am sitting in bed, Marjorie knocks on the door and I tell her to come in, thinking how strange it is that she is asking permission to enter a room in her own house. She is carrying a tray of sandwiches and a mug of hot milk, which she puts on the cabinet beside the bed.

"How are you feeling?" she asks, and I see genuine concern and compassion in her expression.

"Good," I reply, and I mean it. She smiles at me, and gets up to leave. As she walks towards the door, she stops in the doorway as I ask her a question.

"Why are you helping me? I mean, I'm really grateful, but why bother to help me?"

"Because my baby never stood a chance," she says. "Yours does."

And with that she walks out of the room, gently shutting the door behind her.

CHAPTER 6

Dawn

It has been five years since I fainted on the steps of the townhouse, and there is no doubt that Marjorie rescued me that day. Actually, she did more than rescue me; she gave me a life. I say *me*, but I mean *us* – that is, Mary, my daughter, and me. Marjorie, in her own humble way, says we all rescued each other, and as I watch her right now looking shyly up at the man she loves, the man we *all* love, as he places a ring on her finger, I think she is probably right.

Marjorie is wearing a pale champagne-coloured wedding dress. It is a simple and elegant shift style, knee length, that complements her trim figure. An intricate layer of lace overlays the main fabric of the dress and extends to cover her otherwise bare décolletage and arms. Her thick and wavy hair, with its natural grey highlights, has been tamed into a twisted up-do, a pearl hair accessory is hiding the pins and a few loose strands of her hair have broken free and are kissing her cheeks. She looks the most beautiful I have ever seen her, radiant with love; she is age-defying.

The vows have been said now, and the registrar has pronounced them man and wife. "You may kiss the bride," the registrar says in a fun and teasing tone. I think I even saw her wink at them. Marjorie's face is flushed with happiness (and the effects of a little prenuptial champagne) as she is kissed for the first time as a married woman. Mary is jumping up and down in her bridesmaid dress, squealing and clapping her hands excitedly at the sight of Nana Marjorie and Mack kissing. Mack bends down to scoop Mary up into his arms, as easily as one might scoop up a balloon. The sight of all three of them together – Mary in the crook of Mack's arm playing with his tie, Marjorie adjusting Mary's dress so her knickers aren't on show, all of them laughing, happy and content, makes my heart swell. But, as always, the happier I am the more frightened I become. Marjorie tells me often that I need to deal with these feelings before they overtake my life completely and stop me from the actual act of living. She should know, she says.

There is an almost ethereal glow of silver light from the large floor-length window of the ceremony room. It feels like a celestial blessing and it calms me. Caitlin, Marjorie's childhood and most trusted friend, is sitting next to me crying quietly, a sodden tissue to her nose. I assume this is due to happiness for Marjorie, but can't help but wonder if some of it is also regret over her own two failed marriages. There is something about a wedding that can easily make you a little melancholy about your own love life, watching the hope and promise at the beginning of someone else's. Outside the window I spot an advancing army of fat-bellied clouds taking over the sky, holding the sun hostage. The light in the room darkens, and my skin reacts with goosebumps, my mood dimming along with the light. It's all been too good up to now; I have a real sense of foreboding, like something is about to rip it all apart. I can't help it.

"Mummy!" cries Mary, breaking me out of my feelings of doom, her smile bringing me back into the joy of the moment.

Do not dwell on long-term joy, enjoy the simple pleasures that each moment may bring, I whisper to myself. The phrase is highlighted on a bookmarked page in one of the self-help books that Marjorie bought me, and I have been trying really hard to practise the philosophy. It's not easy, but Mary helps to remind me, as each moment with her is such a joy. I feel sure that if I can just conquer the dreams that disturb me almost nightly, I would find it easier. I think last night's dream has rattled me more than most.

I dreamt that I was walking along the shore of the beach and came across a colony of seals. Amongst the colony I spotted Mary playing happily, and I felt secure knowing that she was being protected. As she looked up, she smiled at me briefly before a giant wave rushed in, engulfing her. In my dream, Mary couldn't swim and she was splashing and flailing around in the water. I started screaming her name and as I swam towards her, I saw it, the large insidious fin of a shark circling my little girl.

I woke up before I reached her, so wet with sweat that I could have actually been swimming in that sea for real, and with no way of knowing if I had managed to save her or not. It's just a dream, the rational part of me knows that, so why does it feel so much more than that? It doesn't help that I have had the feeling that I am being watched lately, even though we are all as careful as can be to hide my true identity.

"Hey, Jackanory!" Mack calls out to me in his Geordie accent. He still loves to call me by the nickname he gave me at the railway station the day we first met, the day it all began. I still have the gloves he gave me that day. I treasure them: they are my good-luck charm and a reminder of all the good there is in the world.

"Family photo time, lass," he says beckoning me, and I smile then, outwardly and inwardly, as it gives me such a buzz to think of how far we have all travelled to become a family. We are as diverse a family as it gets in a social sense: our backgrounds, our stories, all so different and yet we somehow managed to converge into our own private, sheltered bay, each of us replacing something missing in one another.

Besides me and Caitlin, there is only one other guest: Philip. Philip had been Marjorie's father's solicitor and is trustee of his will. Although Marjorie was his main beneficiary, her father had created an interest in possession trust, giving Marjorie's mother the right to live in the townhouse until she either died, remarried or chose to leave. A crumbling holiday cottage in Devon and a large portfolio of lucrative investments was left to Marjorie in a trust to be managed by Philip. Marjorie adored her father and had been devastated when he died of cancer at only forty-two. She was just sixteen at the time and his passing meant she was left alone with a jealous, overbearing mother who had never wanted her and whose fury was sharpened by the terms of the will. When a vulnerable Marjorie became pregnant soon after her father's death, it was her mother who made the arbitrary decision that Marjorie was to have an abortion. Not long after, her mother had fallen ill with primary progressive MS and Marjorie was still so young and naïve, still too full of self-loathing and guilt over her abortion, to realise that she deserved better, and before she knew what was happening she had become her mother's full-time carer.

"So often I have wished that I could somehow travel back in time to that young version of me, and tell her not to give up on her baby, to *fight*," she told me once. "That's why, when I saw you stop outside the townhouse, when I watched as your legs buckled beneath you and you started to slide down the steps, I somehow knew you had been sent to me, that you were my one chance to make things right." I know how lucky I have been, that because of Marjorie I was not forced into having to make a similar decision.

Over the years, Philip has become like an uncle to Marjorie, watching out for her as best he can. Today he has the supplementary role of unofficial photographer and he takes this responsibility seriously as he uses exaggerated hand gestures, along with authoritative orders, to move us into the desired poses. After a few shots, Caitlin is summoned to join us, and she stands proudly by Marjorie. She jokingly asks Marjorie to make sure she throws her bouquet at her later – she could do with a third-time-lucky marriage, she says. Marjorie smiles at her, but I know she really wants me to have that bouquet; she dreams of me finding the happiness she has found with Mack.

After the registrar takes charge of the camera for the final few shots to include Philip, we all emerge from the Town Hall building and onto its worn and well-trodden stone steps, into broken sunshine. A few passers-by look up at us, interested and smiling, and I instinctively drop my head so that my face is not in full view. It is a habit I cannot break, and am not sure I ever will. The thought of being recognised, of being found, still terrifies me. I needn't worry today, though, as Mary is stealing all of the attention in her bridesmaid dress, and is revelling in the passing comments of how pretty she looks, how beautiful her russet-coloured curls are. A waiting taxicab picks us up from the kerbside and takes us back to the townhouse. Marjorie and Mack have decided against a reception in a restaurant – it would be far more relaxing at home, they said, where Mary wouldn't have to be on her best behaviour and could run around as she pleased. I had protested, but they were adamant. I feel guilty about that, as I think they are really doing it for me, knowing how torturous I find it being in public spaces with lots of people.

For the last few days leading up to the wedding, we have all been cooking and baking in readiness for the reception. Mary is particularly proud of the fairy cakes that she helped to make, with pink and blue frosting and edible glitter. Figurines adorn the top of two of the cakes – a bride atop a pink frosted cake, a groom atop a blue one – both are at a rather tipsy angle. She is not yet five but can pretty much make fairy cakes on her own now, thanks to hours spent with Marjorie in the kitchen ever since she was able to stand by herself. My contribution has been to decorate the garden, the place that brought Mack here in the first place. It is looking magical with fairy lights and lanterns in all of the trees, and posies of flowers in jam jars set on the old wooden table under the gazebo that Mack constructed a few years earlier. As I sit at the table, watching Mack wiping pink icing from Marjorie's lip before bending forward to kiss her, I can't help but think of the journey that brought him to us.

When I first arrived at the townhouse, this long and narrow garden had been an overgrown wilderness. Marjorie admitted that, whilst caring for her mother, she'd had little time or inclination for it, apart from the south-facing patio area by the kitchen doors where she would wheel her mother out to sit in the sunshine. The rest of the garden had been left to nature, with overgrown bushes that had been taken over by brambles and a large cherry blossom tree whose beauty was hidden amongst the ugly weeds and thistles. It needed brute force to tackle it.

"Mary is already trying to walk," Marjorie had said one day, when Mary was about nine or ten months old. "I think she is going to skip the crawling stage, you know; she needs somewhere safe to play – God only knows what is lurking in all that undergrowth! I'll look into hiring a gardener."

My anxiety levels had risen sharply at the thought of a stranger coming to the house, with all of the secrets that I had brought into it. And then, that evening as I was putting some clothes away, I came across the copy of the *Big Issue* that had brought me here, and the gloves that the *Big Issue* seller, Mack, had given me, and it felt like a sign. I remembered how I hadn't wanted to leave Mack's presence that day, after he'd given me the magazine, the instinctive feeling I'd had of feeling secure around him, and I wondered if maybe he could be the answer and I floated the idea to Marjorie.

"Well, it's thanks to that man that you arrived at my door, Dawn, so if you can find him, and he agrees, I can't see why not," Marjorie had said. I think it also appealed to her philanthropic side, the thought of getting the help you need from someone who could do with a helping hand themselves.

And so I had forced myself to brave the outside world and had made my way back to Victoria Railway Station, not knowing whether he would be there or not. I knew that *Big Issue* sellers tend to work from regular patches, but it had been over a year since I had seen him there and anything could have happened in that time. It had been an unseasonably hot spring day, so different to the bitingly cold day of when I had first arrived, and I wore a peaked cap on my head to protect myself – not from the sun but from recognition. To my relief, Mack had still been there; it had taken me a second to recognise him, his hulk-like frame diminished slightly without the heavy duffle coat that I had remembered him wearing, although even without it he was still imposing in stature. He was wearing a faded khaki T-shirt, and without his beanie I could see his thick brown hair was dappled with the onset of grey, matching the lightly greying stubble over his chin. I stood and watched him for a while, and as he smiled and chatted with a couple of elderly ladies, making them laugh, I just knew my instincts about him had been right and I walked over to him. Mack had looked at me, his startlingly blue eyes pondering me as he tried to process where he'd seen me before. Before I had time to say anything, his eyes widened as his brain appeared to hit its target, and he smiled.

"Jackanory!" he said, pointing as if in affirmation. "My, you look better than the last time I saw you, lass!"

I didn't bother with small talk; I waded straight in with the proposal, and when I had finished Mack was silently rubbing the stubble on his chin with his thumb and index finger, a quizzical expression on his face. He'd looked directly at me for a few seconds, those clear blue eyes scanning mine, trying to work out if there was a catch, and then he simply shrugged and said, "Aye, why not? I'll come and take a look."

I walked away, leaving him with a piece of paper carrying Marjorie's address, and taking away an overwhelming sense of relief.

Mack had turned up at the townhouse the following day and Marjorie showed him the garden. He wasn't fazed in the slightest and had seemed keen and enthusiastic as he talked about how he would tackle it. As I was feeding Mary in her high chair in the kitchen, I remember watching them animatedly discussing planting and landscaping and vegetable patches. It was impossible to miss the chemistry between them, with Marjorie playing with her hair like a teenager, sneaking glances up at Mack when she thought he wasn't looking. Mack had been bolder, more obvious, with the way he looked and smiled at Marjorie.

"Well, Shrimp," I'd said to my daughter, "it looks like Mack may be hanging around for a while." Mary blew a raspberry in response, sending globs of banana yoghurt flying my way.

Marjorie ended up offering Mack a live-in gardening and general handyman position for the foreseeable future, which he happily accepted. He gave up his pitch by Victoria Station and the room at the homeless hostel he was living in, and took up residence in a room on the top floor of the townhouse, bringing with him an old, scuffed canvas duffel bag containing the few belongings that he possessed. It would be a while before he trusted us enough to tell us his story, and we did not pry, although it was hard seeing the heavy weight of sadness pressing down on him when he thought no one was looking.

Marjorie and Mack spent hours together in that garden. Marjorie wasn't averse to a bit of hard labour, it turned out, and it was fun to see her in old jeans and wellies with mud splattered across her face and scratches up her arms. There was a lot of laughter ringing out across the garden and good-natured arguments about what should be done. Then, one day, I was playing with Mary and suddenly noticed that everything seemed quiet. The laughter and banter had become "white noise" for so long that I no longer really noticed it anymore, until it stopped. Curious, I walked to the patio with Mary in my arms and that's when I saw them kissing, Mack's hand cupping Marjorie's cheek. It just looked so right, so natural, although to this day I have never mentioned what I had seen – I wanted that moment to belong to them. They had been standing underneath the magnificent cherry blossom tree, which was in full bloom, the beautiful pink flowers hovering like confetti waiting to fall. I love that this is where they shared their first kiss, under a tree that symbolises the transient beauty of life; a tree that blooms so briefly it serves to remind us that we must be present in the moment to capture the beauty, or we will miss it altogether.

"Look, Mummy!" It is Mary jolting me back to the here and now. She has the bride and groom figurines in her hand. "Look, it's Nana Marjorie and Mack, they are kissing." She has forced their plastic faces together and is making a lip-smacking sound that makes me laugh.

"Why don't you place them under Lucy's rose bush?" I say to Mary. "She would love that." Now Mary is skipping across the garden to Lucy's memorial and places the figurines alongside the wind spinners and fairies that have already found a home there. It had been Marjorie's idea to create a memory garden in honour of Mack's daughter, who died when she was ten. She chose the rose bush as it bore the same name as his daughter, Lucy, and Mack often sits beside it in quiet contemplation. Lucy would have been twenty-seven now, almost the same age as me, and I think that is why Mack is so protective of me.

We have all eaten our fill now, the champagne is flowing well, loosening everyone up, and I put some music on. The intermittent clouds from earlier have dissipated, and the early evening sun is keeping us warm and adding to the good spirits in the way only sun can. Caitlin is flirting with Philip, who was widowed a few years ago – he is seventy-five and his wife was his first and only love. You can see he is surprised and a little bit flustered, which is adding to the amusement of Mack and Marjorie, who keep elbowing each other and side-nodding in Philip and Caitlin's direction.

"Dance with me, Mummy!" Mary commands and I obey, bending over and grabbing her tiny little hands in mine as we twist and turn and jump to the music, Mary leading the dance moves. I feel safe and relaxed with all of the people I love and trust around me – it is a glorious feeling, until, suddenly, I feel as if I am being watched again and my skin prickles despite the warm sun on my bare shoulders. I turn my head and instantly relax once more as I spot Robert from next door leaning on the garden wall, looking at me.

"Good moves, Dawn," he says with a grin. I know that Marjorie is not keen on him, but I have grown to quite like him. He is good-looking, maybe a bit overconfident, but there is something about him. I know he fancies me – Marjorie doesn't know this, but he has asked me out several times and, if things were different, I am sure I would have said yes. But things are what they are, and I am not prepared to start a relationship based on a lie, which means we make do with witty repartee instead.

"Why, thank you!" I reply to him, with a hint of mockery. "But then, as an estate agent, I would expect you to recognise good moves when you spot them, Robert."

He laughs, his way of accepting defeat in the wordplay stakes.

"You really are like a dog with two dicks around my Dawny, Robert. Haven't you realised yet that she is way above your league?"

"Marjorie!" I shout at her, putting my hands over Mary's ears. Although I find it funny, I am actually shocked at her language and even more shocked that she has obviously known for some time that Robert has a thing for me. The way she called me "her"

Dawny isn't lost on me either, and I love her more than ever in this madcap moment.

"Oops," she says, bringing her hand to her mouth as if to push the words back in, or maybe to stop more coming out. "Nana Marjorie is sorry, Mary girl. I think I'm a little squiffy! Did I really just say that awful word? Hic."

Mack's influence on her is clear, and we all laugh. Mack invites Robert over, winking at me as he does so, and I shake my head mouthing "no" but it is too late, the words are out and the invitation has already been accepted.

But, before Robert manages to get here, there is a loud knock at the door, and it turns out I was right to be afraid after all.

CHAPTER 7

Benedict

I am sitting at a table seat on the train from Hampstead to Paddington and I can see I have caught the eye of the attractive, well-dressed woman sitting opposite me. She is staring at me, although not directly, preferring instead to do it secretly by admiring my reflection in the train window. I do the same back, and our reflected eyes meet in that see-through, parallel universe beyond the glass. She quickly averts her gaze, embarrassed at having been caught out, and busies herself by looking in her bag for some fictional item. For a second, I imagine undressing her and fucking her, wondering what kind of noises she would make as I take control of her, until my mind is drawn back to Jeannie, the reason I am here on this train.

I close my eyes; the gentle hum and clack of the train is helping to calm my impatience and I focus my attention on how I am going deal with seeing her again. I have waited five years for this moment – five years of bridled anger and frustration, of *humiliation* – and, although I know I should have waited, gathered more information and prepared, I have done the one thing I have built a career on *not* doing – I have acted impulsively and am making my way to her having no clear, thought-out strategy. She has been an itch I cannot scratch for so long that the temptation to just drop everything and go to her was too much. I hate how she has reduced me to this, to the same undisciplined, primitive level of the people I have to defend on a daily basis.

Not a day has gone by that I haven't thought about her. Although it has been a long time coming, I never doubted for a minute that this day *would* come – not since the Home Office contacted me a few weeks after she went missing.

"I am happy to tell you that Jeannie is on our list of survivors," the young male voice informed me. "She used her passport to return to the UK four days ago."

When I asked whether he had any information about her whereabouts after landing, he hesitated and I could sense he was considering how to answer my question without compromising his professional constraints.

"That's all the information I can give you, sir. No doubt she will be in contact with you soon. You could check with family and friends in the UK, or local hospitals – maybe she felt the need for medical help when she returned."

I didn't bother replying to his patronising attempt at placating me, I simply put the phone down before he had even finished the last word. I learned long ago that there is no point in arguing with a fool; there is no satisfaction to be gained in making an idiot look even more of an idiot. I never told anyone of the truth that I'd learned in that call – in fact, I let everyone believe that Jeannie was among the missing, presumed dead, rather than suffer the ignominy of having to explain the truth. I didn't even tell Charlotte the truth; I didn't want her to think that Jeannie had somehow triumphed in any way. I remember Charlotte screaming at me, "What do you mean, missing presumed dead? I don't understand! Is she missing, or is she dead? How can she be both?" Her mind beginning its downward spiral.

I admit that over the years I became obsessed with finding Jeannie – there was no way I was letting that bitch get away with thinking she had outwitted me. It occurs to me now, though, that there will be some explaining to do once it is known that she has resurfaced, although I will think of a suitable way of dealing with that when the moment comes.

Whilst I obsessed, Charlotte steadily regressed, and these days she is little more than a junkie on prescription medication. She functions, but in the way a robot might, reacting to commands rather than thinking for herself. She has a daily routine that she follows with almost military precision, and generally only speaks when spoken to. Sometimes I hit her, just to remind us both that she's still alive, not that I think she cares whether she is alive or dead anymore. She is of little use to me now except as a release for my frustrations – although, to be honest, she is nothing more than a blow-up doll in bed, practically motionless, her face blank. Still, she lets me do whatever I want to her without complaining most of the time.

There are times, though, that I am tired of Charlotte's submissiveness, tired of being in control, tired of the power I exert every single day. Sometimes I need to let go, to recharge, and for that I have a mistress. By mistress, I don't mean I am having an affair – I have tried that and it becomes messy when the stupid fools fall in love with me and start demanding things that are never going to happen. One affair, though, opened my eyes to something different, a world where I didn't need to be in control. She was a French law student, sexually liberated in the way the French often are. I don't remember her name, but I remember vividly the shock of how turned on I felt when out of the blue she told me to shut up, slapped my face and used handcuffs to restrain me. She worked her way over my body, inflicting a mixture of pleasure and pain, constantly bringing me close to a climax before withdrawing, leaving me begging her not to stop. My body felt as if it was on fire, aching and throbbing with intensity, and when I finally orgasmed it was like nothing I had ever experienced before. The affair didn't last long – like all the others, she thought she meant something to me, that she was somehow *special*, and so I reluctantly had to dismiss her, both personally and professionally. But by then I was hooked on the liberating sex she had introduced me to, and so I did some research and found a discreet agency that specialised in female domination, which I now visit when I need to let go; it means I get what I need without the emotional price-tag.

An unintelligible announcement alerts me to the fact that we are now pulling into Paddington Station. I open my eyes to see the attractive woman opposite me getting up in readiness to disembark. I sense she is furtively trying to see if I am watching her, but I don't bother; my interest in her waned almost as soon as it had peaked. Instead, I am concentrating on the address in my hand – the address of where Jeannie has been living – *hiding* – all these years. It is a good address in a good part of London; I am almost impressed with her. The address was given to me by the private investigator that I hired when I first found out that she was alive. For nearly five years she has somehow managed to remain under the radar with no trace of her existence: no bank accounts, no electoral register, no benefits being claimed – it was as if she had simply vanished off the face of the earth. Still, I paid him to keep checking regularly, knowing that she would have to surface sometime; then, bingo, a hit at the National Archives.

Deed polls are transferred to the National Archives after five years, when they become available to the public, and the PI's recent check showed that Jeannie had changed her name by deed poll to Dawn Kent five years ago. He gave me the details, including her address at that time, but he explained that he had not yet undertaken any other investigative work.

"Of course, it is possible that she doesn't even live at that address any longer," the PI had said when he realised that I intended to go there almost immediately. "At this stage it's just a lead – let me check it out first; that's what you're paying me to do."

But I was not prepared to wait. I have been doing that for far too long already. I don't want anything to spook her, anything to give her an excuse to run if she suspects she has been rumbled; after all, she has managed to evade me for all this time, although I hope she spent that time forever looking over her shoulder, waiting for this day to come. I want to look her squarely in the eyes and let her see the rage boiling within me. I want to see the fear when she realises that she will never be free of me; she belongs to me, and nobody walks away from me unless I let them. She will be coming home with me, of that I am certain – it is one of the reasons I chose to keep hold of Charlotte for all these years, knowing that I could use her as an extra bargaining chip for this very moment. Jeannie no doubt thought she was being clever, believing that, whilst I assumed that she was dead, her mother would be safe. All the power she thinks she wields will disappear when she sees me.

I've arrived at the street named on the piece of paper now. It is a smart terrace of townhouses, expensive, the sort of place I would happily live in; it irks me that she has lived in such comfort. Above me, the sun is about to start setting, bruising the stratus clouds purple and lowering the temperature a degree or so. I scan the number plaques until I find the one that I am looking for, then walk up a set of stone steps to a yellow door.

I think of how much I hate the colour yellow as I knock sharply on the door. It is the colour of cowardice, of betrayal and deceit.

CHAPTER 8

Marjorie

I answer the door to an extraordinarily handsome, middle-aged man. He has salt and pepper hair and hazel-green eyes that are almost hypnotic as they change colour with the light. Although beautiful, his eyes are disconcerting, and his stare feels as if it is demanding something of me, or taking something from me, or both. His eyes wander to my dress – the expression on his face feels like one of mockery and I suddenly feel slightly ridiculous, as if I am a grown woman playing dress-up rather than a bride on her wedding day. The fuzzy warmth of the champagne has gone, my subconscious recognising that I need to be sober for this, that I need clarity of thought. I know that the party is still going on in the garden, but all I can hear is the buzz of silence vibrating the air between this stranger and me. I feel like the prey in a wildlife documentary, my sensory organs on high alert to an unseen danger. The man hasn't spoken yet, but already I want to close the door in his face.

"I'm looking for Dawn," he says in a calm but demanding voice. He is smiling at me as he says it, but I notice the smile doesn't reach his eyes and I know that I am right to be afraid. I'm not just afraid; I panic, too – there is no reason for a complete stranger to know Dawn's name; something is seriously wrong.

"Sorry," I say, my heart thumping so hard it is in danger of jumping out of my chest, "there is no one called Dawn here."

But, even as I say it, I know that I have betrayed Dawn with the tremble in my voice and the tell-tale inability to look him in the eye; I never was a good liar. I attempt to close the door but the man places his foot in the threshold, and his hand on the door to prevent me. He has seen my lie as easily as if it were encased in Perspex.

"Don't fuck with me," he says in a dismissive tone and with a calmness in his voice that is at odds with the threat of the words. Those beautiful eyes have changed to the colour of steel blades and he propels himself forwards with ease, forcing the door into me so that I stagger backwards into the mahogany coat stand, which clatters to the tiled floor of the hallway. I want to scream, but for some reason I can't make a sound.

"Jeannie!" he shouts out with authority, his voice loud and resonant, and I am stunned for a second at the sound of that secret, forbidden name. "I know you're here; I just want to talk to you. You've left your mother hanging, Jeannie, *hanging*, not knowing if you are dead or alive. Do you have any idea what that has done to her?"

Mack has appeared now, his large, muscular frame filling the hallway and blocking some of the light. He looks at me, then to the coat stand, but doesn't say a word; instead, he charges at the stranger like an American football player, catching him off guard and slamming him up against the wall, holding him there. The man is tall and in good shape, but clearly no match for Mack's strength, and he doesn't try to resist him. He is physically powerless, but seems untroubled by this and places his hands up in the air in a mock-surrender pose, a look of defiance in his eyes.

"I only want to talk to Jeannie," he says to Mack, "then I'll leave."

"There is no Jeannie here, man." Mack is practically nose to nose with this man. "You've made a mistake. Now leave. Do you understand?"

"Everything alright?" It is Robert arrived from next door with a bottle of Moët in his hand, staring in surprise at the scene that he has walked into. I notice he has instinctively straightened himself up to make himself as tall as possible, although I am not sure what help he thinks he could be – he is not a fighter, that one.

"Everything's just fine, Rob." Mack doesn't take his eyes off of the stranger in his grasp as he says this. "Just a misunderstanding, isn't that right, mate?"

The man raises his eyebrows and shrugs, still arrogant despite his restraint. Then I see his attention shift to over Mack's shoulder as he appears to notice some framed photos on the far wall ahead of him. He goes still for a moment, detached almost, then his demeanour changes and he is compliant.

"Yes," he says, nodding slowly as he brings his attention back to Mack. "Yes. It's all been a mistake. I'll leave."

Mack loosens his grip on him and lets him walk towards the door. As he passes me, he looks beyond me to the floor and the fallen coat stand, and I notice his gaze hover on Mary's small pink anorak that has been cast adrift from the stand. I look up at the pictures on the wall – the largest of the group is a recent photo of Mary in her new school uniform – and a shiver runs through me that I am certain has nothing to do with the cooling evening air drifting in from the open door.

CHAPTER 9

Benedict

I am filled with it all sorts of emotions as I make my way down the steps and back onto the street. I am enraged at having been unexpectedly manhandled by that Neanderthal – I am big, but he was enormous and, although I had expected to be challenged in some way, I didn't expect *that*. But rage is an instinctive emotion, and to remain in that emotional state would mean I am weak, that my impulses are stronger than my cognitive thought and reasoning, and that is not the case. That man may have physical strength on his side but I have a mental prowess that makes me a ninja-fucking-warrior compared to him. I regained my composure without anyone noticing I had lost it in the first place, although that doesn't mean that the rage isn't still there – it is banked, that's all, ready to be spent later when the moment is right.

My actions are usually measured and premeditated, which is why it is so surprising, even to me, that I made my way here without doing my research first. If I had done so, I would have been more prepared – not just for the physical tackle that I have just endured but for the curveball of the photograph hanging on the wall. It was the colour of the child's hair that drew me to the photo; less than 2% of the world's population have red hair, thanks to a recessive gene that needs to be present in both parents. My hair is naturally dark brown, like my father's was, but my mother's hair was red, which means she will have passed the recessive gene on to me. And so, when I saw the freckled face staring down from the wall, something stirred in my subconscious and it all started to make sense: why Jeannie disappeared, why she abandoned her mother. She wasn't just hiding herself from me; she was hiding my *daughter*. The revelation has stunned me, and, even though I haven't achieved what I came here to do – I haven't even set eyes on Jeannie, let alone brought her home – I know that I need to retreat to consider my next move carefully.

It is approaching dusk now as I walk towards the railway station and, whilst the day prepares for bed, the streetlamps are waking up for their night shift. Their gradual illumination is analogous with what is happening in my mind as I think about what this all means. The little pink coat flashes into my thoughts: it was the right size to fit a child of about five and so the timeline would fit. I am a father, I think to myself, and a strange feeling inhabits me, a feeling I am unfamiliar with. I've never wanted children. I tolerated Jeannie as she came as a package with Charlotte and had been relatively easy to control, but I've always thought of children as pointless adumbrations. Now it appears that I have a child of my own, I feel curious. I made her, she is part of me – it feels like a form of self-preservation, knowing that all I have achieved, all that I am, has been passed on through my genes.

I might not have set eyes on Jeannie tonight, but I know she was there, listening as she hid in her burrow with her cub. Not that she really matters quite so much anymore – Jeannie feels less important than she did just an hour ago; there is someone far more significant for me to focus my attention on than her now. And, besides, I find it gratifying that Jeannie will soon know exactly how it feels to have something that belongs to you arbitrarily taken away.

CHAPTER 10

Benedict

It's been nearly a week since I saw the photograph on the wall and the little pink coat on the floor, nearly a week since I realised that I have a daughter. The discovery has been unsettling and I feel I need to see the child before deciding on my next course of action, so I have been travelling to the child's school each morning, standing at a safe distance each day to survey the comings and goings at the school gates. Until today, there has been no sign of the child, but a car has just pulled up and I can see the Neanderthal that attacked me is driving.

The first person to emerge from the car is the Neanderthal, who I now know is called Mack, followed by a young woman who I realise must be Jeannie. It is my first sight of Jeannie in five years and my stomach does an involuntary lurch. My immediate thought is that she has lost weight – not much, but definitely a little slimmer than I remember. Something stirs in me as I remember her young, soft curves, and I realise that I have not stopped thinking about her as an eighteen-year-old; I'd forgotten that she would be older, that time and running may have changed her.

Jeannie's hair is in a ponytail, longer than it used to be, and dyed blonde, cheapening her. Her demeanour is smaller, diminutive, afraid. She is wearing a baseball cap that is pulled low and covers most of her face so I cannot see the fear I know will be showing there. That's a shame. I would have liked to see the strain the years will have had on her. Jeannie opens the back door of the car and the child gets out. She holds onto Jeannie's hand, then reaches for Mack's hand and begins skipping in between them. Her red hair is braided and she is wearing the school uniform of the prestigious primary school that she attends. It is a good school, there is no doubt about that, but still, it is not one that a child of mine should be attending; a child of mine should be at Thomas's Battersea, where the children of royalty and the elite go.

I watch as the three of them head inside the school building. Jeannie and Mack are gone for quite a while, and I know that they are probably speaking with the head, giving explicit instructions not to let anyone near the child. But that doesn't faze me. Why would it? There are no situations that I cannot charm and manipulate my way out of. I figure that, if it gives them a sense of security, then that can only work in my favour – when you feel more secure you subconsciously let your guard down, become more vulnerable. When Jeannie and Mack finally reappear, it looks as if Jeannie has been crying because Mack has his arm around her and seems to be comforting her. I have no doubt he is telling her not to worry, that everything will be OK, the stupid man no doubt believing his own fallacies.

I wait until Jeannie and Mack get into their car and drive off before making my way towards the school entrance. Inside, the pretty young girl on reception looks up routinely as I approach the desk, and I smile broadly at her, fixing my eyes on hers to command her attention. I immediately notice that her cheeks flush pink: despite the fact that I am probably twenty years her senior, it is abundantly clear that she is attracted to me. I glance at the receptionist's name badge.

"Hello, Sarah, how are you today?"

"I'm good, thank you, sir, how may I help you?" The colour in her cheeks deepens from pink to crimson, betraying her attempts at hiding her attraction to me.

After a short period of flirting and a concocted, innocuous story that she readily accepts, Sarah happily accesses Mary's records for me and reads out a recent report that reveals that my daughter is an exceptionally bright child. That comes as no surprise – she carries my genes after all – but I needed to be sure before deciding on what to do next. I leave with the name of Mary's form tutor – Serena Barclay – on a headed compliment slip, just in case I need to speak with her at some point. I make sure that I brush Sarah's fingers with mine as I take the slip from her hand and thank her, allowing my touch and eye contact to linger a second or two longer than is necessary. It is always wise to leave the door open a crack – you never know when someone could prove useful in the future.

By the time I take the train back to Hampshire, I have made my decision that Mary should be with me. She should be in an environment that befits her, where I can nurture her intelligence. The thought of her mind being contaminated and ruined by Jeannie and her nescient crew is, quite frankly, intolerable and by the time I return home I find myself in a troubled mood. As I enter my house, I notice the red light blinking on the telephone in the hall and a feeling of irritation runs through me that Charlotte has not been answering the phone. I make a mental note to consider adjusting the dose of medication I give her each day – she is spending far too much time sleeping and it is having a detrimental effect on the running of the house. I press "play" and skip through a couple of messages that are no more than the click of a phone being put down, until the final message reveals the voice of my private investigator asking me to phone him as he has some interesting information on Mack that might prove useful.

I phone the PI, and the information he gives me is just what I need. Tomorrow I will send a letter to Jeannie, informing her of my intention to apply to the courts for an enforced DNA test. I have no doubt that the information I hold discrediting Mack will be effective, that I will have no problem in gaining eventual custody of my own daughter. No court in the land would consider that halfway house, with a self-serving runaway and a child-killing ex-offender, to be a better environment for Mary than with me.

CHAPTER 11

Dawn

It has been a month since Marjorie and Mack's wedding and I still shiver uncontrollably when I think about that knock on the door and the shock of hearing that deep baritone voice slicing into me with the name that I buried years ago.

"You've left your mother hanging, Jeannie, hanging, not knowing if you are dead or alive. Do you have any idea what that has done to her?"

On hearing those words I instinctively pulled Mary to me, covering her ears and wishing that I had more hands so that I could cover my own ears as well. Those words still resonate on my conscience. As a mother, I cannot imagine the horror of not knowing what has happened to your child; I haven't allowed myself to think about the suffering I may have caused. My sole priority has been Mary – protecting her, making sure she is safe and happy and has a better life than the one she would have had if I hadn't made the decision I did. Isn't that what a mother is supposed to do? Protect at any cost? What kind of a mother doesn't do that?

The tsunami had been my Genesis flood, wiping out my noxious past and allowing me to regenerate. Only now it feels like a storm has whipped up the waves of the past, churning up secrets in the sand that haven't been buried long enough to be rendered harmless yet and I am desperately trying to shovel the sand back over them. I am *Dawn*, I keep telling myself. Mary's mother. Surrogate daughter to Marjorie and Mack. I refuse to be anyone else.

After the drama in the hallway ended, Mack and Marjorie returned to the garden, with Robert trailing behind them. I don't think they realised Robert was still there and both looked shocked when his voice broke the stunned silence in the garden.

"What the hell just happened in there?" he asked. "Who was that man? Who's Jeannie?"

The questions were uncomfortable and I could see Mack and Marjorie squirm, the truth so long hidden that they no longer knew how to handle questions about it. Marjorie tried to come up with an explanation, but there was really nothing feasible she could say that didn't sound like the cock-and-bull story it really was. It was painful listening to her try and I knew I needed to save her from herself.

"It's OK, Marjorie," I said softly. "Let me do this. Alone." For some reason I trusted Robert and besides, the little he already knew at that point was already too much to be ignored. Marjorie looked unsure, but I could see the resignation in her eyes as she looked at the determination in mine, so she and Mack agreed to take Mary to bed with the promise of a story. As Mack lifted Mary on to his shoulders, my little girl tried to make sense of what had just happened.

"Don't be scared, Grampy Mack, our house is made of bricks so the bad man can't blow the door down."

"Aye, pet, that's right, so you don't need to be worrying that pretty little head of yours." I heard the emotion in Mack's voice as he replied to my brave and wonderful little girl.

"But maybe we should put a cauldron of water in the fire in case he tries to come down the chimney!" Mary concluded as she nodded sagely to herself.

"Ah, what a great idea, Mary, you're a proper clever lass, you are. I'll be sure to do that," Mack replied, squeezing her legs reassuringly.

Thank God for the *Three Little Pigs*, I thought as I heard this exchange. How easy it is to forget that fairy tales are more than just stories; they are allegories helping our children make sense of the world. Never again will I sigh in protest at being asked to read that book for the umpteenth time!

Before Mack and Marjorie walked away with Mary, Caitlin and Philip said their sober goodbyes.

"Come and see me tomorrow, Dawn – you too, Marjorie – we need to talk about this." Philip had reverted from friend to solicitor and, although I never wanted to think about it ever again, let alone talk about it, I knew there was no choice. As everyone left the garden, I felt so sad that such a beautiful day had to end in that way because of me and I struggled to keep my tears at bay. But it was not the time for tears; it was a time to be strong. It still is.

Once we were alone, Robert and I made our way to the cherry tree. Mack had constructed a circular bench around its trunk a couple of years ago, and Robert and I sat there in continued silence for a few seconds as we breathed in the faint scent of lilac and rose and vanilla from the blossom. The dusk light had been beautiful but had brought with it a chill in the air, and Robert commented on my goosebumps, before removing his jacket and placing it around my shoulders. The unopened bottle of champagne was sitting in between us, and I reached out for it and opened it. Releasing the cork seemed symbolic. We hadn't brought glasses with us, so instead we'd swigged directly from the bottle, taking it in turns to do so, as Robert waited patiently for his explanation. Eventually I took a deep breath.

"I'm not who you think I am," I began, before proceeding to tell him my story. I told him about the abusive control; about the abject, paralysing fear; about how, when I saw an opportunity to run, to disappear, I had taken it.

"Wow," was all Robert could manage to say when I finished. The moon had inhabited the sky by then, poking out behind some darkened wispy clouds, and I looked up at that moon and thought that it represented me, partially exposed, partially hidden.

"You can't ever tell anyone. Promise me," I said to him, my voice raised and trembling for the first time. Although I am not quite sure why that bothered me so much now that the past had already come knocking. I guess hiding is a hard habit to break. Robert tipped my chin up so that I could see the expression in his eyes, one that wordlessly confirmed to me that I could trust him. He held my gaze for a second before a smile broke across his face, the same lopsided grin I had seen him use on me many times, right before he was about to say something flirty and witty.

"The thing is, Dawn," he said with devilment in his voice, "I might need some assistance with that. You might need to help me keep my mouth occupied – just to be sure I can't let anything slip out, by accident, like."

He had managed the impossible – to make me laugh in the face of this nightmare – and as he leaned in, I accepted his kiss readily, a little bit of light amongst the dark. His kiss was sweet and undemanding, and sparked up those little nerve endings that had been sleeping under my skin for too long. When we had finished our kiss, Robert pulled me close to him as he leaned back against the trunk of the cherry tree, and I rested my head on his shoulder and closed my eyes, a rare feeling of peace radiating through me, rendering me sleepy.

"You're a warrior, Dawn," he said, kissing the top of my head. "A fighter and a survivor. Never forget that."

When the letter arrived in the post today, Robert's words to me that night were the first thing I thought of.

"I am a warrior. A fighter. A survivor," I say over and over to myself in an attempt to stop myself from falling apart.

CHAPTER 12

Dawn

After the letter arrived a couple of weeks ago, I burst into Philip's house, standing in front of him with the letter burning into my hand. Philip looked shocked at the sight of me and seemed to know instinctively that something was dreadfully wrong.

"What on earth has happened? You are as white as a sheet, Dawn. And what have you done to your hair?"

Changing my appearance is a habit I grew out of a few years ago, when I finally started to feel more secure, but, since Benedict turned up at the townhouse, my psychological need to go to ground has resurfaced, as has the box of hair dye. The only thing stopping me from running has been Mack.

"Secrets are like shadows, Dawn," Mack said. "They never go away. You can't outrun them, pet, you can only keep yourself in the dark corners where the sun will never reach you. You need to stay and find a way to make this go away. For Mary's sake, if not your own."

So, I agreed to do nothing for the time being, although I refused to leave the house. In the end, it was decided that Mary should continue to go to school but on condition that Mack would take her and pick her up. I broke my rule of not leaving the house to go with them on the first day and spoke to the school, giving them explicit instructions that no one except Mack was authorised to collect her. I think we had all hoped that Mack's physical intervention the night of the wedding would have been enough to keep that man away, but the truth is none of us really believed that it would. There had been something Machiavellian about him – he smelt fear, and fear was what fed him.

I always feared Benedict would resurface, but the manner in which he did so, the arrival of the letter, was a shock. By the time I reached Philip, I was shaking so hard that I was afraid to open my mouth to talk in case my teeth fell out.

"This has just arrived," I managed to say eventually, shakily handing him the envelope addressed to: *Dawn Kent, formally known as Jeannie Eleanor Sutcliffe.*

I watched as he opened the envelope, his eyes darting over the contents inside as he learned that Benedict had applied for a court order seeking acknowledgement of paternity of Mary, and I was being ordered to comply with a request for a legal DNA test. Even more disturbing was the accompanying letter from Benedict outlining his intent to seek custody of Mary on the grounds that the "environment in which she is living is putting her at risk of harm". To support this, he enclosed recent photographs of Mack driving Mary to her school, a copy of a court transcript for Mack's sentencing in connection with his conviction for death by careless driving whilst under the influence of alcohol, and some unfavourable local newspaper articles that covered his trial.

I already knew about Mack, of course, as did Marjorie and Philip, but it was still shocking to see it laid out in black and white like that. Innocent or guilty, there is no in-between in the eyes of the law – even less so in the self-righteous, often hypocritical, glare of the general public. But the truth is that sometimes there is a middle ground, a "guilty but…" scenario, that blunts the edges. Mack is definitely in that category, in my opinion at least. The short, shocking, "guilty" version is that Mack had consumed alcohol at a family party before driving his family home the same evening. There was a collision with another vehicle that resulted in his young daughter, Lucy, dying at the scene and his wife sustaining head injuries that left her in a coma for a week. The occupants of the other car sustained injuries that were serious but not life-threatening. Mack suffered broken ribs and lacerations. A breath test found Mack to be over the legal drink-drive limit and he was prosecuted and convicted of causing death by careless driving whilst under the influence of alcohol.

The "guilty but…" version is that the party, and accident, happened in Scotland, where the drink-drive limit is lower than in England, a fact Mack had been unaware of. He had been driving back to Northumberland, just over the Anglo-Scottish border, and had the accident happened there, in England, he would have been under the drink-drive limit according to English law. Furthermore, the accident itself was arguably caused by the driver of the other car, who had come out of a side junction into the path of Mack's car. Unfortunately, however, at the time of the collision Mack had been momentarily distracted by Lucy in the back seat, a fact he'd admitted to, and had he not been distracted he might have had time to avoid the collision, so by definition he was driving carelessly. How many people have been distracted by something whilst driving? How many have dodged that particular bullet, completely oblivious to the potential consequences?

Mack had been sentenced to three years and served eighteen months of that sentence, during which time his wife filed for divorce. When he was released, he had nothing left: no family, no job, no home, just a heart filled with grief, guilt and self-loathing. He drifted and drank to forget until, one day (his words), "I just woke up and realised that I had a duty to live my life better. For

Lucy, who had been denied the opportunity to live any kind of life at all." Mack cleaned himself up, got a room in a hostel and started selling the *Big Issue*. He had no dreams or ambitions as such; he was just living each day as it came. It was the beginning of a long road to acceptance, and one that ultimately led him to me and Marjorie and the unconventional family that we have become.

Benedict's quest to be acknowledged as a father, his flawed notion that blood is somehow thicker than water, made me think about Mack, Marjorie and me, about how incomplete we are when we stand alone, and how whole we are together; about what it truly means to be a family. I hovered over Philip's shoulder, re-reading the letter with him.

"What does that bit mean?" I asked, pointing to a sentence on the page that read *"...If you refuse to provide the samples required for the DNA test, the Court would likely draw an adverse inference against your case."*

"That means the court is likely to rule in Benedict's favour in the absence of concrete evidence – he could be legally acknowledged as Mary's father if you refuse the test. I'm afraid it is a very real possibility." I could hear the trepidation in Philip's voice. "Benedict Sutcliffe is a barrister, a QC no less, and highly respected in his field. He holds a very powerful position."

Philip took off his reading glasses and rubbed the two small welts left on each side of the bridge of his nose. His eyes were closed as he gathered his thoughts. "He has done his homework and clearly knows a lot, but he doesn't know everything," he said eventually. "Leave the letter with me so I can consider our next move. This is my fault and I'll put it right, Dawn."

Philip had tears in his eyes as he said this. He thought it was his fault, but it's not, it is mine for not listening, not being brave. When I first arrived at the townhouse five years ago, Marjorie had approached Philip to ask for his help. He had listened to my story, and his original thoughts were that I should just use the law to challenge the man that I feared so much.

"But if I do that he will know about my baby! You don't know him, what he's capable of!" I had cried. "It won't matter how long it takes; he will find me, find *us*. We will never be safe. He needs to believe I am dead; it's the only way!"

Philip could see how fragile I was at that moment in time, how fear had made me brittle, and he believed me when I said he was dangerous, that I feared for my life. Marjorie was certain that I would run if they didn't help me, and he later said that he had thought about his own daughter, how he would do anything to protect her, and how he realised I had no one to do that for me, no one except him and Marjorie. So, although he knew it wasn't the right thing to do, he agreed to help me to stay under the radar in the hope that at some point I would find the strength to face up to my past.

In the end, it was decided that I would keep a low profile, change my name by deed poll and live with Marjorie, who would support me and the baby. Changing my name by deed poll would enable me to use my new name on the baby's birth certificate when it was born, as this document alone is enough for registering a birth. Marjorie was wealthy and relished a ready-made family, so she was happy to fully support me financially. This meant that there was no need for me to put my true identity at risk by having to use a National Insurance number to apply for anything that could be used to trace me.

Once the deed poll had been signed and witnessed, Philip had left it for his secretary, Harriet, to file. Harriet was young, a new employee who was eager to impress and show her initiative. She had been told that the deed poll was being done as a favour for a friend, that no payment was required, and she simply assumed that Philip would want it enrolled. By enrolling it, she effectively made it available to public records after five years, and Philip said he could only assume that this is why Benedict had turned up now, five years later.

"My failure to make my instructions clear to Harriet was a

small pebble in the pond all those years ago, the ripples from which have only just reached the shore. It is my fault, and I need to redress it."

After I left Philip with Benedict's letter, he decided to call an old associate of his, Doug, a private investigator who he had used in the past to help him gather evidence for cases. His specialty was surveillance and he agreed to tail Benedict for a while – Philip wanted to make sure he wasn't planning another uninvited visit, to make sure Mary and I were safe, but also to see if there was anything at all that he did that could prove useful to us. Philip wasn't expecting much – a man like Benedict is usually good at covering his tracks; he has too much to lose not to – but this morning he received a phone call from Doug, followed by a fax of the photographs he had taken and a transcript of a conversation between Doug and a certain dominatrix – a conversation Doug had taped and kept in his files. It had cost him a fair chunk of money to get close enough to have that conversation, but that didn't matter. Philip was excited by this stroke of luck and called me and Marjorie this morning to ask him to come see him.

As we sit at his desk in his home office, Philip goes to my file to remove the other piece of evidence that he holds that he says he hopes will be enough to stem the tide. He pulls out the old water-damaged letter that has sat there since Marjorie gave it to him, when she first asked if he could help me five years ago. I take a sharp intake of breath as I see the word "Mum" on the envelope and feel sick as I remember it. Philip has always said he understands why the letter was never posted. It is the type of letter that you would think long and hard about sending; the ramifications of its contents are far-reaching. When a letter like that is sent, there is no going back, he says. When I returned to the UK, I made the decision not to send it; it would have been a red flag, a reason for someone to come looking. Now, Philip says, if we play this right, he is hoping it will be a reason for someone to stay away.

Philip carefully photocopies the letter before placing it in an envelope with his own typed reply to Benedict.

"It took me a while to type," he says with a small smile. "My fingers are by no stretch of the imagination fluent on a keyboard, and since retiring I have no secretary to do this for me any longer. Not that I would have entrusted this to anyone else; it is too important. It's not exactly my usual style, either."

He lets me read his reply and I think I understand what he means – the tone of his letter is clearly threatening, or rather thinly veiled blackmail to match the tone of Benedict's.

"I have done my utmost to make it watertight, but I can't help but feel like we are playing a game of chess. I only hope that my reply, my move, is checkmate. If it is, it will be a smothered mate, Benedict's ability to move forward blocked by his own deeds." Philip licks the envelope to seal it, then places a stamp on it.

We are all praying that he has done enough.

CHAPTER 13

Dawn

I am in a raging torrent, holding on as tightly as I can to Mary. The current is so powerful I am struggling to keep our heads above the water as it forces us on a terrifying helter-skelter journey. We are less than a metre from land and safety and, as we hurtle past, I see Marjorie and Mack. They are shouting, although I cannot hear them above the roar of the water. They are reaching out their hands for me to grab, but I cannot reach for them without letting go of Mary; their help is futile. Suddenly and without warning, our relentless momentum stops as I become snagged onto a piece of metal that is jutting out from the side of a building. The force of stopping is sudden and violent and nearly wrenches Mary from my grip, but somehow I manage to keep hold of her as we are pulverised by the continuing power of the water's flow. Then I spot a shadowy figure standing on top of the building watching us, and I scream at him to help us, to save Mary. To my relief, the man reacts to my pleas and dives calmly and gracefully into the water. For a second, he disappears beneath the surface before emerging in front of us, standing upright and still, unaffected by the fast-paced flow of water that rushes around him as if he is anchored there. I see his face for the first time and my relief instantly turns to terror. I start to grab and tear at the fabric that has me hooked on to the piece of metal, in a desperate attempt to free us from this imminent danger, but it is of no use: I am stuck fast. He reaches out and effortlessly takes Mary from me with one hand, and then places his other hand on my head, pushing me under the water. As he holds me there, I can hear Mary's voice screaming for me – she sounds as if she is in a tunnel, far away – and I struggle until my lungs feel as though they are going to explode and little bursts of light, like stars, start to pulse in front of my eyes.

And then, suddenly, somehow, my head is back above the water and I am gasping for breath.

It takes me a couple of seconds for my brain to realise that I am now awake, and to separate my dream of drowning to the very real panic attack I am having. Whilst trying to calm myself, I reach for the paper bag that I keep beside my bed and breathe slowly in and out until my breathing returns to normal. I look at my bedside clock, which glows an eerie green in the coal-black darkness of the room, but I already know what it will say – I wake the same time every morning: it is 3am, just as I knew it would be.

It has been a couple of months since Philip sent his reply to Benedict and, although we have heard nothing in response from him, I still live with the fear that there will be a reprisal of some sort. Every single day I feel like I am waiting for an unexploded bomb to go off. It doesn't help that each time I go to bed my sleep is perforated with dreams of Mary being taken away from me. Philip tells me not to worry; if Benedict was going to do anything, he would have done it before now. Philip's strategy was to bank on humiliation being enough to keep him away from us – he believes that a man like Benedict would never risk losing face, that the threat of sending the information we hold to the tabloid newspapers, of showing the world what kind of man he really is, will be enough. A scandal burns at a fast pace and he would find himself fighting a fire with a cup of water. Even if he did somehow manage to extinguish the flames, the smell of smoke lingers for a long time afterwards and it would cause him irreparable damage, Philip says.

I get what Philip is saying, I really do. It makes sense. I know I am being irrational; I know that whatever happens, Benedict would never be given any rights to Mary. But what if the thought of being a father makes him unpredictable? What if he decides instead to just take her and run, to disappear? I managed to hide for five years – what if he decides to do the same with Mary? Snatch her just when we think we are safe, when we least expect it. Like now. I know that the only way to really stop Benedict, to make him go away forever, would be to step outside of my self-imposed prison and personally face him. But I can't – I am too afraid that it would expose me to an even greater danger.

Along with the crippling anxiety I feel daily, I cannot help but feel sick with guilt and worry that Philip included a copy of the letter that made it back from Sri Lanka with me. The letter wasn't ever supposed be sent – anyone who reads it can see that it was written as a personal catharsis, and part of me wishes I had just torn it up back then. I understand why Philip felt that it needed to be sent, of course I do. His goal was to keep Benedict away from me and Mary, and, although the photographs and transcripts of Benedict's liaisons with the dominatrix are damning and embarrassing, on their own they would never be enough to keep him away. No, a man as powerful as Benedict could easily find a way to explain or dismiss those in some way. At the end of the day, all they really do is expose his sexual predilection and, although it may humiliate him, it does nothing more than hint at the degenerate he really is. But the letter is different. The contents are damaging and powerful – it leaves the reader in no doubt as to his true nature. The consequences of it getting out could be far-reaching for him; even if he tried to refute all that it lays bare, the gold-plated reputation that he has spent years building up would almost certainly be burned away exposing the worthless base metal beneath it. Even though I recognised that the letter was the best armament in my defence against him, I was still upset when Philip told me that he was sending a copy of it to Benedict.

"Do you think he will show it to her?" I'd asked Philip as I ran my fingers across the words *Dear Mum*. Since the night of the wedding, I haven't been able to get Benedict's words, out of my head. *"You left your mother hanging, Jeannie, hanging..."*

"She wasn't supposed to see it," I say. "I don't want her to see it – she will have been through enough."

As a mother myself, I can only imagine the torture of having no closure, of not knowing for certain the fate of the child you gave birth to and loved in the best way you could. Of clinging on to hope with greasy fingertips, because hope is better than nothing. By denying her the truth, this is what I have put her through for five years, and I am struggling to forgive myself for that. I really don't want to cause her any more pain, and I know that the letter will rip her apart; how could it not?

"How can you even attempt to defend that woman, leave alone feel sorry for her?" Marjorie had interjected, her voice raised in an unusual display of anger. "You should not give her another thought, Dawn. A woman who allows those sorts of things to happen to her daughter, whatever the reason, does not deserve to be called a mother. She deserves every minute of any misery that she has had to endure, and then some."

But I believe it is more complicated than that, and find it difficult to judge her too harshly. Doing the right thing is not always as easy as it sounds; the truth is that she was a victim, too, and I can only imagine that her failures were born out of a deep psychological fear. Something I can identify with. Lying to yourself, refusing to acknowledge what is happening, is a coping mechanism, a way of distancing yourself from the truth and any blame. It is a form of basic self-preservation, in much the same way that a child might tell a lie to get themselves out of trouble, even though they know it's wrong and don't really want to tell the lie; in that moment they can see no other way out. An unchallenged lie quickly becomes the truth, even to the person telling it. But Marjorie does not feel forgiving, and I know that the reason is partly due to the pain she feels at being let down by her own mother. And maybe she's right: maybe some people should never become mothers at all if they are not prepared to put their child's needs before their own. But then, how can we possibly know what kind of a mother we will be until we become one? How can any of us be certain of who we truly are, what we are capable of, until we are tested? All I know is that I am damn sure I would fight to the death to protect Mary.

I don't want to think about any of that anymore. I want to go back to sleep but my dream has unsettled me and I have a desperate urge to check on Mary, to make sure she is still there, safe in her bed. For two weeks after Benedict turned up at the townhouse, I insisted that Mary slept in my bed with me every night, until Marjorie told me that it was not healthy for Mary and if I wasn't careful I would end up feeding my anxieties to her. Mary's safe, she told me, no one will get near to her with Mack here, and eventually I gave in and let her return to her own room. The consequence of doing what is right for Mary has been terrifying nightmares every night for me. I pull back the covers and sit on the side of the bed for a second to allow my eyes to adjust to the darkness. I shiver; the air is freezing and the sweat on my body, caused by the nightmare, feels as though it is starting to form a thin layer of ice on my skin. I stand and reach for my fluffy dressing gown, which is hanging on the back of the bedroom door, and quickly put it on and wrap it around me. Then I make my way out of my room and walk as quietly as possible to Mary's.

Mary's door is open and her nightlight is on – she doesn't like sleeping in the dark, and I pray that I have not played a part in her developing this phobia. I stand for a while and watch her. She is so beautiful, her face framed by her silky flame-coloured hair, a dusting of freckles on her perfectly shaped nose. Her eyelids are twitching, and I realise she is probably dreaming, but, as her chest is moving up and down in a calm and peaceful rhythm, I am guessing it is a good dream. I should leave her, now that I know she is safe, go back to my room, but I can't bring myself to do that. Instead, I climb into her bed and pull her towards me, feeling the warmth of her seep into me. She shifts and moans in her sleep, but doesn't wake.

"I love you, Shrimp," I whisper into her hair. She smells sweet, of baby powder, and it reminds me of the nursery rhyme: *"What are little girls made of? Sugar and spice and all things nice..."*

That is the last thing I think of before I drift into a deep and uninterrupted sleep.

***

When I wake, Mary is not in the bed and for a minute I start to panic until I hear her voice filtering up the stairs from the kitchen, where she is helping Marjorie make pancakes for breakfast. Mack and Marjorie are going out for the day today; they wanted me and Mary to go with them, but I am not ready yet to face the outside world and I am not sure if I ever truly will be. My choice to run away five years ago has left me a virtual prisoner. The world beyond the door is hostile for me and it's my fault; I've made it that way.

After breakfast Mary has a rare mini-meltdown as she is told she cannot accompany Mack and Marjorie and it takes me five minutes to calm her down after they leave. I feel so guilty denying her something as simple as a day out, but ever since Benedict's letter, with its threat to take Mary from me, I have not been able to face allowing her out of my sight.

It is late morning now, and a weak winter sun is straining light into the kitchen, where I am preparing some lunch. Mary is upstairs playing in her bedroom and I can hear her little sing-song voice talking to her dolls and teddy bears. I don't need to be in the room to know that they are all lined up in front of the blackboard that Mack made her for Christmas – pretending to be a teacher is her favourite role-play game at the moment. As I hear the "tap-tap-tap" of a ruler on the blackboard, I can't help but wonder if this is a career she will end up in, not that I care what she becomes as long as she is happy. She is very bright and I envy her the freedom she is going to have in choosing her path in life. But I also realise now how powerful choice is, how it has the ability to bring joy, or to destroy. Choices create opportunities, but the wrong choice can leave your future bleeding in front of you until the life finally drains away from it, and that's it, you are stuck forever in the place where that one bad choice left you. When she is old enough to really understand, I intend to make sure Mary knows the power she holds over her own future, the power that can be contained in one simple choice; I want so much more for her than I have allowed myself to have.

A tap at the window startles me out of my thoughts. The unexpected sound has set my already-jangled nerves on edge – my instinct these days is to view anything unexpected as a potential threat. I look up, afraid of what, or who, I might see and immediately jump at my own reflection before spotting the robin perched on the window ledge. Marjorie loves to feed the birds in the garden, and to her delight this one has become particularly tame, tapping on the window occasionally to ask for some scraps. I open the window, letting the sharp cold air in, and throw out a slice of buttered bread; the robin trills his now-familiar "chzip" sound as he takes flight after it. Marjorie once told me that robins are said to be the spirits of loved ones who have died, coming to pay a visit. She finds comfort in that, hoping it might be her father still watching over her, but I don't; I feel haunted enough by the past as it is.

As I close the window, a little shiver works its way down my spine. I know it is just a reaction to the cold air left behind, but for some reason it feels more sinister and my mind involuntarily wanders back to last night's dream. I put the kettle on the stove to boil some water for a cup of tea to help me warm up, and to distract me; the sound of the kettle starting to boil drowns out the sweet sound of Mary singing a song to her dolls and teddies. Before long the kettle starts its low whistle, gradually building into a long, monotone scream, forcing me to pay it some attention. As I remove the kettle from the flames and switch off the heat, I hesitate, momentarily confused as my mind registers that the screaming hasn't stopped like it should have. The blood instantly drains from my extremities, its retreat as cold as ice in my veins, my body going into automatic fight-or-flight mode. It's Mary! I drop the kettle back onto the stove, spilling water onto the hot ring, which hisses in protest. As I turn to run out of the kitchen, my hand knocks the kitchen knife and plate of sandwiches that I have prepared off the countertop, sending food and crockery to land and smash like abstract art across the floor.

I scream out my little girl's name as I bound up the stairs, two or three treads at a time, grinding broken crockery into the carpet from the bottom of my shoes.

"I'm here, Mary, Mummy's coming" I shout. I need her to know I am here, that I am coming for her.

I reach her bedroom in seconds – the door is open and I can see Mary sitting on her bed with her knees up in front of her. Her back is pressed into the wall as if willing herself to become intangible, to bleed into the wall and beyond, through to the safety of the other side. The blackboard is lying askew on the floor, trapping one of her dolls beneath it and creating a barrier between her and me. Mary's face is contorted with fear, and I am instantly struck by how fear has made her look more like me than ever before. Her large honey-coloured eyes are fixed to a spot behind the bedroom door and as I follow her gaze, I feel physically sick when I see the elongated shadow on the wall that betrays the person lurking there. My mind is desperately trying to process how this has happened. He must have been watching the house, saw Marjorie and Mack leave and knew we were alone. But how did he get in? The front door was locked. I know because I checked it, I always check it several times a day, every time I pass it. But it doesn't matter how he got in, I need to act, do something right now, only I suddenly realise that I don't know *what* to do. I have thought about the possibility of something like this happening a thousand times, and every time I have been brave, fearless, undefeatable; I have done whatever I needed to do to protect and save my child. But, to my horror, all those hours of playing out different scenarios in my head have counted for nothing. Instead of being ready to fight and defend, panic and fear are a venom seeping like osmosis through my skin and flesh, into my bones, paralysing me, making me fail in my duty as a mother. The only thing I have left at my disposal is my voice.

"What do you want from us?" I scream at him. "Why don't you just leave us alone? I've called the police!"

I want my voice to sound firm and in control, but I know the opposite is true – it sounds out of control, weak and afraid, as pathetic and useless as the person I have turned out to be. I hope he doesn't realise that I am bluffing, that I hadn't even considered calling the police until this very moment. Oh God, is that the kind of mother I am? One that can't even be relied upon to call for help when it's needed? I wait for a response, but none comes. I know what he is doing: he is using the power of silence to heighten my sense of dread, knowing it will disarm me. And it works, to my shame, I feel the warm trickle of urine making its way down my leg, bleeding into the fabric of my jeans. I hate myself right now, more than I ever thought was possible.

Mary suddenly screams again, and points as she shouts, "He's coming, Mummy!" The sound of Mary screaming breaks me out of my paralysis, and I immediately look around for something that I can use as a weapon. I cannot believe my own stupidity – just a few minutes ago I had a kitchen knife in my hand and yet I ran to defend my daughter empty-handed! *What was I thinking?* Before I can find something to use, the intruder shows himself, emerging from his hiding place behind the door and I am immediately stopped in my tracks. It's not Benedict. A large spider is scuttling down the wall towards a crack between the wall and skirting board. Mary was screaming because of a *spider?* Surely that can't be it. Despite my fear, I somehow find the courage to quickly swing the door back, but the only thing it reveals is a dressing gown hanging from a hook on the back, and I realise that this is what caused the elongated shadow on the wall. There is nothing more sinister in her bedroom than a spider and a dressing gown.

I drop to my knees, sobbing with relief, disbelief, shame, my body heaving violently as I try to catch my breath in between adrenaline-fuelled sobs. I am having another panic attack – my heart is beating so hard and my chest is so tight that I can hardly breathe. I feel as though I am going to die; I *want* to die right now. Then Mary runs to me, her little arm outstretched with a pink and white candy-striped paper bag; the sugary sweets it held have been tipped out onto her bed.

"Breathe, Mummy," she says. "Don't be scared, the spider's run away now. He won't hurt us no more."

I am stunned that she knows what to do. How many times have I subjected her to this, for her to know what to do? I take the bag from her and place it to my lips, allowing it to act as bellows to my lungs, helping me to replace the carbon dioxide that I need, until slowly my breathing returns to normal once more. I am exhausted. My hair, damp from sweat, is clinging to my forehead and the jeans around my crotch are wet with cooling urine.

"You 'kay now, Mummy?" my precious, intelligent daughter asks me, her head leaning to one side in a precocious display of concern as she looks at me. I am a mess, emotionally and physically, and I hate that Mary has to see me like this.

"I'm fine, baby," I say, although I am far from fine. "Come here." I pull her into a tight hug to comfort her; or is it to comfort myself?

"Ugh! Mummy you're all wet!" Mary says pushing me away and wrinkling her nose.

Her comment makes me laugh through my tears; a weird dichotomy of emotions is running through me right now. And then the absurdity of what I have just allowed to happen hits me, and I start to laugh even harder, throwing my head back in abandonment of all the negative emotions that I have been holding on to, seeing it all for what it really is: that *I* am my own worst enemy. I have created an environment so dense and foggy with fear, that I can no longer see where the danger lies within it, nor the light that shines beyond it. Mary is looking at me, not quite sure why I am laughing so hard, but then she joins in, proving the old adage that laughter really is infectious. When the laughing eventually subsides, I get up off the floor and pick up the candy-striped paper bag that Mary had given me just a few minutes ago. My eyes wander to her bed, where the sweets are scattered.

"Where did you get the sweets from, Shrimp?" I ask. I am teasing her, really, interested to see how she responds. I ration the number of sweets she has, but I know that Mack secretly gives her some every now and then with a little wink. I don't mind, Mack is her grandfather to all intents and purposes, and that's what grandparents are supposed to do – secretly spoil. Mary's cheeks flush as pink as the stripe on the bag as she tries to think of what to say that isn't a lie and doesn't betray the culprit.

"Don't be cross, Mummy, it's not his fault," she says, and I smile. I love that she has such an honest and generous heart.

"Of course I won't be cross!" I say, ruffling her hair, but nothing can prepare me for what she says next.

"My daddy gave them to me."

CHAPTER 14

Benedict

When I received Jeannie's response via her solicitor, I admit I
was shocked. The smug tone of the letter infuriated me. I looked
at the photos and read the transcript of the conversation with
the dominatrix that I visit, and a heat coursed through me.
Fucking bitch. But, although it wasn't great, if that was all they
had I could have easily mitigated it. No, it was the copy of the
letter that Jeannie had written for her mother that was really
damaging, something I could never have anticipated.

They played their move well; I'll give them that. If they had
simply threatened to go to the police with the letter, I could
have handled it. I would have been afforded anonymity and,
besides, it would never have reached the Crown Prosecution
Service, thanks to the fraternity that I am a senior member of.
No, threatening to go to the papers, to make it public, was a
clever move – the premise being that my reputation would be
irreparably damaged regardless of whether I managed to clear
my name. I was raging at the audacity of the threat against me
but, having already learned my lesson on acting on impulse, I
knew it was wise to stay calm, be patient and lie low whilst I

tried to figure out a new plan. After a week of deliberating on what to do next, I still hadn't come up with anything feasible and, despite my former resolve, I found my thoughts becoming increasingly more frenetic, twisting into an obsession. Mary was my child. *Mine!* Jeannie might have believed she had won, that she could keep me away from what is rightfully mine, but she was wrong. No one was going to tell me I couldn't be with my own fucking daughter. And then I remembered the compliment slip that the receptionist had handed me at Mary's school, and instantly I thought of a way that I could get to Mary. Serena Barclay, Mary's form tutor.

Women are so weak, so easy to control with compliments and blackmail, and Serena was no exception. Serena is thirty-nine, married ten years to her dull accountant husband, Clive, and has two young children: a boy and a girl. Until I came along, they lived a comfortable, middle-class, suburban life. I imagine their evenings were occupied with trite conversations about what had happened that day, about music lessons and sports events, and discussing whose turn it was to host the next neighbourhood BBQ. Without those things to talk about, they would probably suffocate in their own silence. Serena was so accustomed to her banal existence, so numbed to pleasure, that she didn't even realise how bored she was, how sexually frustrated and desperate for excitement, until I appeared.

Having an affair was something a woman like Serena would never ordinarily have contemplated – she would never risk the status quo – but I am far from an ordinary proposition. Once I had established the wine bar she frequented every Friday after work, I found a way into her social scene. My subtle, flirty advances seemed to stun her at first, as if it were the last thing she had expected, and she had no idea how to handle the attention. This was a novelty to me. I am used to women succumbing to me immediately, but she was like a shy virgin. I was patient with her, making her gradually unfurl and open up, until there was no part of her left that was out of bounds to me. All it really took was for me to listen to her thoughts and opinions as if they mattered, for me to tell her how beautiful she was, how sexy, how *irresistible*. I showed her how alive you feel when you do something reckless and, in less than two weeks, I cracked the uncrackable and was fucking her in a hotel room, although I'm sure Serena would have called it "making love" in her deluded, bucolic state of mind.

It didn't take long before she predictably started talking about leaving her husband, making plans for our life together. I let her have her moment of hope and happiness and then I watched her unravel as I told her about Mary, the little girl in her class, my estranged daughter, and what I wanted her to do for me. Serena suddenly realised that our affair was built on quicksand, that she was no more than a means to an end and had meant nothing to me. As soon as she realised that, her once dull and boring life with Clive – a life she had been so happy to toss away – suddenly seemed solid and dependable, worth hanging on to. If she didn't do as I asked, I told her, Clive would have the full, sordid details of what I had been doing with his wife. As would the school, whose policies probably didn't include teachers fucking the parents of their pupils. Fear of being alone is a powerful weapon against a woman, and Serena knew that, if the details of our affair was exposed, Clive would be too humiliated to stay with her – how on earth could he ever face the neighbours again, knowing how they would be gossiping? He would leave her, of that there was no doubt, and she would be left to play by herself on the seesaw of life. And so, today I get my reward for having had to suffer this tedious affair: I get to see Mary.

It is the afternoon break, and I am headed to Serena's classroom, where she has agreed to keep Mary behind for ten minutes. As I approach the classroom, I can see Serena through the glass in the door. She is sitting on a chair beside my daughter's desk and it serves to exaggerate how small both the desk and the child are. Serena looks ill, pale and drawn with dark circles beneath her eyes, no doubt coloured in by lack of sleep. Mary is looking up at her and talking, but I can tell she is not concentrating on what the child is saying; her troubled mind is elsewhere. I open the door to enter the classroom; I don't bother knocking and Serena jumps up and out of her chair, startled.

"Ben!" she says, stating the obvious, as if she is surprised to see me, which of course she's not. She looks like she might cry. Women like to cry, I've found; they often use it as a tool to try and manipulate, but this time I think it's real, I think she really does want to cry. She knows she has messed up.

"You can leave now," I tell her but she shakes her head.

"No. It will look strange if anyone sees you alone in here with her. I have to stay. You have five minutes, Ben, no more."

I shrug in acceptance. What she is saying makes sense; I don't want to arouse suspicion.

I have been practising what I might say to Mary. It is difficult for me, speaking to a child. If Mary had been living with me, she would most certainly be accomplished in her vernacular by now, but I have to accept that she has probably been held back, her language simple, and so I will have to keep my language simple, too.

"Hello, Mary," I say, as soothingly as I can muster, and Mary looks to Serena for reassurance that she can speak to the stranger before her.

"Go ahead, Mary, it's OK," Serena says and I can see that it really was a good decision to allow her to stay.

"Hello," the child replies shyly as she bites her bottom lip. Her voice is sweet-sounding; I guess you would call her cute if you were so inclined.

"Do you like sweets?" I ask as I remove a pink and white bag from my pocket. Again, Mary looks to Serena, who just nods in reassurance.

"Mummy doesn't like me to have too many sweeties," she says, "but Grampy Mack sometimes lets me have some when Mummy isn't looking."

"Ah. So, you know that some secrets are OK, then?" I say and Mary seems confused.

I extend the bag of sweets again, and this time Mary takes them from me. "Thank you," she says politely and then opens the bag to peer inside.

"Do you know who I am, Mary?" I ask and the child lifts her gaze back to me and stares; her large eyes are quite beautiful. Mary shakes her head to indicate she doesn't know who I am.

"I am your daddy," I say.

"I don't have a daddy," she replies, furrowing her brow in confusion.

"Everyone has a daddy, Mary," I say. "And I'm yours."

"Why don't you live with us, then?" she asks.

"Because Mummy doesn't really like me very much. It's complicated, Mary, grown-up stuff that you won't understand. But it's not my fault that I can't live with you." I turn my head towards Serena, and Mary follows my lead. "Mrs Barclay knows that it's not my fault and she thinks it is OK for me to see you and to give you sweets, do you understand?"

Serena can tell that this is her cue to nod, and she does so, although I can see the resentment manifest itself in the stiffness of her movement. Mary thinks for a moment before she says, "Freya's daddy doesn't live with her, and he gives her sweets. So, I s'pose it's OK."

"That's right, Mary, you're a clever girl. But you mustn't tell your mummy. Not yet, do you promise me? Because, if you do, she might stop me from coming to visit you, from bringing you sweets and presents, and that wouldn't be fair. It's not my fault that I can't see you, remember. Promise me?"

Her face twists at this and I can guess it is because she has been told not to keep secrets and make promises. Her conscience is telling her something is wrong; her analytical skills are strong.

"Ben!" Serena's tone has gone up an octave with anxiety at what she has just heard me say. "You told me this was a one-off, we agreed…"

She is right, that is what I agreed, but that was before I met my daughter, my little girl who shows such promise. I ignore her protest as if she had never even spoken, and kneel down to be at my daughter's level.

"Promise me?" I say again. "You would like to see your daddy again, wouldn't you?" And this time she nods and blinks.

"That's my girl," I say, and the pride I feel in those words takes me by surprise.

I walk out of the classroom then, and without even looking in Serena's direction I say, "Same time next week, Serena."

CHAPTER 15

Charlotte

Ever since he received the brown envelope, Benedict has been acting strangely. I'd placed the envelope on his desk with the rest of that day's post and I could see it piqued his interest, which was unusual. Curious, I watched him through a gap in the door to his study as he opened it.

I saw colour creep into his face as he began to read a typewritten letter, something I had never seen happen before. Then he reached into the envelope and removed some photographs and the colour in his face deepened. I couldn't see the images from where I had been standing, but they clearly provoked a reaction in him. He placed them back down and then fished out what looked like a handwritten letter, which he began to read. The letter was several pages long and as he was reading, I recognised the subtle signs that betrayed the rage it roused in him – a slight tremor of the hand, nostrils flaring, deeper breathing, finger-tapping. Whatever was in that letter, in those photographs, had unsettled him.

When he finished reading, he took a deep breath as if to calm himself and then placed the letter and photographs back into its envelope before placing it into the desk drawer. He sat silently for a while; he was staring ahead at nothing, his gaze cloudy with thought, his fingers drumming on the green leather top of his antique writing desk – things he does when he is angry, when he needs to think. When I heard the wheels of his expensive Herman Miller chair start to roll back on the wooden floor, I scurried away, not wanting to be caught watching him and risk a beating. Later that morning, after he had left for work, I tried the drawer, but it was locked.

This morning I was dusting the desk in the study and accidently knocked over the table lamp, revealing the key to the drawer hidden underneath. I put the key in my pocket and carried on dusting, telling myself I would put it back later. That was a couple of hours ago and I know I should put it back, forget I've even seen it, but that small key is heavy with the weight of my curiosity. Something is telling me that there is something important in that envelope, something that I should know about, and I find myself in his study again.

I know Benedict won't be home for hours, but my heart beats wildly as I place the key into the drawer and unlock it. I hear a sound and I freeze, my nerve endings crackling with fear. I listen, barely trusting myself to breathe, but hear nothing more. I am unnerved and I know I should quit now while I'm ahead, but I also know I'm not going to do that. Even so, before I open the drawer, I listen out again, just to be sure, but all I hear is the buzz of white noise and the tick of a clock, so I open the drawer and pull out the envelope.

The first thing I pull out are the photographs. I cringe when I see them – photos of Ben in sexually submissive poses. In one he is lying on a bed, tied up like a hog with a ball-gag in his mouth; in another, he is blindfolded and handcuffed to the same bed. In each photo he is clearly aroused. I am finding it hard to accept that this is Benedict, the man I know to be so sexually violent and dominant. I place the embarrassing photographs onto the desk and as I do so the ridiculousness of how he looks hits me and I afford myself a rare smile, a chuckle even, as I realise how mortified he must have been when he first saw them.

I take out the typewritten letter next and as I read it, I can feel the blood draining from me as I realise what that bastard has been hiding from me: *Jeannie isn't dead.* Jeannie is still alive and she has a little girl. My chest begins to heave in and out as my breathing gets out of control. I try to slow my breathing down, but I can't; I want to scream, but my brain has frozen like a spinning circle on an unresponsive computer screen. Then it happens, the spinning stops, my brain re-engages and I emit a noise like nothing I have ever heard before. I know it is coming from me, but it sounds like it is coming from somewhere else, from something else. I pick up the table lamp and throw it against the wall, needing to release some of this energy I am feeling, and then I slump to the floor. As I land, the envelope and its contents flutter down from the desk and scatter on the floor around me and that's when I spot it, the envelope with "Mum" on it in Jeannie's handwriting.

Shaking, I fetch the letter off the floor and kiss it as if by kissing the handwriting I am kissing her. I don't want to read it here like this, sitting on the floor surrounded by the filth of his face in those photographs. I collect the photographs and put everything except Jeannie's letter back into the envelope – being forced to keep everything tidy is a hard habit to break, even now. Then I get up and walk to the kitchen and start the coffee machine. I know that what I am really doing is a delaying tactic. I want more than anything to read the words that Jeannie has written, but I am scared of what they might say.

The coffee is ready now, it is time. I sit at the table and open the letter.

Dear Mum,
    There is so much I need to say, but I don't know where to start.

I'm afraid, too. Afraid to say the things that have been pulling at the edges of my subconscious for some time now. I know that to do so will change things between us forever – I will lose the mother that I believed I had and I am not sure if I am ready for that.

No matter what, you are my mum and I love you. I need you, too – probably now more than ever – so believe me when I say that ignoring the truth would be way easier. But it wouldn't be right. It would make me no different than you, and right now I need to know that I am different. I need to know that I am better.

When it was just you and me, before Benedict, things were good, weren't they? And I mean really, honestly good, not pretend-good. Do you remember the prayer we used to say together when you tucked me in to bed each night? It went something like:

"From ghosties and ghoulies and long-legged beasties and things that go bump in the night, may God protect us."

Do you remember that? I was, what, four or five years old? And that was the last time I truly felt safe and loved. The last time I didn't need to pretend that life was normal.

If only that prayer had been enough to protect us from the "beastie" that you brought into our lives, Mum, enough to have protected us from Ben. How different things could have been, eh? But God didn't protect us, did he? He was never going to protect us, because I have come to realise that God doesn't exist. God is no more than a concept – a lie to give false hope to the weak. A lie to make people give second and third and fourth chances to those who don't deserve them, and call it forgiveness.

To be honest, I miss believing in God. A world without God is heavier and full of responsibility. It is a world where you have to carry your own burdens, your own blame; a world where you are responsible for your own decisions and the consequences of them; a world where you cannot hope for "footprints in the sand" or hide behind "God's will". What about you, Mum? Do you still believe in God? Was it the thought of His will that allowed you to turn a blind eye, to be so accepting of the unacceptable? Did it help you to let go of any feelings of responsibility over what was happening to me? Are you counting on the power of God's forgiveness when your time comes? For your sake, I really hope with all my heart that I am wrong about God.

Don't get me wrong: just because I don't believe in the forgiveness of God, it doesn't mean I don't believe in the act of forgiving. But, before I can forgive, I need to acknowledge the truth, accept and understand it. And, to do that, I need to dig up the bones of the past and lay them out in the open to dry. So here goes:

I was five or six years old, a baby really, when I first realised that life was never going to be the same again. We had been living with Benedict for just under a year, and I guess you must have done something to anger him because he pinned you to the wall and tried to strangle you. I don't know why he did it, but I remember vividly the awful sounds you made as you desperately tried to suck air into your lungs, and how white your knuckles looked against your purplish face as you gripped and pulled at the hands around your neck. I remember that our eyes met and I was scared because you didn't look like my mum. Your eyes were bulging and bloodshot, with tears running down from the outer corners, and I knew that you were pleading silently with me to help you, but I was terrified, I thought Ben had been possessed by the devil. Then I saw the very moment when the fight left you, and as soon as your hands started to slacken and you stopped resisting, Ben let you go. Looking back, I think that was the exact moment he had been waiting for – he needed to *know just how far he could push you before you gave up. To be honest, you didn't fight very long for yourself, Mum, and I wonder now if maybe that is significant, that maybe you were simply born weak.*

After Ben released his grip on you, he simply walked out of the house and I remember that you slid down the wall to the floor. I ran over to you, crying, but you pushed me away and told me to go to my room and stay there. That night, when you came to tuck me in, there was no prayer – that prayer was never to be said again – instead you told me how important it was for me to be good and quiet, and not upset Ben. You told me that Ben loved us both very much, and we should show him how much we loved him by being good. If we were good, good things would happen, you said, and I believed you. I tried so hard to be good, I really did, but it seemed I was never quite good enough.

Although he never went as far as that again, the incident seemed to stir something in Ben and I regularly witnessed the beatings you took from him. It wasn't every day, or even every week, but it might as well have been. The apprehension of not knowing what was going to tip him over the edge, when he would snap, was a daily invisible attack every bit as vicious as the real thing. Although he never once physically struck me, I was told, and believed, that many of your beatings were my fault. Ben forced me to apologise to you and you accepted my apologies. It has only just occurred to me that you never once told me it wasn't my fault – even in those moments where we were alone together without Ben, you never reassured me. Instead, you would tell me to be quiet, be a good girl, make myself scarce.

Did you really believe that getting me to change my behaviour would somehow protect me, protect us?

The truth is you just reinforced the message that the consequences of not doing those things well enough, made what happened to you all my fault. I honestly believed that you were taking my punishments for me, but you weren't really doing that, were you? You knew those beatings would happen regardless; some other excuse would have been found. Lying to yourself made the beatings easier to take – it allowed you to think of yourself as some sort of martyr, taking the thrashings so I didn't have to. Am I right, Mum? If so, how did you justify the time he tied me up and locked me in the basement? Or the time he killed my puppy? Where was your self-sacrifice then?

But, to be honest, I could forgive you all of that. I think I even understand it in a way. But understanding or forgiving you for what was to come is much harder. The night of my sixteenth birthday. Do you remember that, or have you wiped it from your mind? Because no matter how hard I try, I cannot erase it from mine. I was just sixteen, a virgin, and he pinned me to the bed and forced himself on me. Raped me. Yes, Mum, that is what he did to me, that is what you chose to turn your back on.

Every night when I close my eyes, I am back in that moment. I see him looming over me, the urgency in his eyes, his quickening breath turning to ice on my bare skin. I hear the grunt of his efforts and smell the faint odour of sweat mingling with his aftershave. I feel the relentless burn of him inside of me. I cried for him to stop, begged him, but he just kept going; "teaching me a lesson", he called it. But, however much it hurt me, it was nowhere near as painful as the agony of knowing that you did nothing to stop it.

I cried out for you, Mum. I needed you to be a mother and to make it stop. I know you must have heard me. I used to hear your cries when he beat you, so if I heard *your cries and your pleas, how could you not have heard mine? But you never stopped him and, so, when he told me that it was my fault, that I deserved it, that I brought it on myself, I believed him. What else could I think? Surely you would have protected me if it hadn't been my fault?*

That was the first of many times that he "punished" me by raping me. But I am pretty sure you already know that. In the end I did the same thing you did – I pretended to myself that you never knew what was happening to me. It was the only way I could cope, because the alternative was to accept that I didn't mean as much to you as I should have.

I can't help but wonder, though, what you did when you heard me crying out for you that night. Did you put your hands over your ears to block it all out? Did you busy yourself with some chore to distract you from the noise? Did you at least hesitate and consider coming to my rescue? Maybe you thought about picking up one of the knives in the kitchen, or maybe you picked up the phone to call the police? If so, what stopped you? That question has gone round and round in my head lately, and I cannot think of anything that could explain it, let alone justify it. You made a choice to do nothing and whichever way I look at it, you let me down in an unimaginable way. Doing nothing is not the same as doing nothing wrong, Mum.

I'm sorry if this is hard to read, but believe me it is nothing compared to the shame I carry for the things he made me do and the guilt that I have had to endure, wondering why I didn't do enough to make it all stop. But what could I have done? I was sixteen with no experience of the world, no friends to confide in. All I had in the world was you. And if you, my own mother, was not prepared to accept the truth, how could I possibly expect anyone else to?

But that is all in the past now, and the past cannot be rewritten. What I want more than anything now, Mum, is for you to take the baton of guilt from me, tell me that it was never really mine to hold, that it was always yours. But I am scared to ask that of you, scared in case I don't get the apology from you that I deserve, leaving me once more wondering if I really do deserve one.

These last few months in Sri Lanka have helped me see things more clearly. That, and the fact that I am going to be a mum myself. Yes, that's right, Mum, I am pregnant with Ben's baby. I wasn't sure at first whether I could find it in myself to keep it, knowing that it wasn't conceived out of love, but out of something brutal. And then I realised that this baby is as much of a victim as I have been. It didn't ask to find itself growing inside of me, it doesn't know the evil that helped shape its existence, and, although I am terrified, I have decided to keep it. I have decided to be a mother. And that is why I needed to write this letter, to dig up the bones and examine them – to understand and make sure I never make the same mistakes that you have made.

I am crying as I write this, Mum. Crying at everything I have had to endure. Crying out all the feelings of hurt and anger and disappointment that I didn't even know I carried in me. Crying in fear of the kind of mother I might end up being, no matter how hard I try, because I know in my heart that you never set out to be the kind of mother you became. But I am also crying because I know that I will never see you again and I will miss you. In spite of everything, I will miss you so much. You see, I'm not coming home, Mum, I can't. I am walking away – it is the only way to keep this baby safe from Ben. If he knew the truth about what is growing inside of me, there is no way he would let us go. I'm afraid for you, Mum, afraid of *what he might do to you, but my priorities have changed now, they have to, and I hope you can understand that.*

Anyway, the truth is, you will never get to know any of this, Mum, because you won't ever receive this letter. I realise now that I was never going to send it. To send it would risk Ben finding out about the baby, but there would also be the risk that you would not accept that you have been less of a mother than you should have been, that you might deny me the chance to forgive you and move on. I also don't want to hurt you, Mum, can you believe that?

No, this letter has been written for me, a therapy letter of sorts, to help me find closure. To safely find acceptance of what has passed and make my peace with it, without fear of rejection or recrimination. It's a way to say goodbye, I guess.

So, goodbye, Mum. I hope you find some remnants of strength left within you to leave him, but if you can't, then stay safe.

I love you. Always will.

Jeannie

Xxxxxx

CHAPTER 16

Benedict

I have been visiting Mary at the school a few times now but I know that I am playing a dangerous game. I have made Mary promise not to tell her mother, made her believe that I will get into a lot of trouble if she does so, but I know it is only a matter of time before she trips up.

Since visiting my daughter, I have established that she does not have a passport, which is rather convenient. I intend to apply for one and then use it to take her out of the UK – I have influential friends in Dubai and that is where I intend for us to go. I applied for a copy of Mary's birth certificate a week ago and it arrived today at my office. It incenses me when I see the blank space where my name should be, but I am placated by the thought that Jeannie will soon pay the price for dismissing me so readily.

My phone is ringing and a feeling of antipathy runs through me at the sound of Serena's voice. I have grown to find her whiny victim act repulsive, but I am due to visit the school again this afternoon and it makes me concerned – why can't whatever she wants to say wait? I drum my fingers on my desk as she tells me that Mary is not in school today and her voice starts to crack when she admits that Mary hasn't actually been in school for a week, that her mother had phoned in to say Mary was unwell. There is a silence that I don't intend to fill, and it clearly makes Serena uncomfortable as she starts to talk again, tries to justify why she has waited until today to tell me.

"I never told you before – I just assumed she would be back by today. I'm sorry, Ben."

She is clearly afraid of my reaction, and she is right to be afraid, I am boiling with rage. She can kiss goodbye to her pathetic little life with her pathetic little husband and pathetic little job, but I don't tell her this. I end the call without saying anything, simply press the *end call* button on my mobile phone, and it feels so unsatisfactory. Mobile phones deny a person the satisfaction of slamming down a receiver in frustration.

I sit whilst drumming my fingers and reflecting on what Serena has told me. Despite what the school has been told, I'm certain the child isn't ill. Something is wrong, I sense it. I have already cleared my diary of appointments in order to visit Mary this afternoon, so I decide to go home instead and consider my next move. I also need to release some of my anger.

I grab my coat and make my way home. It is a sunny afternoon, one that should lift a person's mood, but it is doing nothing for mine. I reach the house and enter, placing my coat neatly on the stand. The house is quiet, but I can smell the distinctive aroma of fresh coffee as I enter the kitchen. Charlotte is sitting at the kitchen table; tears are streaming down her puffy cheeks; she looks grotesque. In her hand is Jeannie's letter and I realise the dirty whore must have broken into my desk. How *dare* she.

She looks up at me. "She's *alive*, Ben," she says. "Jeannie's alive and you *knew*."

Her tears are mingling with her snot; she is repulsive.

"Give me the letter, Charlotte," I say slowly and she knows by the tone of my voice that I am not messing about. I am not in the mood to wait for her to do as she is told.

She looks at me and there is something in her eyes, a defiance that I haven't seen in her before. It is a look I remember in Jeannie all those years ago and, although it is disturbing, it is somehow arousing. I walk towards her and as she tries to back away in the chair I lunge at her and grab the letter from her hands and the envelope from the table. I realise I was stupid to have kept them at all, but I really didn't think Charlotte had it in her to be this brazen or devious.

I walk towards the kitchen sink, open the cutlery drawer and pick out the candle lighter that is kept there. I drop Jeannie's letter and the envelope containing the photographs into the sink and set fire to them. The fire is hypnotic as it eats into the paper, the flame dancing and changing colour as it consumes its prey. Behind me I hear Charlotte crying and my anger increases. First Serena, now Charlotte: I am surrounded by weak, repulsive women. I walk over to her and grab her by her hair, dragging her as she screams and cries, to the sink, where the remains of the letter and envelope are smouldering and turning to ash.

"Leave me alone!" she screams at me as I force her head under the tap and turn it on. The cold water makes her gasp and she bangs her head on the tap as she tries to wriggle out from my grasp, begging me to stop.

"Someone needs to clean you up, you stinking bitch. It's your own fault, Charlotte. You have done this to yourself. Rifling through my things? You are nothing but a petty criminal. I should have you thrown into jail."

I am enjoying feeling her struggle, overpowering her. She has had no fight in her for so long that I have barely bothered with her, but right now I am aroused, my erection pressing into the small of her back. I turn off the tap but keep her body pinned under me as I reach down for my zip.

CHAPTER 17

Charlotte

The fog that has been as thick as soup in my brain for so long has been clearing since I stopped taking the tablets Benedict has been giving me for years. He has no idea that I have been spitting them out and for the last couple of months I have been able to actually hear things again. I can hear the birds sing as they herald in each morning; I can hear the words to the songs on the radio.

I can hear him unzip his trousers.

I realise he is going to rape me again. Normally I am too out of it to really care, my mind shuts off from what is happening to me. But today my mind is too clear for me to shut this out. I am not going to let him do this to me again, today, or ever. The sun is shining cheerfully through the kitchen window, and I can't help but wonder how can it be so bright and cheerful when such dark things are happening? Then I notice the long arm of the sun's rays pointing, telling me what to do, picking out the one to do it with, as the long steel blade glints in the sun's spotlight. Benedict notices what I am looking at, and reaches out to pick the knife from its magnetic holder, taunting me with it.

"Is this what you want, Charlotte?" he says, putting the knife to my neck, his mouth twisted in sarcastic hatred. "Is this what you want to do to me?"

I can feel his erection growing along with the feeling of power the knife is bringing him.

"I should kill you right now, you slut," he says as he puts his other hand beneath my skirt and pulls at my underwear.

"No!" I scream and that's when I reach into my pocket and take out the silver letter opener that I put there earlier, and with a strength I never realised I possessed I twist around and stab it into Benedict's neck.

Benedict drops the knife and it clatters into the sink. He puts his hand to where I have stabbed him; his eyes are filled with a mixture of surprise and something I have never seen in him before: fear. He pulls the letter opener out of his neck and there is a pumping arc of blood spraying from the wound, spraying the kitchen like one of the Jackson Pollock paintings he is so bloody fond of. Benedict is silent; he staggers and falls against the sink before sliding to the floor and as I watch him, I feel a sharp stinging and something warm running down my neck. I hadn't felt the sharp steel of the knife he had been holding slice into me as I'd twisted out of his hold. As the warm blood leaves my body, I feel cold and weak. I drop to the floor beside Benedict.

It is cold on these Italian tiles and I feel so tired, but I don't want to die here beside this monster. I know I need help and I muster all the strength I have left to crawl to the front door. The floor feels slick beneath me and I am making slow progress, like a snail. I don't look behind, but I know that if I did I would see the snail-like trail of my own blood across the tiles. I reach the front door and stretch out for the handle, but I can't reach it. Then I hear her: Jeannie. She's calling out to me. I try to call out, to let her know I'm here, but I don't have the strength.

I'm so tired I need to sleep. I close my eyes, just for a minute; she'll be here for me in a minute. My Jeannie will be here.

CHAPTER 18

Mary

That day, fifteen years ago, when Benedict walked into my classroom and told me he was my father, everything changed.

"He's not your daddy!" Mum screamed at me when I confessed as to who had been giving me the sweets she had found. "Do you hear me? He is not your daddy. Don't ever call him that!" She actually shook me, as if she wanted to shake any thought or mention of him out of me, and I started to cry.

As this was happening, Marjorie and Mack returned from their day out and I heard Mack's heavy footsteps bounding up the stairs at the sound of Mum's raised voice. Mum never shouts, even when she is really cross, so I can only imagine what must have been going through their minds as they burst into my room to the scene before them.

"Whoa! You're scaring her, lass," Mack said as he bent down and gently removed me from Mum's grip, picking me up and cradling me in his giant's arms. I threw my arms around his neck and sobbed into his shoulder, breathing in the warm pine notes of his aftershave. His voice, his smell, always calmed me as a child, made me feel safe. I'm twenty years old now, but Mack still has that same effect on me when I need him.

"What on earth is going on, Dawn?" Marjorie had dropped to her knees beside Mum, who was by then in the throes of another panic attack, but all Mum could say in between short, ragged breaths was "Benedict."

Mack took me downstairs and tried to distract me by making me help him prepare dinner whilst Mum and Marjorie remained upstairs until Mum had calmed down. That night, after Mack had put me to bed and read me a story, I heard Marjorie and my mum talking in hushed tones in the dining room. I couldn't make out what they were saying, but I could hear the distinctive glug of liquid being poured, and I knew without even being there that it was the sound of wine being poured into the crystal glasses that Marjorie kept in a cabinet in the dining room. Mum and Marjorie often had what I thought of as "secret conversations" like this. When they thought I was asleep, I would hear the cabinet being opened, a delicate chink as a couple of glasses were taken out, followed by the gentle "thud" of a cork being removed from a bottle. Then I would hear snippets of words and sentences that I did not really understand but sounded grown-up and important, until I would finally drift off to sleep. That night was different, though. Mack joined them and their voices were fast and urgent and I heard parts of sentences, words that I recognised but had no idea what they actually meant.

"Time to face up, to tell the truth…"

"Never…"

"… have to leave."

"It's the only way."

"… never be safe."

"The country house…"

When they had finished, Mum came into my room and climbed into my bed. I pretended to be asleep, but I was glad she was there. Mum stroked my hair and kissed me on the crown of my head. "I love you," she whispered. "I'm so sorry, I didn't mean to shout and scare you. It wasn't your fault, darling, it was mine. I won't ever shout at you again. I'm going to make sure you are safe. Whatever it takes." Then she climbed back out of my bed and I heard her open my wardrobe and take out a suitcase. I sat up, forgetting I was pretending to be asleep. "What are you doing, Mummy?"

"We are going on a trip, Shrimp," she said. "Why don't you help me to pack your favourite things?"

And so it was that in the middle of the night Mack threw our suitcases into the boot of the car and drove Mum and me away from the townhouse forever.

"Where are we going?" I asked excitedly, my body straining against my seatbelt as I stretched to look out of the window at the sights and sounds of nocturnal London. I had never been outside that late before and I was so excited, blissfully unaware of the gravity of the situation.

"To a new house in Devon. It is in the countryside and there are sheep and cows and the sea. You will love it, Mary," Mum said to me.

"What about Nana Marjorie? Is she not coming with us?" I remember my excitement being replaced with anxiety as it hit me that Marjorie wasn't in the car with us.

"Aye, lass, she'll be coming soon enough." It was Mack's soothing voice, making everything alright. "We just need to get you and your mummy settled first. Now why don't you count some sheep and have a nice magic sleep, eh? You'll get there quicker."

Magic sleep is what Mack always used to call sleep on Christmas Eve. "It's magic because it makes Christmas Day come around more quickly than if you stay awake," he used to say. It always worked at Christmas, so, excited by the prospect of this place called Devon, I trusted what he was saying, nodded sleepily at him and yawned.

Mum had brought along the pillow and duvet from my bed. She placed the pillow behind my head and settled me against it as best she could within the confines of the seat belt before covering me with the duvet. I remember putting my thumb in my mouth and waiting for the remonstration that would follow from Mum – *only babies suck their thumbs, Mary! Your thumb will shrink!* – but this time she just smiled at me and stroked my head, allowing me to indulge in my childish comfort for once. Mack cranked up the heating and the car fell silent except for the drone of the tyres against the road. The combination of the darkness, the warmth in the car and the purring of the tyres soon lulled me to sleep and, when I woke, it was to the rose-gold glow of dawn.

A glance out of my window revealed a moving patchwork of green fields, stitched together with fences and hedgerows and dotted with fluffy sheep that I was certain were the same ones that I had counted in my mind a few hours earlier to get me to sleep. I was entranced. Soon the fields started to show signs of human habitation, with farm buildings and houses rising out of the fields. We reached roundabouts and drove through towns where the traffic was light enough that I had time to count the number of cars that we passed on our way, until eventually we reached signs for the village of Abbotscliff, our final destination.

It was still early in the morning as we drove slowly through the main village. The road was flanked by a verge of short hedgerows and spindly trees, beyond which were miles of open fields. "Look Mary!" I remember Mum exclaiming as she pointed to the bobbing white tails of rabbits as they scampered and darted for cover in the fields, the noise of the car engine having disturbed the peace of their early-morning foray. We passed several bungalows, which soon gave way to a terrace of pretty stone houses in the heart of the village. Lights emanated from some of the windows of the houses, causing puppet-like shadows of the people inside as they went about their morning routines, oblivious to their audience passing by. It was strange and it was wonderful. Mack pointed out the local school on our left and I twisted my head to take a look at the old stone building where I imagined I would soon be playing with new friends. I remember Mum fell silent, and I saw Mack glance at her and Mum subtly shaking her head, although I had no idea what that all meant.

Eventually, the robotic voice of the sat nav directed us to turn right up a steep, narrow lane. I listened as Mum read out the names of each house and farm that we passed along the way, until the lane narrowed some more and we reached the final house and stopped. Up ahead we could see a drystone wall that marked the end of the lane to vehicles, although walkers were invited to continue into the field beyond by way of a wooden stile.

"Abbotscliff House," Mum announced. "This is it, we're here."

Abbotscliff House, or just Abbotscliff, as we call it, is perched on the crest of the hill and has an incredible view across miles of sheep-hewn fields down to a rugged coastline. The view was lost on five-year-old me, though – my attention was firmly on an old rusty swing hanging from an apple tree in the overgrown front garden. We parked in the driveway and got out of the car, Mack stretching and commenting on how stiff he felt after such a long drive.

Mack glanced around the outside of the property and rubbed his chin, something he always does when he's thinking. "This is all a bit déjà vu," he'd said as he looked at the wilderness that was the garden confronting him. I remember wondering what déjà vu meant but was too excited to ask as that would mean waiting for an answer, and there was no time for that. I ran to the swing and clambered on, the old chains giving an elderly groan at my uninvited weight.

"Push me, Grampy Mack," I called out, and as Mack did my bidding, and I soared up into the sky and looked down at the foaming sea in the distance, I was the happiest little five-year-old in the world. After a few pushes, Mack stopped and when the swing had slowed down enough I jumped off and followed Mum and Mack as they started to take the suitcases from the car into the house.

Inside, the house was cold and smelled old and stale. Mack and Mum dropped the suitcases in the tiled hallway before making their way into the kitchen, where I followed them. The kitchen had a thin layer of ubiquitous dust covering its surfaces, including a long wooden farmhouse table. Several of the doors on the pine kitchen cabinets had dropped, no longer sitting squarely on their hinges, which gave the kitchen a higgledy-piggledy feel. To me, it felt like it could have belonged in a fairy tale; I loved it! As Mum started opening the wonky cabinet doors to check the cupboard contents, hoping to find some cleaning fluids that were still OK to use, Mack took himself back outside to look in the outbuildings for things like brooms and buckets. I decided to turn my attention to the rest of the house and scampered around, investigating each room like it was an adventure, stirring up years of settled dust that swirled around me, angry at being disturbed from such a long sleep.

Abbotscliff has been in Marjorie's family for several generations, and it was where she had spent her school holidays as a child during those long, hot summers of folklore. It was fully furnished but had not been used since the death of her father decades ago so all of the furniture was covered in mushroom-coloured dust sheets, which I took great delight in peeling off to reveal what lay beneath.

For the next month, Mack and Mum concentrated on bringing Abbotscliff back to life. Mack mended the wonky kitchen cabinets, sorted out rusty plumbing issues and fixed broken and missing roof tiles, along with various other tasks that were required, whilst Mum concentrated on decorating: rubbing down woodwork, stripping wallpaper and painting each room. Mack slept in the room next to mine and late at night I would hear him talking and laughing softly into the phone to

Marjorie, who had remained in London facilitating the sale of the townhouse with the help of Philip. She eventually sold it for what she called "an obscene amount of money that will see us all through to Judgement Day and beyond." It was sold with all the furniture included, "Lock, stock and barrel", as she put it. I didn't realise at the time that it meant it was gone for good and I would never go back, but to be honest I never really thought about it much. It is just a fond memory now, and maybe one day I'll return to see it as a memory-tourist. Abbotscliff is my home – I love it here; it has seeped into my soul.

During the month that Marjorie was away, I missed her so much. She was a constant in my life – I had never had a day away from her before – so that month felt like forever to me. Every day I would ask, "When is Nana Marjorie coming?" and every day I would get the same reply from Mack: "Soon as, lass, soon as." The morning that I woke up to find Marjorie watching me from the doorway of my room, I screamed with delight, catapulting myself out of my bed and into her arms. Mack had driven a round trip through the night to collect her so that she could surprise me when I woke up. Marjorie told me much later that she had never felt so loved in her life as she had in that moment; I'm so glad about that, that she knows just how much I loved her then, and still do.

Once Marjorie had arrived, the outside transformation of Abbotscliff began. After everything had been cut back and cleared, the first job was to create a new memorial for Lucy in the garden. Marjorie had brought the rosebush and its trinkets with her, the only things to make it to Devon from the townhouse, and this was carefully replanted. A simple bench, made from driftwood from the beach, was placed beside it, and I re-adorned the area with the old wind spinners and ornaments and added some of the shells and pebbles I had collected.

As well as its large garden, Abbotscliff has two one-acre fields. In one Mack and Marjorie created a fabulous vegetable garden, but the other one was just a meadow until the animals started arriving. It started with chickens – former battery hens that were to be slaughtered if they couldn't find a home. Mum cried at the thought of the life that those poor hens had endured, just to be slaughtered at the end – she couldn't bear it – so she never turned any down. Mack built a chicken coop and hen house and they gave us all so much enjoyment – not just from the eggs they eventually started to lay but from how entertaining they were; chickens really do have their own personalities.

After the chickens, the rescue dogs arrived: a springer spaniel puppy, Charlie, old Ned, a Labrador cross who was near blind and deaf, and two-year-old Queenie, the Shih Tzu with definite delusions of grandeur.

Before long, Mack found himself building a paddock and stables as we somehow found ourselves fostering a couple of rescued donkeys and a gorgeous Exmoor pony named Teeny Tiny that I learned to ride on. Pot-bellied pigs and a beehive eventually completed our animal family. We didn't need a cat – we informally inherited several from neighbouring farms who seemed to enjoy spending lazy days stalking mice in the fields around our house and leaving them for Marjorie to find in the kitchen.

Naturally, over the years many of our much-loved animals have died and have been replaced with others in need of rescue, but we still have our beloved Charlie, although he is now a stiff and arthritic fifteen-year-old. He spends most of his time in his bed by the equally age-weary Aga in the kitchen. The Aga is chipped and scarred at the edges, with tarnished steel top plates, but is a thing of beauty to me. I think back to the new, electric one that sat shiny and resplendent in the kitchen at the townhouse, but it doesn't compare to this oil-fired ancestor that is the beating heart of this home. In fact, the Aga is rarely off. As well as being an incubator for all manner of delicious foods – cakes and bakes and biscuits in the summer; curries and roasts and casseroles that bubble away for hours in the winter – it also has an integral central heating boiler, making the kitchen the best place to sit and warm up after a frosty winter walk.

Whatever the time of year, it never gets boring walking across the sloping fields, past sheep and grazing cattle, towards the gorse-edged cliffs and down a stony incline onto the beach where we go mooching to see what the tides have regurgitated onto the shore. A couple of years ago I found a perfectly preserved triggerfish, quite rare for our waters, which had been mummified by the sun's rays and warm sand during an unusually hot summer. It is now propped on a mantelpiece, and each time I look at it I remain fascinated by its human baby-like teeth. My favourite find, though, is a real-life message in a bottle that I found bobbing in the shallows of an incoming tide when I was about ten. It is a small white plastic bottle, a scintillation vial, the word "open" and an arrow pointing to the screw top written on it in black marker pen (although the "o" and arrow were so faint as to have nearly disappeared). Inside the bottle was a scrap of paper with the following message:

This bottle was released in the ocean off Cape Hatteras, North Carolina, USA, on June 16, 2010.

An address followed and *Please write!* had been circled next to the address as a sign of encouragement, which I did not need – I couldn't wait to write. Mum took me to the village store and I picked out a postcard that showed the stretch of coastline at Abbotscliff where I had found the bottle, and sent it to the address on the note. We included our own address and the reply we received explained that the bottle had been released by a thirteen-year-old boy, who, along with his father, used fishing trips to release bottles as an experiment to see how far they might travel. Mum and I looked on a map to see just how far that little bottle had come. I learned about the Gulf Stream that had carried it across the Atlantic Ocean to our shores, and that led to other questions about waves and currents and longshore drift, culminating in a bit of an obsession with all things marine. It is the reason that I chose to study oceanography at university, and the reason I am in the study room at Abbotscliff now, looking for my birth certificate. I need it to apply for a passport as the final year of my degree includes a residential trip, and the option I have chosen is a placement in Indonesia.

I have never had a passport as I have never been abroad before; never been anywhere, really. Mum rarely leaves Abbotscliff and, when she does, I see the way she hides behind hats and glasses, as if she is afraid to be seen. I know it has something to do with my father but, ever since the day Mum found out that Benedict had visited me in school, the subject of my father has always been shut down, taboo. Even as a young girl, I sensed a fragility in Mum, as if asking her would be like hitting a pane of glass at its weakest point, shattering her into a thousand pieces, and so I've never pushed it. Besides, I didn't feel the need for a father. I felt lucky with the family I had.

I know that Marjorie keeps all sorts of documents in the right-hand drawer of the writing desk, and so I am looking for a key to the drawer, which is locked. I know I should wait and ask, but I also know that the thought of me going abroad will provoke a fit of hyperbole in Mum, and quite possibly Marjorie, too. It just seems easier to apply for my passport first, then find a way to break it to them gently later.

Mum and Marjorie have gone to pick up some more ex-battery hens from Brenda at Hen Picked, the local hen rescue, and Mack is out on a long, solitary walk along the coast path. It would have been Lucy's forty-second birthday today, and each year Mack takes himself off to be alone with her in his thoughts. I remember the year I overtook Lucy in age and how strange it felt that I was born a long time after her, yet she would now be forever younger than me. Although he's never said it, I think it has been hard for Mack, watching me grow older in a way that Lucy never will. It is Mack's way not to talk openly about her and we all respect that; we all just give him the space he needs when he needs it.

It doesn't take a genius to find the key, which is in the unlocked left-hand drawer of the desk! Having unlocked the drawer I find that it is neatly organised into headed hanging files, and I reach for the most obvious one, the one that is marked "Family Papers". The house is eerily quiet with no one here except me. I can hear the clock ticking away on the mantlepiece: the tick-tick-tick sounds like tut-tut-tut at my transgression and I feel my face pinken slightly as if I have been caught in the act as I pull out the file. My birth certificate happens to be the first document in the file and I lift it out and examine it. The place where my father's name should be recorded is blank, and I don't know why, but that has surprised me, made me feel weirdly incomplete. It has also made me wonder why Mum would do that, leave it blank; what awful thing must he have done that she doesn't want him to exist in any form, not even as a name on a document.

Having retrieved what I had come for, I close the file and start to place it back in the drawer. As I do so, I casually scan the other files and stop when I see one marked "Jeannie". It isn't a name I recognise, yet at the same time there is a familiarity about it, as if I have vaguely heard it somewhere before. Intrigued I fish the file out, and inside I find an old wrinkled and damaged passport. I open the passport and look at the photo, but it is too water-damaged to be very distinguishable. I can make out the name, though, *Jeannie Eleanor Sutcliffe*, and then the next of kin, *Benedict Sutcliffe*. My heart lurches at the sight of Benedict's name. It was missing on my birth certificate, yet it appears here on a mysterious passport. I'm struggling to understand what this all means. Is Benedict related to Jeannie? I hadn't thought about that before, the fact I could have other family out there somewhere.

There is also a letter in the file, so I place the passport down onto the desk and sink into the swivel chair to read it. Maybe this will shed some light on who Jeannie is. As I sit down, a sudden, unexpected shaft of light bursts through the only window in the room, the sun's rays having been temporarily released from behind the clouds. As I open the letter, little dust motes are freed into the air and begin flying busily around in the light like little planes looking for a place to land.

"Dear Mum," the letter begins and what follows is so awful I can barely bring myself to read the letter to its conclusion. Benedict was Jeannie's stepfather. He raped her and she became pregnant. I decide to look through the files again, to see if there is anything else to do with Jeannie, and I find a copy of a deed poll. Jeannie changed her name to Dawn Kent. Shit! Jeannie is Mum? It would explain why she doesn't want anything to do with Benedict, why she didn't want his name on my birth certificate, why she has been so jumpy and protective of me all my life.

I feel shell-shocked and stare at the letter for a bit, as if willing it to reveal more, and then I jump as I hear the familiar sound of tyres on gravel and the slam-slam of car doors. Mum and Marjorie are back from Hen Picked. At first, my instinct is to quickly file the passport and letter away and lock the desk drawer before I am caught in the act of snooping. But for some reason I don't do that. I sit and wait until Marjorie calls out to me from the front door.

"Mary, darling! Come and see our new feathery friends – there are some proper characters!"

I hear Mum drop the back of the pick-up truck and I know she will be reaching for the cat carriers that will have been used to transport the chickens. I get up from the chair, still clutching the letter, and make my way to the open front door, where I see Mum lifting the last of three clucking carriers onto the drive and Marjorie talking in animated baby-fashion to the new arrivals.

"Who is Jeannie?" I ask, although I know I have already worked it out. Both Mum and Marjorie stop what they are doing and go as still as statues, as if the question is a giant pause button.

"Mum?" I say in an attempt to resume play, and Mum and Marjorie look at each other. The blood has drained from Mum's face – she is the colour of alabaster and I can see her visibly shaking as her eyes stray to the letter in my hand. Marjorie reaches out to touch Mum's arm as if to remind her she's not alone.

"Where did you get that?" Mum's voice is barely above a whisper, but the atmosphere is so charged it feels as noisy as radio static and none of us has heard Mack return from his walk.

"Seems like it's finally time for the truth, lass," he says to Mum, almost nonchalantly as he passes by and walks into the house. "I'll pop the kettle on." I don't know why, but I get the feeling he has been waiting for this, whatever this is, for a long time.

I look back at Mum, my heart thumping. If there is a truth to be told, it stands to reason there will have been lies, too.

"Are you Jeannie, Mum?" I ask.

Mum closes her eyes as she takes a big intake of breath as if she needs inflating to deal with this. She seems almost taller when she opens her eyes to look into mine.

"No, Mary," she says, her voice stronger now. "I'm not Jeannie. My real name is Anna. Let's go inside and talk. I'll explain everything."

PART II

"Only death can part us"
Jamie

CHAPTER 19

Sri Lanka – twenty years ago

Dawn

I wake to an eerie stillness and for a moment I am confused. I look around and it takes a while for me to adjust to the horror of realising that the bright-coloured fabrics I can see around me contain dead bodies. I feel panicked, I need to get out of here. I stand up, weak and shaking, and spot a flash of purple by my feet and I remember.

> *I see the young woman, her red hair plastered to her pale face as she looks up at me. I feel our hands gripping on to each other and I am screaming at her to hold on tight as I try to pull her towards me. I feel her grip weaken and I can see in her eyes the very moment she gives up and she lets go. I make a grab for the bag that she is wearing across her body in an attempt to keep hold of her, but the strap breaks and the bag is the only thing I am left holding on to as I watch her being sucked, unresisting, beneath the debris-strewn water.*

The whole thing took no more than a few seconds – just a few seconds for that young woman to go from living to dying. How can that even be?

I had somehow managed to keep hold of her bag as I hauled myself to safety onto the roof of this building, and I now feel a strange sense of responsibility for it. I couldn't save her, but I can keep a part of her with me so long as I have her bag. I pick the bag up, knot together the broken strap and place it over my head to wear it cross-body in the same way she had done.

As I look down from the roof of the building, I can see that the water has subsided, leaving a mud-pit of disaster in its wake. I climb my way down over the collapsed buildings and makeshift ladders of accumulated debris, over bits of concrete and cement, palm trees and splintered wood, broken furniture – all slick and slippery with thick, salty mud. I slip and my sarong snags on a sharp piece of wood – part of an old fence that has been whittled into a giant toothpick – and as I roughly tug at the sarong it rips a long tear into the fabric. I don't notice that the piece of wood has also scratched at my thigh until I see a scarlet patch of blood seeping along the torn edge of the sarong.

I reach the ground and everything is chaotic yet strangely almost silent. As I stumble through the chaos, I feel my ears pop and a trickle of water leaves them; I realise now that the silence was a trick played on me by the water carried in my ears. Now my ears are clear, I can hear the grief and shock and desperation as well as see it: names being shouted out as people desperately try to locate their loved ones; lifeless eyes and twisted limbs rising out from the rubble and the sounds of people digging through mud and ruins to get to them; the terrifying noise of unstable buildings collapsing and creating yet more death and destruction; and the worst noise of all, the wailing. I've seen scenes like this before, as entertainment on screens in cinemas with a tub of popcorn on my lap. But this is not a disaster movie, it is not entertainment, it is real and harrowing and impossible for my brain to process.

Suddenly someone grabs my arm and twists me round. Jamie has found me. But, to my surprise, it's not Jamie, my husband; it is a man looking for some other woman, not me, and the disappointment in his eyes is of the same intensity as the relief will be in mine. In that moment, I realise more than anything that I do not want to be found.

A butterfly movement in my tummy startles me and I place my hand on my stomach as I think of the impossible baby that is still growing inside of me, the one that Jamie has no idea about. I can hardly believe it has survived after everything it has been put through. A month ago, I started cramping and bleeding heavily, passing large clots of blood – I had suffered a miscarriage before, so I had no doubt as to what it had meant, that I had lost our baby. When I told Jamie that I had miscarried again, he blamed me. He accused me of not resting enough, of eating the wrong things, of being too uptight. He was right, it *was* my fault, but not for any of those reasons. It was my fault because I had *prayed* for it to happen. I was suffocating, slowly drowning in his warped version of love, and I had slowly come to realise that, with a baby, there was even less chance that I would ever be able to get out. A baby was never going to change things for the better; a baby would make me more trapped than ever.

But last week I was devastated when the pregnancy test kit I bought secretly at the airport pharmacy confirmed what I had begun to suspect, that I was still pregnant. I can only guess at how this could be. Maybe the miscarriage I thought I had suffered was actually a twin, or maybe I'd suffered a ruptured placenta. There are plenty of stories like this online when you look for them, but, whatever the reason, this baby is still here, clinging on to life. I haven't found the courage to tell Jamie yet because telling him will make it real, and until now I haven't wanted it to be real; I've wanted it to go away. But now I am not so sure. This baby is a fighter – it has been through so much already and survived; maybe it deserves its chance to be born.

I carry on walking, although I have no idea where I'm going; there are no landmarks for me to follow anymore. The ground beneath me is uneven – I say ground, but it isn't the ground, not really, it is a layer of flattened rubbish lying over the top of the ground – and I trip over something and fall to my knees. A hand appears in front of my face and I hear a voice speaking to me in a language I don't understand. I grab the hand and am hauled back to standing.

"You OK, lady?" the man says, switching to broken English, but my vocal cords are paralysed and I just nod, let go of his hand and stumble on. He doesn't try to stop me; there are too many people needing, and accepting of, his help.

I walk until my bare feet hurt too much and then I sit down. I want to cry, but for some reason I can't. I pull the velvet purple bag around my body onto my stomach and hug it for comfort, as if it is my baby that I am hugging. Then the tears finally come; I finally start to cry at the senselessness of it all. Why I managed to hold onto the girl's bag but not onto her. Why I should have been the one to survive when my life is not worth living.

After a few minutes, I calm down and stop crying. It has occurred to me that the bag may hold clues as to who the girl was, clues that will at least help me to find her family and let them know what has happened to her. I unzip the bag and tip out the contents. A purse, a passport and a carrier bag fall out. I open the passport. I can make out the name – Jeannie Eleanor Sutcliffe – and a date of birth that tells me she was just eighteen. Water has seeped into the photograph – it is possible to see her flame-red hair, a similar colour to my own, but her features are obscure. I don't need the photograph to see her face, though, I can see it plain enough in my memory.

I turn my attention to the carrier bag, which I find is holding a beach dress, a peaked cap and pair of flip-flops, size 7. I am size 6 and have nothing on my feet, so I gratefully slip on the flip-flops; they fit OK, not overly big. The remaining items in the carrier bag are an open return air ticket from Colombo Airport to Heathrow, and an envelope addressed "Mum". I don't know why, I know it is wrong, but I open the letter. The carrier bag has protected the letter a little from the water, so it is damp but legible. By the time I finish reading, I am shivering, in a state of shock at some of the parallels between Jeannie's life and my own. It seems inconceivable that she and I, of all people, could have ended up thrust together in this way.

I re-read the parts where Jeannie talks about the baby growing inside of her:

> ... *this baby is as much of a victim as I have been. It didn't ask to find itself growing inside of me, it doesn't know the evil that helped shape its existence, and, although I am terrified, I have decided to keep it. I have decided to be a mother.*
> ... *I am walking away – it is the only way to keep this baby safe from Ben. If he knew the truth about what is growing inside of me, there is no way he would let us go.*

I have decided to be a mother... I am walking away... There is no way he would let us go. I read those words over and over – I understand them, I *feel* them. Jamie is obsessed with me, to the point that I feel like his possession. He believes ours is a perfect relationship, that I am a perfect wife, and he cannot handle anything less. So long as I avoid situations that might leave him insecure or upset, so long as I don't do anything that he might disapprove of, so long as I don't disagree or question him, everything is OK. But, if things aren't the way he feels they should be, if *I* am not as perfect as I should be, he changes, becomes angry. Not physically violent with me, never that, but he rages inside. I can see it in his eyes, how he struggles to contain himself, to control the anger invading him, and it has been getting worse since he decided we should have a baby.

I was so young when we met, I didn't know what loving someone was supposed to look like. When Jamie told me that we were soul mates and were destined to be together, I wanted to believe him – I *did* believe him. He was romantic and loving and wanted me all to himself, which I found sweet at first, before it became suffocating. One by one my friends disappeared and then, when my parents died, I found myself completely reliant on Jamie. He dealt with the estate and controlled the finances, putting the money from the sale of their house into his own bank account and, when I queried it, he looked hurt.

"Why do you need your own bank account, Anna? We're married – you don't need a separate account anymore, you only have to ask if you want something. You make it sound like you don't trust me. Is that it? Don't you trust your own husband?" His eyes were an odd mix of anguish and anger. He made me feel like I was the worst wife in the world, like I was accusing him of stealing the money and so I left it, just accepted that that he was my husband and would take control for us both.

My inheritance meant that we had enough money that I didn't need to work, but, ironically, without my own regular income and no social contact, it made me even more dependent upon Jamie. He gave me a credit card but it came with a credit limit that was only just enough for me to pay for food and bills. Despite the sale of my parents' house being over £300,000, I had to ask if I needed any more money. Without friends, family or income, he had complete control over my life. I couldn't leave him – I had no one to turn to and no access to money. Most of the time I just accepted that this was how it was, but every now and then resentment would raise its head. Jamie always somehow sensed when this was happening and he would do something extravagant to spoil me and show how much he loved me, and I would be left feeling guilty that I had ever thought badly of him.

But, since Jamie decided he wanted us to have a baby, things have changed and I feel very afraid of him. I cannot tell him how I feel, what I want, as I can sense something dark rising in him when I do. I realise that there is something very wrong with him. He is like a bottle of poison, harmless so long as the cork is in tight; but the cork is disintegrating, and if I shake the bottle, even a little, the poison trickles out. I want to leave him, but I just don't know how.

I think of the day no more than a month ago when I told Jamie that I had miscarried for a second time. I knew I didn't want to try for another baby and somehow in that moment I found the courage to tell him. I told him that I'd had enough, that I needed some space. I didn't quite have the courage to say I wanted to leave him, but I was opening that door and Jamie knew it. Just remembering how he reacted makes the panic rise within me again; my heart is beating so fast I am struggling to breathe. He tilted his head to one side and looked at me in silence for a few bottomless seconds, his pupils wide and dilated as if his eyes were ingesting me. When he finally spoke, his voice was slow and calculating, as if he didn't want any part of what he was saying to be missed.

"Love is a form of ecstasy, Anna. Did you know that?" he said, his eyes strangely dispassionate. "It is beyond all reason and self-control." He reached out to lightly brush my cheek with the back of his hand.

"A man can descend into madness because of love. He is capable of *anything* in the name of love."

He moved his fingers across my face to my mouth and started playing with my lips. The action was slow and gentle, but menacing and I didn't dare move.

"God, I love you, you're so perfect," he said, moving his fingers down over my chin to my neck, spreading his hand briefly around my throat, applying gentle pressure, before weaving his fingers into the hair at the base of my skull. He pulled me in to him, kissing my unresponsive lips, then kissing my neck, before moving his mouth to my ear.

"If you ever tried to leave, Anna, I'd have no choice but to find you," he whispered and I could feel the heat of his breath inside my ear pervading my body, making my skin prickle. "Because love is forever. *We* are forever. Only death can part us."

He hadn't hurt me physically, he hadn't raised his voice, he hadn't made any direct threat to my life, but I was left in no doubt as to what he was implying. And then he took in a deep breath before letting it back out long and slow, and with it a change in tone.

"You know what?" he said brightly. "You're right – I've been unfair. You need a break, we both do. I'll book us a holiday. Recharge our batteries. We've got one embryo left – we can try again when we get back." Then he kissed the top of my head, got up and walked out of the room, whistling as he went, as if nothing in the world was wrong.

His words resound in my head now: "*Only death can part us*" and suddenly everything seems to come into focus. I could disappear. People go missing in disasters all the time – they are never found and are presumed dead. I just need to make Jamie believe that I am dead.

I remove my blood-spattered sarong, and the money-wallet containing my passport from around my waist, and place them on the ground. I pull off my wedding ring and I try to remove my watch but my hands are shaking so much that I cannot work the clasp, so I wrench it from my wrist and toss it. Jamie gave me the watch on our wedding day and it has become a shackle around my wrist ever since – it feels good to be free of it. I know these things will be gathered up eventually and, I hope, used as evidence to support my death.

I slip Jeannie's beach dress over my bikini, put her peaked cap on my head and reload her passport and letter into the purple bag. I remove the cash that is in her purse, alleviating my guilt by telling myself she of all people would understand and would want me and my baby to have it, and then I toss the purse in the hope that it can be picked up and used to identify her later. Her mother may not have protected her as she should have done, but she still deserves something of her daughter back. In the distance I can see people making their way up to higher ground, to what looks like a temple on a hill. I head for that, where I hope to find a way to get myself to Colombo Airport and on a plane back to London using Jeannie's airline ticket and passport.

I have no idea what I will do when I get there; I just know that this is the only chance I will ever have to be free.

CHAPTER 20

Jamie

I had another dream last night. It's strange because I rarely used to dream at all, at least none that I ever really remembered, but since it happened I dream regularly about her. In the dream, I found Anna's broken body face down in the water, bobbing rhythmically with the residual current, her bright blue sarong billowing out around her like a deflated and defeated life jacket. I turned her over and recoiled as her beautiful face had been destroyed – the place where her striking amber eyes once sat were now just cavernous black holes, no more than hiding places for creatures of the sea. I desperately scanned the shallows for her eyes, knowing that if I could find them, and return them to her face, she would be alright. Then I spotted them! Jubilant, I scooped them up before realising that they weren't her eyes after all; they were just little amber gemstones. I started screaming in frustration, but then the frustration turned into fear as tentacles reached out of her eye sockets and turned into chubby little fingers that snatched the pebbles from my hand.

I woke screaming and I lay frozen for a few seconds, my mind trying to process what had just happened. There was a time that I would have had that sweet dawning that comes after a nightmare, the realisation that it was only a bad dream, not real, but, as my heart rate subsided and the sweat on my body turned cold, I was forcibly reminded yet again that this wasn't a nightmare but a variant of the truth. She did die. She is never coming back to me. No one told me that grief could last forever.

In the beginning – I've just realised that this is a strange choice of words to describe an event that ended everything for me – I was in a state of shock, denial. Stage 1, apparently, of the five stages of grief, according to the grief counsellor I had later been persuaded to see. All I knew was that I had been left wondering what the hell I was supposed to do, how I was supposed to *feel* when the very thought that she had died was unimaginable. I can't tell you much about those first few months after returning home, if I am honest. I don't remember eating or sleeping, although I must have somehow managed to do enough of both to just about keep me alive. Normal life was played out in my peripheral vision, blurred actions belonging to muffled sounds that I was aware of in the way you might be aware of someone standing nearby, waiting to speak to you whilst you are involved in another conversation. Whatever they want to say has to wait; normal life had to wait. Although in denial, I couldn't ignore the fact that I would never be the same again and I found myself looking straight ahead into the shattered mirror of my life, wondering which of the distorted images staring back was the real me, the new me.

By the time of Anna's memorial service, I had crept into the next stage of the so-called grief cycle: anger. I was surprised at how many people were at her service. Anna was a quiet person, who never really accumulated friends in the way that some people do. Among the mourners were my parents; my brother, his wife and children; friends from our life together; and what felt like an invading army of her relatives: ageing aunts and uncles and some cousins whose faces I vaguely recognised from her parents' funerals that had taken place years earlier. She had been an only child and, not long after we had married, her parents had died in a car accident. When the pain of losing them had subsided, we used to joke that I had become her complete universe: husband, friend and entire family rolled into one, and so I had all but forgotten about the larger extended family that now sat sniffing and coughing in the pews behind me.

I remained quiet and still on my pew, listening to the sounds and whispers around me, echoing and exaggerated by the natural acoustics of the church. I was in the privileged front pew directly facing the vicar, a privilege I would rather not have had to endure, and it occurred to me that this position protects you from putting your grief on display to the rest of the mourners, all of whom I was certain harboured a morbid curiosity as to what my grief looked like. That thought made me self-conscious about whether I looked grief-stricken enough and I wondered whether maybe I should exaggerate my display of distress for the benefit of others. It may not have been visible, but I could feel my inward agony tightening its grip on me and slowly twisting into something dark and angry, something fearful.

Out of nowhere, a butterfly fluttered into the church and landed on my forearm. It was a cabbage white, the white of its wings emphasised against the midnight-blue of my suit. The suit was the one I had worn on our wedding day, a wool-and-cashmere number that had been custom made for me, or rather for the "me" that I was the day we married. The "me" that was sitting in that front pew facing the reality of "till death do us part" was a shrunken version of the man that had so flippantly said those words only three years before. It seemed like a good idea at the time to wear it to say goodbye, but as I sat there it suddenly felt as wrong as it looked on me. Loose and unstructured around the muscles that once gave the fabric definition, it looked borrowed, which I guess in a way it was –

borrowed from the old me – and the bagginess was a reminder that without her I was less than I used to be.

When the service began, the vicar commented on the "sea of people" before him, not realising how perverse and insensitive that metaphor was considering how she had died. I was so angry that I wanted to drown him in the ornate christening font that I had become fixated on the minute I walked into the church, the one that would never be used for the baby that we had been trying for before she died, but instead I let the anger slide slowly down my face in the form of a single corrosive tear. During his sermon, the vicar read from John 10:27–28 "My sheep hear my voice, and I know them, and they follow me. *I give them eternal life, and they will never perish, and no one will snatch them out of my hand..."*

Eternal life. Never perish. Snatch. Those words reverberated inside my head, bouncing off the walls of my skull. I cannot describe the anger I felt that she had been snatched from me, or what I would have done to have given her eternal life. After the service, I stood and I watched her family, people I didn't really know, hugging each other awkwardly, not knowing how to balance being pleased to see each other whilst somehow remaining respectful of the reason they were seeing each other at all. Their facial expressions were doleful, their brows furrowed to emphasise their sorrow. At first, they whispered to each other (as if the dead care how loud you speak!) "How are you?" "Good to see you, such a shame it's under such awful circumstances. I still can't believe it, so *tragic*". But the truth is, whispering requires much more effort than talking freely, and those people, it seemed, had so much to catch up on that, before long, the hushed tones gradually raised themselves back to normal, even some *laughter*, which cut right through me.

"These days we only seem to get together at weddings and funerals..." I heard one woman say, and it seemed clear to me that they were using Anna's memorial disingenuously, simply to catch up with each other rather than to mourn her. My hands were so tightly furled into fists that my knuckles ached with the desire to punch something. I have never been a physically aggressive person, but it took all my effort not to lash out.

A few nameless friends from various stages in her life-before-me, people she had not seen for years before she died, approached me to offer their trite and overused platitudes and I resisted the urge to call them out as the fakes I felt they were. As far as I was concerned, they were not true friends, they were no more than taphophiles, tombstone tourists playing on the spurious fame of having once known the tragic dead person. There is something about dying young that elevates a person to celebrity status for the briefest time. These "friends" were not there through the multiple miscarriages that she suffered, or the gruelling rounds of IVF that began with hope and ended with despair. Only I was. I was the only person that really cared for and loved her in the end.

Out of the corner of my eye I spotted a woman I recognised, and felt the full weight of her glare on me. I turned my face and met her gaze in a challenge to see who might blink first. Predictably, she did; after only a few seconds she turned her head and walked away. She was as easy to get rid of in that moment as she had been when I first met Anna. Anna had thought she was her friend, but I showed her just how much of a friend she was – she walked straight into my honey-trap, right through to the other side, far away from the only woman I would ever truly love. It nearly killed me to see how upset Anna was, how *betrayed* she felt, but I helped her to understand that I had done it because I loved her, and when you really love someone you help them to see the hidden truths that they are blinded to, however much that may hurt. How could she possibly ever trust me if I didn't act on the things I could see so clearly? If there had been any other way to prove to her how toxic her friendship with that woman was, I would have taken it, and eventually Anna realised that and loved me all the more for it, I think.

I hadn't given that woman a second thought until she had the temerity to turn up at the memorial, and I haven't thought about her in the twenty years that have passed since. *Twenty years.* The time has flown by and yet has also passed interminably slowly, if that is even possible. During that time, I have learned that grief is a toxic companion that becomes strangely addictive. You need it, because without it you fear that the object of your grief will somehow become less important or even disappear completely. Grief reminds you of them daily; it is the conduit in which they continue to exist. Even now, all these years on, the grief is still there, albeit a shadow hiding in the wings of the new life I have created. It surfaces at night, invading my dreams, or when my guard is down it manifests itself in the face of a stranger taking on her features, so that for the briefest moment she lives again.

I glance at the clock – it is 4.30pm. Last night's dream has distracted me for most of the day and I haven't managed to get anything productive done. I am self-employed and work from home these days. The front door suddenly bursts open, letting in a slew of cold air that is quickly followed by Amber, my fifteen-year-old daughter. So far Amber hasn't turned into the archetypal teenage nightmare you see mocked in sitcoms. She isn't moody and uncommunicative; she is bright and chatty with an intelligence that makes her stand out from the majority of her peers. Rarely have I seen her angry, except when listening to political debates on social issues. She has a strong sense of social justice (which I am fairly sure is due to nature rather than nurture as I have little interest in such things) and she has joined her school's debating team.

"Hi, Dad," she says breezily as she dumps her school backpack onto the kitchen table. I can feel the cold air from outside clinging to her like an invisible forcefield, and for some reason it makes me think of the old Ready Brek adverts, those that show a warm orange glow around the kids, only right now I imagine a blue one around Amber. My heart warms, despite the coldness in the air, as it always does when I look at her. She is so like her mother it almost hurts.

"Whassup?" she says quizzically, as she notices the way I am looking at her.

"Nothing, Anna," I say, quickly realising my slip of tongue, but Amber has not registered my mistake; instead, she has her head in the fridge hunting out a pre-dinner snack. My slip makes me wonder how much longer I can keep the truth from her.

CHAPTER 21

Jamie

People used to tell me that time heals, but I didn't want to heal. Instead of fighting my grief, I learned to welcome it in some strange way, because a life without grief would mean accepting a life without Anna. I didn't want a life without Anna. I wanted to give her eternal life, like the sheep in the vicar's sermon at her funeral. Then I stumbled across Hannah and I just knew, I realised that she was the answer, that I could still have everything I thought I had lost. That I could have Anna back.

I remember the day I first saw her; she literally stopped me in my tracks with her likeness of Anna. She was working as a waitress in a coffee shop and I was passing the window when I saw her bending over her order pad and laughing with a customer. I was caught off guard, and shocked enough to say Anna's name out loud, which gained me some strange looks from passers-by. Despite already running late for an appointment, I walked into the coffee shop and sat down, unable to take my eyes off of this woman. On closer inspection, I could see that there were obvious differences – Hannah had brown hair, whereas Anna's had been auburn; Hannah's eyes were a light brown and unremarkable in comparison to Anna's – but her bone structure, the shape of her nose and curve of her mouth, the way her thick hair fell from her parting when she leaned forward, although not exact, reminded me very much of Anna. Eventually, Hannah approached me and smiled, her pen poised on her pad as the repetitious question was on her lips: "Hi, what can I get you?"

I kept her chatting for a bit about the menu so I could examine her some more. She was slightly taller than Anna, but by no more than an inch; her shoulders were marginally wider, her breasts fuller. Up close I could see she was a little older than Anna had been when she died, the corners of her eyes showing the faintest signs of the deep lines that would form on her face in the fullness of time. Lines that Anna will never have to fret about. I had taken for granted that Anna and I would gradually grow old together, but instead I have been forced to grow old without her. She will forever be suspended in time as a young woman, whilst I will slowly accumulate all the physical baggage of old age as I grey and wrinkle and sag with each advancing year. Before long, the image of her – young and unlined – will no longer be compatible with the old man that I will become.

From her accent, I deduced that Hannah was probably a local, born and bred, which likely meant she had very little ambition or experience of the world outside of the town she lived in. I checked her ring finger – it was bare – and I wondered if she spent her evenings watching the sort of films that offer romantic hope to the romantically hopeless, wondering when her turn to be swept off her feet would come. Hannah didn't look like she would have a difficult time finding romance, so it was my guess that she had fallen so hard for the idea of love portrayed in those films, that the reality of romance never quite matched up to her expectations. If it doesn't look or feel like the love in those films, it can't *be* love, and she would rather have no love at all than the wrong kind. I just knew that all I needed to do was give her the fake love she craved, and she would be mine. If I wanted her.

I went home, and that night I had a dream. I was standing at the water's edge and on the horizon I could see a body, this time floating face-up in the water, a bright blue sarong flapping around it like the wings of a manta ray. With each set of waves, the body gravitated nearer to shore, until eventually it was close enough for me to wade out to it. When I reached it, I could see it was Hannah and my heart sank with the realisation and despair that it wasn't my Anna floating there. As my eyes spontaneously filled with tears, salty as the ocean, she spoke.

"Don't be disappointed," she said, only it was Anna's voice coming from her mouth. "Our dream is still alive."

I woke crying, then, with a strong sense that meeting Hannah had not been a coincidence; it was fate, and Anna was giving me her blessing. A few days later, a letter arrived in the post and it was the final sign, the confirmation I needed. It was time to begin the process of immortalising Anna.

CHAPTER 22

Jamie

Getting a woman to sleep with me has never been a problem – I'm good-looking, keep myself in shape and intrinsically know how to flirt. But I didn't need Hannah to just sleep with me; I needed her to fall head over heels in love with me and that was a whole different ball game to the one-night stands, the release of sexual tension, I had preferred since Anna had died. The thought of sleeping with the same woman more than once made me feel sick, like I was betraying Anna somehow, but I knew that there was no other way if my plan was to work.

It was easier than I thought in the end, in part because I was drawn to Hannah – not just for her physical similarities to Anna but also because I actually did come to like her. Her naivety, her lack of harsh edges, appealed to my protective side. Someone like Hannah will always end up manipulated and bruised, whether physically or metaphorically, and so in many ways she was lucky that *I* had set my sights on her, rather than someone who would not appreciate her. I may not have been able to truly love her but I would make sure she was looked after. Safe.

I started to visit the café once a week and always on a day

that I knew she would be working. I would take my laptop on the pretence of work whilst I sat for a couple of hours at a table tucked in a corner. I knew that one day a week would mean my plan would take longer than I would like, but I needed to do this properly and I was worried that any more could be seen as strange, or even stalking. The café was a small, family-run business, under the control of a matronly septuagenarian called Olive. The kindest way to describe the place would be nostalgic, although a more accurate description would be a museum. It had remained essentially untouched since the 70s and was a warts-and-all depiction of a 1970s greasy spoon, so beloved by the family that they could not bring themselves to update it in any way. If we were talking hairstyles, the café was still sporting a pudding-bowl cut.

It was usually around 10.30am when I arrived at the café, a little bell above the door announcing my arrival. At that time of day, the café usually had a few patrons, but finding a table to sit at was never a problem. My preferred table, tucked quietly away in one corner, was usually available and I would head directly for that, following the pale pathway worn into the orange vinyl floor by years of foot traffic. Despite the café's tired and worn décor, it was spotlessly clean and you could see the wet lines recently left behind from a damp cloth on the shiny, green Formica surface of the table. If the air had not been filled with the greasy smell of sausages and bacon, I just knew I would be breathing in the lemony scent of cleaning fluids.

The menus were the old-fashioned wipe-clean, laminated type, somewhat sticky from the last wipe-over, and the fare on offer was predictable. I always ordered the same thing: filter coffee, black, with a Danish pastry, making sure I smiled and made eye contact with Hannah when ordering. She wouldn't hold my gaze for too long, looking shyly down at her pad as she wrote my order, which was a good indicator that she found me attractive, at least. Each time I left, I would leave a generous tip

– I wanted to make sure I really stood out from the rest of the customers and make her look forward to my return.

After a few weeks, Hannah would make a point of acknowledging me when I walked in the door, mouthing "Hi" with a broad smile and "I'll be over in a bit".

"No rush," I would always reply, which, after a few more weeks, I cheekily extended to "No rush – you're worth the wait!" This made her blush, making her look even more radiant. I would sit at my table, drinking my coffee and eating my pastry, whilst seemingly engrossed in my work, but secretly I would be watching Hannah work the room, listening to her conversations with the customers, soaking up any valuable information I could on her, recording my findings on my laptop.

It is amazing what information you can learn about a stranger just by casually watching and listening. I learned that she lived a few streets away from the café in an area that was well known locally for being less than desirable. She flat-shared with a girl called Tammy, a short and skinny redhead who came into the café occasionally for a sneaky free cup of tea in return for gossip. I learned that Hannah had a boyfriend called Toby, who sent her flowers to apologise when he fucked up (which was quite often). Despite the fact that he was obviously a prick, her eyes lit up when those flowers arrived, and I just knew she would forgive him practically anything so long as he made overtly romantic gestures. I learned that she would love to dine at La Cucina Italiana, but it was too expensive on her waitress wages, and, despite numerous hints, Toby still hadn't taken her there, not even on special occasions. One of the most important things I learned, though, the one thing I really needed to be certain of, was that she loved children.

Whenever a baby or child was brought into the café, she would make a beeline for them, making a fuss of the infant and complimenting the mother on producing such a beautiful child. When asked if she had any children, her reply was always the same: "Not yet", which told me she wanted them. The fact that Hannah had a boyfriend was a problem I needed to overcome, but it turned out not to be such a challenge after all, when she came in one day with red and puffy eyes after she found out he had been cheating on her. We had enough of a rapport by now for her to feel comfortable telling Olive this in front of me, and I could tell by Olive's reaction that she was thinking the same thing I was – why was Hannah the only person that seemed surprised by what Toby had done?

"He must be blind or a fool!" I blurted out from behind my laptop. "Or maybe a blind fool!"

She turned to me, mildly astonished by my remark, and then promptly laughed, a tinkly, girly laugh that suited her. I had broken the waitress/customer dam between us, and the water seemed warm, so I continued.

"I'm a good listener," I said and invited her to join me for a coffee during her next break, which she did. She opened up about Toby and his loose fists and even looser morals, and I helped convince her that he was a low life that didn't deserve her, which was true. In return for her openheartedness, I offered her a little piece of my story. I told her I was a widower, but didn't elaborate on the hows and whys, just saying that I couldn't see how I would ever find myself in a relationship without feeling guilty. I could see something shift in her eyes then; it was the romantic movie-script moment she had been waiting for: she was wondering if maybe she could be the special woman that heals my broken heart. When it was time for me to leave, I left my money on the table along with my usual generous tip. On the bill I wrote *"Don't forget, you deserve better!"* and drew an amateur caricature of my version of a blind fool.

The next week I noticed that she had started to pay more attention to her appearance and I felt on safe territory to offer small compliments.

"Have you changed your hair? It suits you. The colour you are wearing really brings out the colour of your eyes." If I had said these things too soon, they would have been dismissed as cheesy, or even creepy – timing in these matters is crucial. Hannah seemed to enjoy them and beamed her appreciation back at me. I liked making her smile, it made me feel good. One day she jokily asked me, "What do you do on that laptop? Are you writing a book?"

"Well," I said, "that would be more interesting than the truth! If I was writing a book, what type of book would you like it to be? What do you like to read?" Without hesitating she responded, "*Wuthering Heights*."

This took me back. *Wuthering Heights* is a tragic tale of love; dark and powerful, not the fluffy, light romance that I had imagined her to read. For some reason, it almost stopped me in my tracks. I considered giving up, thinking I had completely misread her, until she continued with the words "I love Jane Austen" and I realised immediately that she had never read *Wuthering Heights*; she was simply trying to impress me.

"You do know," I said in a mock-serious tone, "that Jane Austen did not write *Wuthering Heights*?" She laughed her tinkly laugh before saying, "Busted! Will you still like me if I admit to a bookshelf full of Danielle Steel?"

"You are impossible not to like, Hannah," I said, making her cheeks pink up. And I meant it. She was sweet, good-natured, the type that picks up snails to move them out of harm's way. But she was also naïve and vacuous enough to believe only in a fairy-tale version of love, and that was her greatest weakness, and my way in.

This time, along with a generous tip, I left my phone number on the bill. The next week we went on our first date.

CHAPTER 23

Jamie

Hannah had waited three days before calling me, which I admit surprised me – I had expected her call much sooner. For our first date I decided to take her to the cinema to see *Pride and Prejudice*. It seemed fitting – it was Jane Austen, after all, our first little in-joke – and it was romantic, which I knew would press her buttons.

The date went well and when I took her home at the end of the evening we lingered a little awkwardly by the beaten and graffitied communal door-entry to her flat. I knew she wanted me to kiss her, it was palpable. But I needed to be her Mr Darcy, and Mr Darcy would not be kissing after a first date, let alone doing the other things my mind was imagining doing to her. Hannah was the first to break the silence:

"Thank you for a great evening," she said. "I would invite you up for a coffee, but Tammy's home and…"

"No problem," I said, "there's no rush for coffee." I hoped that she understood the innuendo. I leaned towards her then, and brushed back her hair, securing it with my hand to the back of her neck, before I kissed her slowly on the cheek. "I'll wait here until you are safely in your flat," I told her. "Wave at me from the window when you get in. You can't be too careful – you don't know who is lurking about in corridors these days." I could tell that my concern for her welfare had replaced her disappointment at not being properly kissed.

Hannah and I spoke on the phone a few times after that first date, flirty phone calls continuing to build on the chemistry between us, before we met up again. I was leading the pace, and made sure we took things slowly. I wanted to build it up in the way a romance builds in a film, but I also needed time to adjust to being with a person other than Anna.

We went for several walks at night – Hannah loved the smoky dusk light, and I must admit it was easier to talk, somehow, under the cover of darkness. When it became chilly, I would put my arm around her to keep her warm, and one night I absent-mindedly kissed the top of her head, something I used to do when walking with Anna. When I did that, Hannah looked up at me expectantly, and, although I didn't feel quite ready, I had no choice but to kiss her properly then, and so I did. It was a short kiss, under a pool of light cast by a lamp post, my hands cupping her face in a deliberate gesture of tenderness. When I pulled away, Hannah's eyes remained closed and in that fraction of a second I could see the purity of her feelings for me. I hugged her to me then, protectively, and wished that I could feel the same back, knowing I never would.

After the kiss, it felt like the right time to quicken the pace a little. During this time, we kissed and we caressed, but I stopped short of making love to Hannah. I didn't want to make it all too easy and risk losing her once the novelty had worn off, but I also knew there was a fine line between building anticipation and getting bored of waiting. So, I gave her my bleeding heart to mend, telling her that I would understand if she couldn't wait, but that I needed time to make sure Anna was out of my system. This wasn't really true, of course, as no one could ever take Anna's place in my heart. When Anna died, I not only lost the only woman I would ever love; I also lost the dream we had shared of having a baby together. I knew I could never resurrect Anna, but it might be possible to recreate our dream. And for that I needed Hannah to be wholly committed to me.

The fact was, I already knew when I would be "ready". I had it all planned – it was going to be on her birthday. I was going to give her an expensive cocktail dress and lingerie, then take her to La Cucina Italiana to wine and dine her, after which we would return to my place. On the day of her birthday, I had her gift delivered to her flat, along with a note telling her to wear what was enclosed and I would pick her up at 8pm. The dress was a beautiful designer label – off the shoulder, mid-length in black silk that I knew would skim Hannah's curves perfectly. The underwear, black satin and lace, was sexy, but in an elegant rather than overt way. Both the dress and lingerie were individually wrapped in tissue paper, and had been expertly dry cleaned and pressed so that Hannah would never know that they had once belonged to Anna. I also included a new bottle of Chanel No.5, Anna's favourite perfume. It was important to me that Anna was part of this process, although Hannah could never know.

When I picked her up, I nearly cried. She stepped out of the communal entrance to her flat onto the pavement outside, her expensive-looking beauty incongruous with the grey and grimy street. Her hair was placed into a chignon, just like Anna used to do with hers, and I had not been expecting that. It could easily have been Anna standing there, and I felt a sob form in my throat, the familiar guttural pain hitting me like a punch to the solar plexus, making it difficult for me to breathe. I did my best to compose myself and jumped out of the taxi to open the door for her, unable to take my eyes off of her. She looked at me and smiled, her smile fading to concern when she noticed my eyes were shiny with unshed tears.

"You look so beautiful; you are moving me to tears," I told her by way of an explanation before kissing her, and with that her smile was back, even brighter than before, as she slid into the back seat of the taxi, leaving the scent of Anna in the air.

We arrived at La Cucina Italiana, and this time Hannah emerged from the taxi into a world that befitted her. We walked towards the restaurant, my arm around her waist with my hand resting on her hip, my palm gliding over the familiar silk of the dress with the ebb and flow of each step. As we entered the restaurant, I noticed Alessandro, the maître d', do a double-take in our direction. Anna and I used to visit this restaurant several times a year, enough times for Alessandro to recognise us whenever we arrived, and make us feel welcome. To be honest, I hadn't even thought about Alessandro – I had no idea whether he even knew that Anna was dead and I suddenly felt a little embarrassed, exposed. Alessandro approached us with arms outstretched and a broad smile, and I knew instantly that he didn't know, that he thought Hannah was Anna.

"Signor Attwood," he said, in a softly anglicised Italian accent. "It has been too long." Then he turned to Hannah and for a split second, so fleeting that no one but me could have noticed, I saw his smile falter and confusion in his eyes, before he deployed an expert cognitive shift.

"Signorina," he said to Hannah, "may I say how beautiful you look this evening. Is this your first time at La Cucina Italiana?" Hannah's face lit up with the compliment, and she nodded.

"Then we shall do all we can to make you feel very welcome and special," he said, leading us to our table, Anna diplomatically consigned to the past and my fingernails digging into my palm in silent protest.

After our meal, we got into a taxi to make our way home. "Where to, mate?" the driver asked. Anna proceeded to give her address, but I stopped her and gave mine instead, looking directly into her eyes as I gave it so that she would know exactly what this meant. Her eyes were wide, pupils dilated like little black holes determined to pull me in before I could change my mind. I could see her breasts moving rhythmically with her increased heart rate and I felt a crackle of anticipation, which took me by surprise. I placed one hand around the side of her head, my fingers burrowing into the soft hair at the back of her neck, my thumb brushing the hollow of her cheek, and gently drew her to me, kissing her slowly, tasting the sweet champagne that was still lingering on her lips.

When we arrived at my house, we entered the entrance hall, and I closed and locked the front door as Hannah took in the surroundings. She had not been to my house before – we had always gone out on our dates, after which I would make sure she got home safely and usually ended the night with a coffee in her flat. My house was a world away from Hannah's make-do flat, which had second-hand furniture and appliances that were on their last legs and I could tell Hannah was impressed with the clean, minimalistic lines that both Anna and I had worked hard at achieving in our home.

As we walked through the hallway into the lounge, I saw Hannah's eye being drawn to a photograph on the wall. I had already taken down some photos of Anna in readiness for this moment – Hannah would be expecting me to have some memories of Anna around, but she wasn't aware of the physical resemblances between them and I didn't want to scare her in any way. A few of the photos in the house had captured their differences rather than their similarities, and so these stayed in situ, amongst them a black and white image of Anna and me taken on our wedding day, which had caught Hannah's eye. It was taken by a friend of mine, who I always thought had a soft spot for Anna. In the shot I am looking straight ahead at the camera, my stare challenging the lens, whilst my arm is firmly around my new wife's waist. Anna's right arm is draped around my neck, her hand still holding her bouquet of white lilies, and her focus, her full attention, is on me as she leans in to whisper in my ear. It is quite a serious shot for a wedding photo, but Anna looks exquisitely beautiful in it.

"You both look so young," Hannah said, and to distract her from the photo I walked up behind her, placing my hands on the curve of her waist and kissing her on the neck, making the baby-fine hairs at her nape stand on end. She started to turn around but I stopped her, releasing her hair from its chignon, allowing it to cascade to her shoulders before unzipping her dress and letting that fall to the floor.

"You are so beautiful," I whispered, before turning her around, pulling her close and kissing her with intent, rather than with romance. We had sex on the lounge floor, where I learned even more about Hannah by the moans she gave up in reaction to my touch as I navigated her body. Afterwards, she lay in the crook of my elbow as I stroked her hair and contemplated silently on how strange it was that Hannah could look so much like Anna, yet act and feel so different when I was inside of her. At first, I admit that I felt a little disappointed. I think I wanted it to feel like Anna was back with me, but I knew that I was being unrealistic and it was unfair to try and compare them in that way. Anna was here, all around me – in this house, in the lingerie and perfume Hannah was wearing – and that would have to be enough for now.

After a while, the temperature in the room started to drop and so I got up off the floor and helped Hannah to her feet. She had goosebumps on her flesh, so I picked up my suit jacket, crumpled from having been discarded on to the floor a short while earlier, and placed it around her shoulders, before lifting her up in my arms to carry her into my bedroom as if I were carrying her over a marital threshold. As I laid her down onto the bed, naked and vulnerable, I bent over her, holding her arms above her head, and looked into her eyes. She looked up at me, her eyes so bright with trust and happiness she reminded me of a little child. Then I lied to her.

"I think I'm falling in love with you," I said.

The next morning, I woke in my bed with Hannah beside me. I felt strangely replete. I turned onto my side, propped up on my elbow, and faced her. I brushed an errant strand of hair away from her face and took a moment to take in her beauty. She really was beautiful – maybe even more beautiful than Anna had been, except for her eyes; nothing could ever compare to Anna's eyes. My hand moved from her face, down her neck to the curve of her shoulder, slowly working its way down her arm until it reached her elbow, which was resting on her waist. From here my hand left her arm and travelled the path of her hip to her outer thigh. The flesh of Anna's thighs had yielded beneath my fingers when I had caressed them, but Hannah worked out and hers were firm and solid to my touch, different but not in a bad way. She moaned as my hand crossed over her knee to the inside of her thigh, working its way back up and I felt her body stiffen slightly in anticipation, relaxing again when my hand merely brushed past the area of her excitement and landed gently on her stomach, where its journey ended. Anna's stomach had been soft and feminine, perfect for storing a baby, whereas Hannah's was flat and taut and I couldn't help wondering if it would be capable of stretching to accommodate a new life.

"Do you want children?" I asked her as my hand rested on her belly. Of course, I already knew the answer, although Hannah didn't know that. The question took her by surprise, the significance of it ramped up by where my hand was placed as I asked it.

"Yes." There was a second's silence before she asked, "What about you?"

She so badly wanted me to say yes, I could hear it in her voice, for that's what happens at the end of all the best romantic fiction – a couple fall in love, have a baby and live happily ever after, although no one ever gets to see what happily ever after actually looks like; it is always left to your imagination at the end.

There are probably millions of different versions of happy-ever-after floating around in the minds of the hopelessly romantic. They have no idea that, for some, happy-ever-after can be short, harsh and brutal, and I envy them their ignorance.

"I can see a future with a baby in it," I'd said, and kissed her tenderly on the lips, working my mouth down in little kisses along the same route my hand had taken, only this time not brushing past the area that excited her.

CHAPTER 24

Jamie

In the end it had taken about six months for Hannah to completely fall in love with me. I wasn't in love with her, of course, but it felt good having someone to look after and protect again, and so not long after her birthday she moved in with me. I persuaded her that she didn't need to work at the café any longer, that it was my job to take care of her. Soon her tastes and habits started to change for the better and she started to become more refined and less rough around the edges, as I introduced her to a more cultured world.

After she moved in, she naturally wanted to put her stamp on the house, mark out her territory a bit, and I started to panic. That was not part of the deal – the house was perfect the way Anna and I had arranged it – but I had to be careful not to drive her away and so I let her have a few small victories. It would be worth it in the end, and, besides, the house would have to change before long anyway.

Apart from a few little blips, living together was good in the beginning. I liked to spoil her and she liked to be spoiled. The only setback to my plan had been Tammy's presence in Hannah's life, but, once I'd managed to convince her that Tammy would only ever be a reminder of a world she no longer fitted in to, they soon started to drift apart. Once Tammy was no longer on the scene, I felt that the time was right to take things further.

One evening, we found ourselves walking through the park. The light was rapidly fading and a chill wind was acting as a dance master to the trees, which were swaying rhythmically to the hollow sound the wind was making. I pulled Hannah in closer to me, grabbing her hand in mine before placing both of our hands into one of my pockets for extra cosiness. As we snaked through the park's walkway, we passed a young pregnant woman sitting on one of the benches. She looked to be close to her due date, her coat stretched around her burgeoning abdomen, the buttons straining at the thread. She was rubbing her belly and talking to the unborn child – an intimate moment that stirred something in me. I stopped walking and leaned against a tree, where we could watch the expectant mum from a safe distance. Then I manoeuvred Hannah to stand in front of me, and wrapped my arms around her, taking hold of her hands and strategically placing them on her stomach, my hands protectively over hers. I could feel Hannah's heart beating, the vibrations carrying through her back on to my chest, and I noticed that our hearts started to beat in sync with each other.

"What do you say we make a baby?" I whispered in her ear.

That night we had the most incredible sex, we were so turned on by the thought of what we were planning to do. I felt happy in that moment, I really did. The next day, Hannah threw away her contraceptive pills and we made love whenever we got the chance. The best part of it all was that I realised I no longer felt guilty, like I was betraying Anna; I felt that I was doing this all *for* her, for *us*.

Like most people trying to start a family, there is a naïve expectation that getting pregnant will be easy, and Hannah was no exception. I knew from experience, of course, that this is often far from the case, and I tried to manage her expectations as much as possible, without damping down her enthusiasm. When it didn't happen as quickly as she'd hoped, she did some research and turned to something called the *basal body temperature* method, hoping to get a more accurate record of her ovulation, and the days that she would be most fertile.

"A woman's temperature rises by around 0.2°C when ovulating – I'll be most fertile in the couple of days leading up to this," she had told me, along with informing me of the fact that my sperm would remain active for up to five days inside of her, which meant that the few days either side of her calculated ovulation dates were pretty frantic in the bedroom, to say the least.

I've heard it said that treating sex this way can make it feel clinical, a chore, but I found it rather fun. Maybe this was partly to do with the fact that I knew that these things would be futile, so it felt like a bit of a game to me. Hannah also took to lying on her back with her legs raised for twenty minutes after we'd had sex. Anna had done this, and I remember feeling so proud of her for how hard she was trying for us both, and I had taken to lying down beside her for the whole time as a show of solidarity. "We are in this together," I would say. But, when Hannah did it, it just looked faintly ridiculous, to be honest, and I had to walk out and leave her to it.

One thing that wasn't fun, though, was Hannah's disappointment each month when her period arrived. Even though I was prepared for it, it still depressed me to remember the despair I had gone through when Anna and I had been trying, and I did feel some guilt at putting Hannah through that. She became so stressed, and more than a little obsessed with worrying that there was something wrong with her. She assumed it must be her, as she knew that I had undergone tests when Anna and I had been trying for a baby, and my semen had been given the all-clear: champion swimmers apparently.

Then, after nearly ten months of trying, it happened: Hannah missed a period. I was stunned. You see, I knew that it was practically impossible, but if the impossible had somehow happened, it would ruin everything.

CHAPTER 25

Jamie

The missed period turned out to be a false alarm, but it had rattled me. I had been waiting for the right moment, but I very nearly let things go on for too long.

The veiled truth was that I'd had a vasectomy when I first decided Hannah was the one, specifically to avoid a situation like that, and, although common sense told me not to worry, I had still held my breath in a different kind of anticipation to Hannah's when she had excitedly taken a home pregnancy test. When it came back as negative, I breathed a secret sigh of relief, but Hannah was so distressed that she was rendered silent, almost in a state of shock, having already convinced herself that she was finally pregnant, she was going to have our baby.

She'd made an appointment to see her doctor later that day, who confirmed what the pregnancy test had shown – she was not pregnant. The doctor had told her that she needed to relax, that it was probably the stress of trying to conceive that had caused her to miss a period. She needed to be patient, let nature take its course – she wanted it too badly and that was having an adverse effect on her body. By the time she returned home, her period had arrived, heavier and more painful than normal, and she cried through the night, big heaving sobs; there had been no consoling her.

The next morning, Hannah was exhausted, pale and withdrawn from a night with no sleep. I took her some hot buttered toast and a cup of Earl Grey on a tray, along with a small glass of water and some paracetamol.

"I don't deserve you," she said, swallowing the tablets with some water. "You deserve someone who can give you a baby."

I didn't respond to that. I knew I should have reassured her, told her that I loved her with or without a baby inside of her, but I hadn't wanted to lie to her about that, hadn't wanted her to see a different kind of future for us. Besides, I sensed that the near-miss was actually the perfect opportunity, whilst she was brow-beaten and vulnerable, to present her with my solution.

"I'm disappointed, too," I lied, "but there is another way, Hannah."

She'd looked up at me quizzically, her brain fuggy from sleep deprivation and grief, not understanding. But then, she couldn't possibly have been prepared for what I had been about to suggest to her.

"I already have a child waiting to be born," I said. "It just needs a mother. It needs you to help it live."

At first the penny didn't drop, which was understandable. "What do you mean?" Hannah asked, her brow furrowed.

I put my hand in my trouser pocket and pulled out a neatly folded letter, which I handed to her. The letter was from the NFFC (Nucleus Foundation Fertility Clinic) and was letting me know that the storage duration period that Anna and I had agreed on when we started the IVF process was coming to an end.

Hannah read the letter in silence before speaking. "You and Anna were going through IVF?" she asked, her eyes still scanning the letter. "Why didn't you say something? I don't understand." She looked up at me, a single crease between her eyes demonstrating her confusion.

Hannah knew that Anna and I had struggled to conceive; she knew that we had both undergone tests that established that I was fine, but Anna had a problem which made it difficult for her to get pregnant; she knew that Anna had finally become pregnant, but had miscarried at seven weeks and, before we had a chance to try again, she had died. But I hadn't told her that Anna had only managed to get pregnant with the help of several rounds of IVF. So I filled in the gaps of what she already knew and told her how we had endured four failed attempts to implant tiny eggs that had been fertilised by my sperm, two of which never attached and two of which ended in miscarriage. Four tiny little life-forms, all part of me and Anna, that had died before they had had a chance to live. I hated the words "failed attempts" as if they were somehow to blame for not trying hard enough. I grieved for each and every one of them.

After the fourth attempt ended in miscarriage, we had just one remaining fertilised egg left to implant. I wanted to try again immediately but Anna was emotionally drained and needed a break from trying. What I didn't disclose to Hannah was how begrudgingly I had made that decision. Secretly, I was angry at Anna; I had felt that she was being selfish, but I agreed to it as I knew that she would come around before long – she always saw things my way eventually. But then she was gone, and the life was ripped out of me, almost as if I had miscarried *her*, and the last tiny little life form we had created together was denied its chance of life.

I explained to Hannah that Anna and I had a clause in our original IVF consent paperwork that, if either of us should die, any frozen embryos that had been stored would legally transfer to the living partner. This meant that I now had full control over what happened to this one remaining embryo, the last tiny living piece of Anna. I could choose to discard it, let it thaw out and perish, which was definitely not an option I was prepared to consider. I could extend the storage duration (technically frozen embryos can be stored for up to fifty-five years). I could donate it for research or training. Or I could use it, with the help of a surrogate.

When I had finished, I looked at Hannah and could see the tracks of her tears on her face, a pear-shaped teardrop still leading the way on her right cheek, which she brushed away before it had chance to fall off her chin.

"Oh my God, Jamie," she whispered, her eyes wide, her tone incredulous, "please tell me you are not suggesting that I become a surrogate for your dead wife! Please tell me I've got it wrong!"

I sat down on the bed and removed the letter from her before gently taking her trembling hands in mine. "I love you, Hannah. You know that I love you more than anything in the world, right?"

The words had come easily, devoid of meaning, but I'd prayed they would be effective. When she never responded, I persevered, my voice more coercive but still gentle, my eyes searching hers, unblinking, until I had my answer.

"Tell me, Hannah, tell me that you know I love you more than anything in the world, that I would never do anything to hurt you. Tell me."

"I know you do," she croaked as her gaze shifted down to our hands and I remember feeling a slight pull as if she was trying to free her hands from mine.

"I can't put you through what Anna had to endure. I can't do that to you, Hannah. It nearly destroyed her and I won't let that happen to you."

"But it won't happen to me. I will get pregnant soon, you'll see. I will."

"Oh, Hannah, darling, you forget I've been through all of this before – I know the signs and it is happening all over again. We will keep trying and keep trying, and each month nothing will happen except that the pain will get deeper and our relationship will become hard and permanently scarred for it. I can't bear it, I can't. You know it's true – you are not going to get pregnant naturally or you would have by now. Can you really go through another disappointment like yesterday? Do you think it is fair to put *me* through it all again?"

Hannah looked at me as if she was trying to figure a way out of the reality that I had placed in front of her.

"But it won't be *mine*," she pleaded, in the way a child pleads with a parent when they want to get their own way. "Why don't we try IVF for *our own* baby?" she'd pleaded, hope filling her voice in vain. I tried to hide the sick feeling that came over me at that thought, the thought of having a baby that wasn't part of Anna.

"Two years," I said, almost harshly, fighting to disguise my rising temper. "They make you try naturally for *two years* before they even start any tests. Then they will try all kinds of fertility treatments that we all know won't work but they are obliged to try anyway, before considering whether we are even suitable for IVF."

I have no idea if I was telling the truth or not; the information was purely anecdotal – Anna and I never used the NHS; we paid privately for our tests and treatment. I was close to tears, then, from a mixture of frustration and repressed grief.

"Why go through it, Hannah? Why, when there is a child waiting to be born, to be held and loved by us both? What difference does it make if it is biologically yours?"

"For something that doesn't make a difference, it seems to make a whole lot of difference to you!" she snapped, and I nearly hit her then, the closest I have ever been to hitting another person, and close enough for her to flinch even though I never even raised my hand. Maybe in that moment, something in me reminded her of Toby, the blind fool she had been involved with when we first met. If so, I can't say I was proud of that. I have never really understood why men hit women. It shows a complete lack of intelligence, if the only way you can get someone to comply is by beating them. I looked straight at her, letting her hands drop to her lap with a dull thud and began to walk out of the room. Hannah didn't try to stop me – I think her instincts had told her to just let me go and calm down.

"Think about it, Hannah," I said as I closed the bedroom door, and in an attempt to make her think about what she had to lose I added, "I honestly believe it is the only way we can survive."

As I walked out of the house, needing to get some air, I was shaking with the effort of not screaming at her. I had known it wasn't going to be easy to convince Hannah, but what I hadn't realised was how much I had invested emotionally in this working out the way I needed it to. I had underestimated her basic instinct to have a child of her own, which was self-contradictory, I know, when I consider my own reasons for asking her to become a surrogate. For the first time I was truly scared that she might not concede, that everything I had worked hard for was in danger of being cast adrift, and I was forced to contemplate the possibility that she would not agree.

After walking aimlessly for a few hours, I returned to the house to find Hannah in the kitchen making some tea. She turned her head as I entered the room, and I caught a glimpse of her pale face and the dark circles under her eyes, before she turned back to the task at hand. She looked shocking, and I was surprised at the sense of shame I felt in knowing how much I had contributed to that. But shame is a weak contender against need and desire. This wasn't about Hannah; it was about my baby, my child, and giving it a life. It was about bringing Anna back in the only way possible, and during my walk it had dawned on me that I still had a trump card to play.

I walked over to Hannah, who had now turned her back to me as she squeezed the life out of a teabag, and I put my arms around her middle, cupping her right breast in my left hand as I nuzzled my face into the curve of her neck and shoulder. I could feel the downy hairs on her neck rise to attention as I kissed her in that soft spot just beneath her ear.

"I'm sorry," I murmured, "forgive me. I've been an idiot."

She made a move to turn towards me, but I stopped her, continuing to plant gentle kisses into her neck. I felt her body yielding to the touch of my lips and to the stroke of my thumb against her nipple, which began stiffening underneath the material of her dress. She let the spoon holding the teabag clatter down as her hands pressed into the work surface to steady herself. A moan escaped from her as I moved my right hand down her body until it reached the hem of her dress and made its way underneath, searching for the part of her that I knew was aching for me right then. She came quickly, the orgasm dissipating the tension from earlier, helping her to reconnect with me emotionally. I knew that in this post-orgasm state she was at her most vulnerable, more open to suggestion, less resistant.

"Marry me," I whispered to her then, as her body was still pulsating, her mind weakened from pleasure. I knew that this was the one thing she wanted as much as a baby of her own, the one thing I had left to barter with. My trump card.

"What?" she asked, turning to face me as if she couldn't quite believe what she had just heard. Her face was flushed, her eyes were searching mine for confirmation of what she had heard.

"Marry me," I said again, hoping my eyes weren't betraying how sick I really felt at the idea.

"But what about the embryo, the baby...?" she said, not quite knowing how to address the issue that had seemed insurmountable only hours before.

"Forget I ever suggested it," I said. "We love each other and I just assumed that our love would have no boundaries – I never appreciated the gravity of what I was asking from you. It was selfish."

I was playing a dangerous game, and for a moment I saw relief in her eyes.

"It just devastates me, that's all, to see the joy and hope slowly leaching out of you each month. When the letter from the clinic arrived, it seemed to be fate. I've always thought of that embryo as a living child, always mourned the fact that it would never have a chance to be born, and this seemed like the perfect solution. For both of us."

I could see Hannah's expression start to change, becoming uncertain and so I continued.

"I would do anything for you, Hannah, *anything*," I stress for effect. "But I realise I cannot expect the same back from you. It is unfair, unrealistic, to think that there are no lines that you would not cross for me, that you could ever love me in the way that I love you."

Hannah is a good soul, one who always strives to do the right thing, who always puts the feelings of others before herself and I was gambling on that side of her nature prevailing, especially as she would still be in the throes of her dopamine-induced feelings of love for me.

"Your happiness is more important to me than my own. I want to be with you forever, and if that means letting my baby go, letting it *die*, then that is the sacrifice I have to make. If nature doesn't give us our own child, then so be it, we will always have each other and that is enough for me."

I could see her prevaricating as her mind wrestled with what I was saying. The joy of that longed-for proposal of marriage repressed by the guilt of the sacrifice she thought she was forcing me to make by abandoning my own child. And, on top of that, my message, although subtle, was clear: this baby or no baby at all.

Silence filled the room for a few seconds that felt like minutes, during which Hannah held her hand over her mouth as if she couldn't trust herself to speak, or maybe to stop herself from being sick.

"I'll do it," she said. "I'll marry you and I'll carry your baby."

I think I almost loved her in that moment – at least it felt something like love, rather than just the mechanics of sex when I made love to her that night. We came together this time, my sterile semen flooding into her, and afterwards I felt her tilt her pelvis ever so slightly upwards under the sheets and I realised that she was still holding on to a secret hope that only I knew was a barren one. I should have felt guilty, I know, but the truth is I just felt happy.

CHAPTER 26

Jamie

When we attended the clinic for our initial consultation a few weeks later, we were told that the chances of IVF producing a live birth for a woman aged under thirty-five is less than 25%, a fact I already knew, of course. Anna and I had used four out of our five embryos, none of which had resulted in that much-wanted live birth. Statistically, the fifth should have worked had we been given the chance to try. I decided to think of the statistics in terms of the number of embryos implanted, that the womb into which that fifth embryo was to be implanted would be inconsequential. I needed to believe that this would work. Hannah, on the other hand, seemed to take a different view – that *she* had less than a 25% chance of the IVF working – and I swear her mood was lifted by that thought.

As I already knew most of what the consultant was discussing with us, I was barely listening to what he was saying, instead concentrating on the nuances of Hannah's reactions, and it disturbed me to think that she had seemed buoyed, rather than deflated by, a worst-case scenario. But I barely had time to register my annoyance before I was brought back into the moment by something that he said that I *hadn't* known, that I hadn't been expecting: if the IVF was successful, Hannah would automatically be classed as the legal mother of the child.

The consultant explained that, under UK law, the person that gives birth to a child is the first legal parent, regardless of whether they are biologically related to the child. This threw me. I had incorrectly assumed that, as I was the only living biological parent, and I was consenting for my fertilised embryo to be implanted, that Hannah would have to apply for a parental order after the birth to become a legal parent, and I would have to agree to it. This angered me on two levels – firstly that Anna would never be legally acknowledged as the baby's mother, and secondly that this gave Hannah rights that I never anticipated she would have when I eventually left her. Although this caught me off guard, I had no choice but to accept it as a price I would have to pay until I could figure something out.

We left the clinic with a handful of information leaflets and consent paperwork for us to go over, and a date on which to return to the clinic to set the wheels in motion. On the drive home, Hannah was chattier and more positive about the whole procedure than she had been on the way to the appointment, and I couldn't help but think that this was down to a secret belief on her part that it wasn't going to work. I felt my mood darken at this thought, but then I rallied as I realised it really didn't matter what she secretly hoped, the important thing was that she was going through with it and *it would work*, I just knew it.

Several weeks later, after all the paperwork had been signed and some tests had been carried out on Hannah, she was given a course of drugs for weeks to help prepare the lining of her womb, to make sure it was in the best possible shape for the transfer of the embryo. Hannah withdrew into herself a bit during this time. I think the reality of what she was about to embark on was hitting home and I was fearful that she might back out. But she didn't, and before long it was the day of the embryo transfer process. I felt sick with a mixture of excitement and fear: this was a one-shot chance and there was no plan B to fall back on if it didn't work.

After the transfer, all I could do was wait during the longest two weeks of my life to find out whether it had been successful, whether the dream I'd had with Anna, for us to have a baby together, was either about to come to life, or end up as dead in the water as she was. We had been advised by the clinic to do a home urine pregnancy test at around fourteen to seventeen days after the transfer, after which a blood test at the clinic would be done to confirm the results if the urine test was positive. I decided we would do the test on day 14, and, if it wasn't positive, we would do it again on day 17 just in case. Day 14 was warm and sunny and this boosted my mood and confidence as it was hard to imagine a negative result on such a beautiful day. The house was flooded with light, and I noticed dust motes hanging in the air. Normally this would have annoyed me, thinking the housework wasn't being done properly, but that day it just felt as if the motes were a crowd of well-wishers waiting for the result. I escorted Hannah into the bathroom to sit with her as she did the test, not able to wait a second longer than necessary to find out, not wanting Hannah to be the first person to know if my baby was beginning to thrive – that was not *her* prerogative.

I sat on the edge of the bath as I took the pregnancy test stick out of its packaging, and watched as Hannah pulled her trousers and knickers down below her knees and sat on the toilet. The skin of her thighs was white, paler than the skin on her arms, and I noticed that her thighs softly spread across the toilet seat, less firm than normal, as if she had put on a little bit of weight. I was hoping that was a good sign. She had a strange look on her face as she took the stick from my hand, avoiding looking me in the eye. She positioned the stick into place and before long I heard the steady stream of her urine passing over it. When she had finished, I took the stick from her and held on to it so that only I could see the little display window that would give me the answer I desperately needed.

Then we waited.

The instructions told us to wait for three minutes, and those three minutes felt like the longest of my life, with both Hannah and me suspended in silence. I noticed Hannah was trembling and I knew that I should have gone to her and put my arms around her as a show of togetherness, but I couldn't bring myself to do that; this moment wasn't about her. Eventually I watched as that longed-for blue line appeared in the test window and for a few seconds I just stared at it, not quite daring to believe it could be true. Then I looked up at Hannah, not saying a word because I didn't have to, my expression told her all she needed to know, just as the change in her expression told me all *I* needed to know:

"It's positive, isn't it?" she said, her voice not much more than a whisper, in a tone that suggested bad news, and it was clear to me that she had been expecting, hoping, that this would fail – after all, Anna had had two embryo transfers that had not made it this far, so why should she succeed at the first attempt? I realised, then, that I had to tread carefully; I had won the battle, but the war was far from over.

The embryo, that beautiful mix of me and Anna, the very last part of her to ever exist, had attached itself to Hannah's womb straight away, but its tenure was still fragile and the risk of miscarriage was high. The risk seemed even greater in the knowledge that Hannah appeared to be reluctantly pregnant. She had more control than I did over whether the pregnancy actually succeeded, and I hated that thought. I realised that I needed to acknowledge her feelings about this baby and somehow find a way to change how she felt about it. Besides, I couldn't ignore the fact that it would never have been possible without her.

"Look, I know you don't really think of this baby as being yours, Hannah." I decided to be honest and direct with her, and

I could tell that she was taken aback by this. She tried to protest.

"It's not that…" she started, her eyes downcast, not knowing how to finish the sentence in such a way as to not lie. Hannah isn't the sort of person who lies, except maybe to herself.

I knew that I needed her to have a reason to bond with this baby.

"I spoke with the clinic a while ago – did you know that, as it grows in you, you will pass on some of your DNA?" Hannah looked up at me at the mention of her DNA and by her expression I could see that she looked lifted by the thought.

"Really?" she said, her voice thick with hope.

Although what I'd said wasn't strictly true, it wasn't a complete lie. I had discussed it privately with the clinic and was told that, although a tiny amount of Hannah's genetic material can, in theory, get through the placenta, the amount would be negligible, its presence insignificant amongst the crowd of legitimate DNA. My baby's DNA was already in situ from the egg and sperm – its genetic future was already mapped. It would be mine and Anna's; Hannah was just an incubator.

"Really," I said as I kissed her tenderly on the lips. "Now, shall we call the clinic, *Mummy*?"

That word, although necessary in that moment, had been hard to use on Hannah.

The rest of the pregnancy passed without any other dramas or surprises. When my baby moved inside of her, Hannah would stop what she was doing, grab my hand and place it where the movement was happening so that I could feel how strong my baby was becoming. I almost loved her in those moments, when she shared what was going on inside of her with me, and I tried to imagine making it work with her, about the three of us becoming a real family. But as hard as I tried to love her, I knew that what I was really feeling was nothing more than gratitude. She might have looked like Anna, but she could never *be* Anna – she was nothing more than a cheap copy, her presence serving only to emphasise everything I had lost, like replacing a stolen Lowry with a child's stick drawing. At night, when the stillness in the room was disturbed only by my thoughts, I felt as overcome in my grief as I had when I first lost Anna. I would watch Hannah sleeping, her face comfortingly familiar and yet so alien at the same time, and despite myself, I found my gratitude slowly starting to twist into resentment.

But, when Amber was finally born, for a moment everything changed, a light shone for the first time in a long time, lighting up the shadowy corners of my grief and exposing the cobwebs ready for dusting. The moment I saw my little girl's head start to crown, everything else lost focus and I was oblivious to any other sights or sounds in the delivery room. When she finally gushed out, bloodied and beaten from her journey to me, she was truly the most beautiful thing I had ever seen. I cut the cord, and it felt somehow ceremonial, finally being able to cut the physical tie between Hannah and my baby who didn't belong to her.

I had previously instructed the midwife and obstetrician that I was to be the first person to hold my baby when it was born, but the midwife had objected, spouting something about mother and baby skin-to-skin contact and bonding. But I couldn't have cared less about what she said or thought; I was paying for the privilege of expensive private maternity care so I could insist on whatever I damn well pleased.

"Oh, Anna," I said, as I'd cradled my baby for the first time, "she's perfect." And I ignored the tiny sobs and the whispered "Hannah. I'm *Hannah*" that came from the hospital bed.

It took another couple of years before Hannah was out of our lives in any meaningful capacity. My mind went to some dark places in my desire to get her out of our lives but in the end she made it easier on me by pressing her own self-destruct button. Since then, it has been just me and Amber, and that has been enough for both of us; until recently at least.

Amber is fifteen now and looks more and more like Anna every day. I thought that my grief was under control, but Amber has become a constant reminder, a living ghost of what I've lost and every now and then it hits me like a breaching whale and I feel like I am drowning in Anna's absence again. I've been feeling angry, too, as Amber has started asking questions about Hannah, the woman she thinks is her mother, questions that I really do not want to answer. As far as I am concerned, Hannah is irrelevant, she does not exist. Amber would feel the same if she knew the truth about who her real mother is, but I haven't told her the truth yet – I have been waiting for the right time. The trouble is, the longer I leave it, the harder it is to explain, and now I worry I may have left it too long. It doesn't help that Amber has become distant with me lately, and I am fighting the feeling that history is repeating itself.

I am beginning to feel like I am living in a proverbial house of cards, that everything is folding in on me, and I can feel a dark panic rising at the thought I'm losing my little girl.

CHAPTER 27

Hannah - fifteen years ago

I have been feeling Anna's presence for some time now.

It started with just a feeling of being watched – the kind where you sense someone is watching you but, when you turn around, no one's there. At first, I tried to ignore it, I put it down to an overactive imagination, to being tired, to being scared that I will never, ever measure up or be good enough.

To being constantly compared to a dead wife.

I mentioned it to my midwife, although only in passing as I didn't want to make a great deal out of it, in case she thought I was going mad. She said it was postnatal depression, that it was perfectly normal, especially considering the stressful circumstances of my pregnancy.

At first, I thought maybe she was right. Jamie constantly compares me to Anna, compares everything I do to what *she* would have done, tells me that I owe it to Anna to do things right, the way *she* would have done them, that I'm selfish to want to do things my way. It's no wonder it feels like Anna is here, inhabiting the house, watching me. But in the last few days, things have changed and I no longer just sense her, it has become more than that and I am afraid.

Although I can't see Anna, I see the shadows shift and I know she is there, hiding and watching me, disapproving and resentful. It is not my imagination, it is real, and she is getting bolder, closer. I feel her cool breath on the back of my neck when I feed Amber, and I know it is her because Amber reacts, stops sucking for a second and gurgles a smile. Sometimes I think I can hear her, too, a distant voice in the far reaches of my mind, no more than a whisper – less than a whisper, even. I can't tell anyone – no one would believe me; I hardly believe it myself. I can't even trust Jamie anymore – her eyes have inhabited his, so when *he* looks at me, *she* is looking at me. They are coalescing into one person with one agenda: to take Amber away from me.

It is exhausting. I need to sleep, but I can't sleep, I have to keep watch. I don't know how much longer I can take this. I feel so alone.

CHAPTER 28

Amber

I vaguely remember Dad taking me to visit Mum in hospital a couple of times when I was really little. At least I think I do. It might be a false memory based on what I've been told, as that can happen, apparently – you see a photo, or are told something, and your mind takes it on as a memory as if you were actually there. Isn't that weird?

Anyway, I never really thought about my mum much – it was always just me and Dad growing up, and I never really felt I was missing out on anything. I do remember asking him once, when I was really little, why I didn't have a mummy like the other children at school. Dad had said it was because he had more love to give me than a thousand mummies ever could, and that there were other children who needed mummies more than I did. I simply accepted that explanation in the naïve way only a child can. Anyway, it never really bothered me much until I started my periods and then I missed having someone I could talk to about girl things.

That was when I really started to become curious about her, but the only thing Dad would tell me was that she was in a secure mental hospital and not well enough for visitors.

"She has no idea who we are, Amber; it's best to just forget about her." But I wanted to know more, wanted to know why. Every time I asked a question, though, Dad would get agitated and wouldn't really talk to me about her. Then one day he snapped at me.

"Why do you keep asking me about her now, Amber? You've never bothered before. I've tried to give you everything you need, to be both a mum and dad to you. I couldn't do any more if I tried – are you saying that I haven't been good enough? Is that it?"

That made me feel guilty. I love Dad. I know it has been hard for him bringing me up on his own. He's been a great dad and the last thing I wanted to do was make him feel I didn't appreciate everything he does for me, so I stopped asking for a while. Then last year at school we were learning about genetics in science and my curiosity grew again. I needed to know more about her, more about why her "mind had gone", so I asked again.

"This isn't going to go away, is it?" Dad said. "You asking me about her?" Then he sighed. "Look, Amber, it's difficult for me to talk about this. I love you and my instinct is to protect you. The truth is your mother did – or tried to do – a terrible thing, and I need to know you are ready to cope with the truth, that you are mature enough to understand that it had nothing to do with you, or me, and everything to do with her being very, very ill."

Then he told me as much as he thought I needed to know, the bare bones about her illness and what she had done, but, as shocking as it was, I could sense that there was something more important that he wasn't telling me. That night I cried myself to sleep, wondering how my mother could have done what she did.

After that, Dad refused to talk about her anymore, and when I asked if I could go and visit her he became angry.

"No, Amber!" he shouted. "I've told you all you need to know! Hannah is no more than an empty shell. She's not what you want her to be; she is incapable of being your mother – seeing her will just upset and confuse you. Just let it be."

But I couldn't just let it be, and so I contacted the hospital myself to ask if I could visit. Dad was furious when he found out and we had our first ever big fight, but by then I had set the ball rolling and he did not have any reasonable excuse that he could give to refuse permission. I am nearly sixteen and it wasn't solely up to him – the decision to accept or deny my request would be made by an approved social worker. Apparently, it is because of something called *safeguarding* – they have to make sure that it is in my best interests, that I am strong enough to cope with seeing her.

The social worker that interviewed me was a large man called Tom. He had a deep, soothing voice, and for some reason I immediately liked him. There was a metal table in the room with grey, plastic chairs on either side of the table. I sat on one of the chairs which felt cold even through my jeans, and Tom grabbed the other chair and dragged it to the side so that the table was no longer between us. On the wall behind me was a white plastic clock ticking noisily away, and I noticed Tom glance at it as he sat down. I wondered how much time I had been allocated and hoped it wasn't going to be too long.

Tom started by asking what I knew about my mother. I told him that I knew she was sectioned when I was two years old but I didn't remember much about her. I think I may sometimes have flashes of memories when something pokes at my subconscious. Like when I was watching a film once and a character in it started singing "Hush, Little Baby", I suddenly had a feeling that Mum used to sing that to me and I could feel her stroking my head. Tom smiled when I said that.

I then told him what Dad had recently told me: that Mum had become mentally ill after I was born. That she had something called *puerperal psychosis*, a sort of extreme postnatal depression that made her hallucinate and do weird and sometimes dangerous things, a bit like schizophrenia. That it was a rare condition, and, although most people make a full recovery, for some reason Mum didn't. I also told them about the terrible thing she'd done, the thing that Dad had wanted to protect me from – she had tried to kill me, and that is when it was decided she was not going to get better and needed to be sectioned. Tom had been writing all of this down as I was talking, nodding as he wrote, but he stopped and looked up at me when I mentioned the trying to kill me part.

"So, you know about that?" he said in his gravelly voice. "How do you *feel* about that?"

I shrugged when he asked that question. "I don't know," I said. Then I thought for a bit. "Sad, I guess. Like she didn't really love me. But I don't blame her. I know she wasn't well in her mind. I don't know how she tried to kill me, though. Dad won't tell me. He says it doesn't matter, she didn't succeed and that is all that matters. I have tried my best to remember, but I was only two years old and Dad says that is too young to remember anything. But, if I can remember my mother singing to me, why can't I remember something as dramatic as that?"

"Sometimes, things we think of as memories are not really memories," Tom said. "Sometimes, what you 'remember' is what someone has *told* you, and after a while, when you think about it, you place yourself into it, believe you were actually there. It is a false memory."

"Oh," I said, and felt a pang of disappointment that the only memory I have of my mother – of her singing to me – was maybe not even real.

"I'm not saying that it never happened – it is possible that it did happen." Tom seemed to pick up on my disappointment. "It is just more likely than not that you have created a visual memory from the things you have been told. Actual memories of events that happened before the age of three are quite rare."

"Do you know how she tried to do it?" I asked. "How she tried to kill me?"

"Yes," said Tom. "Do you want me to tell you what happened, Amber?"

I nodded. Stupid question – of *course* I wanted to know!

"Your mother was very ill," he began. "There is no doubt from the evidence we have that when you were born she loved you very much. But, as you already know, she had psychotic episodes where she suffered from dangerous hallucinations that made her lose her grip on reality. During one of those episodes, she tried to drown you in the bath. In her unstable mind, it wasn't *her* doing it. Thankfully, your father caught her in time to save you."

"Oh," I said again. I didn't really know what else to say. And then I had a flash of a memory, only now I wasn't sure if it was a real memory or not.

My head under water; of not being able to breathe; thrashing my arms and legs; the sound of my mum's voice screaming in a faraway land; of my dad's hand pulling me up by my hair; of Mum tearing at him with her hands; of him slapping her to the ground; of sirens and flashing blue lights…

I tried to stop it, but a tear rolled down my cheek then. I didn't want to look weak in front of Tom in case he denied me my visit.

"Are you OK, Amber?" he said. "Do you want me to call your dad?"

"No!" I said, wiping my eyes. "No. I'm alright. I just feel guilty, that's all, like it was my fault, somehow."

"What do you mean, Amber? In what way do you think it could have been your fault?" Tom's head was tilted to one side as he asked this, his eyes sharp and focussed as if they were doing their best to read my mind.

"Well, if I hadn't been born, she wouldn't have become ill," I said. "You only get puerperal psychosis if you have a baby, so it *was* my fault, in a way…"

"No, Amber, it—" Tom was going to try and tell me it wasn't my fault, but I cut him short.

"It's OK, I know it wasn't, like, *really* my fault," I said. "But you get what I mean! And I'm scared, too, that it might happen to me if I have a baby one day. I know it can be hereditary, I googled it!"

I looked at Tom as I said this, and I noticed him hesitate slightly, as if he didn't quite know what to say next.

"Have you spoken to your dad about that? About that *particular* worry that it might be hereditary?" he asked. His eyebrows were knitted together, and I don't know why, but I felt he was tiptoeing around something with that question.

"I've tried to talk to Dad about it, but he changes the subject," I said. "He tells me not to worry about that now, that I shouldn't even be thinking about babies at my age! He says we will talk about it when the time is right. But when will that be? Because to me it feels like the right time is right now!"

The meeting went on for another five minutes with Tom asking me more questions, ones I can't even remember now, and me answering them, until finally he said, "I need you to know, Amber, that your mother is still very ill. She is heavily medicated and not very communicative. She thinks you are still a baby and is not likely to recognise you. Do you think you can handle that?"

Suddenly I felt a pull of hope and anticipation that I actually might be allowed to see her.

"Yes!" I said in reply. "She's still my mum, no matter what's happened. I want to be able to understand more about her, that's all. Maybe seeing me will even help her a bit. Does this mean you are going to let me see her…?"

"I need to discuss it with her psychiatric care team first, but my recommendation will be that you are allowed a visit. You will have to be accompanied by an appropriate adult from the care team and your father will be allowed to accompany you, too, of course."

"I'd rather do it on my own – I mean, I know someone will have to be there, but I'd rather my dad wasn't. Dad doesn't really want me to go, and it will be awkward with him there. Is that OK, can I see her without him?"

Tom said he would discuss this with the team and I would be sent a letter confirming any decisions that were made. A week later I had a letter with an appointment date for me to visit my mum at the secure hospital where she was a patient. The letter acknowledged my request to see her on my own without Dad, and it said that a psychiatrist would be present during the visit to safeguard both me and my mother.

Today is the day of the visit, and Dad has just dropped me off at the hospital. He is still angry with me. Angry that I contacted the hospital in the first place to ask to visit Mum without discussing it with him, and angry that I want to do this alone. But what else could I have done when he is so unwilling to talk to me about her?

Dad grabs my arm to momentarily stop me as I open the car door to get out. My heart is thumping so fast.

"Just remember, Amber," he says, his voice serious. "Your mother is crazy and says crazy things. She is delusional. Don't take too much notice of what she says, do you hear me? I love you, baby."

I nod and swallow hard as I get out of the car and then run to the hospital entrance to avoid the big, fat drops of rain that are coming down hard. He seems scared. I've never seen him like that before, and I wonder if I should be even more scared than I am right now.

I have the appointment letter in my hand, now splodged with rain, which tells me that Mum's clinical psychiatrist is a lady called Janice Dumal. I hand the letter to the hospital receptionist, who looks unimpressed at the soggy state of it. She then picks up the phone to dial Janice's extension, letting her know that I have arrived, before asking me to take a seat in the waiting area. As I wait, several people are milling around. Some are clearly visitors and some appear to be patients whose interactions and conversations, normal to them, are bizarre and frightening to me. I look down and study my fingernails, uneasy with making eye contact with anybody. I wish now that I had let Dad come with me, but it is too late for that – he left after he dropped me off and told me to ring him when I was ready to be picked up.

"Hello, Amber." The voice belongs to Janice, who is standing before me, greeting me with a wide smile and holding out her hand for me to shake. I've never had to shake someone's hand before and it makes me feel important, like an adult. It has helped me feel a little bit braver, too.

"How are you feeling?"

"A bit scared."

"Well, that's completely understandable," Janice says. "We have spoken to Hannah about your visit, but to be honest it is hard to say how much she's taken in. She has withdrawn from the outside world, and lives in her own version of reality which is based very much in the past. She is unlikely to have any concept of who you are, and may not even acknowledge you are there. You can try and engage with her – talk to her – but for your safety I must ask that you do not attempt to touch her as she can become very agitated when approached. Are you OK with that, Amber?"

I nod. My mouth is so dry with nerves now that I am not sure I can speak.

"Good girl," Janice says and with those two words I am instantly demoted from an adult who shakes hands to a child again.

Janice chit-chats with me as we walk to my mother's room, but I am struggling to take in what she is saying, as all I can think about is what I am going to say to my mother when I see her. I hadn't thought about that before Janice had said I could try and engage with her; isn't that strange? Suddenly Janice stops.

"Here we are," she says as she knocks on a door and opens it without waiting for any acknowledgements.

"Hello, Hannah! You have a visitor!" she says to a woman who is sitting in a rocking chair in a sparsely furnished room. The tone of Janice's voice is loud and overly cheery, but the woman doesn't respond; it is as if she hasn't heard a thing.

For a minute I am confused – I wonder who this woman is, and then it dawns on me, and I am shocked at the sight of this woman, my mother, and my first instinct is to turn around and run. I thought I was ready, but now I'm not so sure. My heart is hammering in my chest and I feel sick. The image I have carried of my mother has come from a single photograph beside Dad's bed. It was taken in the days after I was born, and she is holding me and smiling up at the camera. In that photo she is young and beautiful, her skin soft like peaches. In real life, she is much fatter, her frame straining against the cotton nightdress she is wearing that must have fitted her once, I guess, and her unbrushed hair is so long she is almost sitting on it. Her hair, although tinged with grey at the temples, is brown and that surprises me. In her photographs her hair is more auburn, and I realise for the first time she must have dyed it in the past. Her face is creased like an un-ironed shirt, but is still pretty, I can see that, and I search it for any similarities to my own face. Disappointingly, I can't really find any, but then she doesn't resemble the person she used to be in that photograph, either – madness and medication have taken their toll on her features.

She is cradling a plastic doll and is rocking back and forth singing "Hush, Little Baby". Instantly it brings back my memory, false or otherwise, and I just know that she thinks that the doll is me. I'm not sure what to do now, what I should say, but Janice steps in.

"This is Amber, Hannah. You know who Amber is, don't you? We talked about her the other day."

At the sound of my name, my mother moves her head in my direction. Her shadowed eyes, unblinking and empty, latch onto mine and I see them suddenly widen and come alive as something appears to register in her broken mind. For a second, I think she must recognise who I am, but then she starts to make a strange sound – a sort of guttural moan, one that starts low and gets louder and louder with what appears to be a mounting distress. She is clutching the plastic doll tightly to her chest and hunches herself over it, as if to protect it, her rocking becoming almost frenzied. Janice looks worried.

"Hannah?" she says. "What's wrong, what's the matter? Can you tell me why you are upset?"

My mother points at me without looking at me, purposely turning her head away as if by not seeing me she is somehow safer. She is still rocking with the doll against her chest.

"Anna!" she says. "Anna wants my baby!"

That name. The one Dad keeps calling me when his guard is down: Anna. He doesn't think I notice, but I do. At first, I thought he was calling me Hannah, which wouldn't be that unusual given it is Mum's name. But then I realised he was actually saying *Anna* and, although I wanted to ask him about it, something about the whole situation didn't feel right. It felt like a secret I wasn't supposed to know about, a girlfriend, maybe, so I never questioned him. The fact that my mother has just called me by the same name has spun me out.

"Who's Anna?" I ask, turning my head to direct my question at Janice.

"I think we need to leave; this is upsetting your mother."

"*No! No! Please! Let go!*" my mother screams randomly as I leave the room. Those words echo around the room and something in me stirs, poking at my subconscious.

CHAPTER 29

Jamie

I have just dropped Amber off at the psychiatric hospital. I cannot believe that this is even happening, that she has been allowed to see Hannah without me being there. It is raining hard and the windscreen wipers are moving furiously against the windscreen, the rubber squeaking in protest. I turn the radio up to drown out the noise, but also to help fill my head with something other than the thoughts that are oscillating through my mind.

I haven't seen Hannah for years – well over a decade, in fact. When she was first sectioned, I would visit from time to time, partly because it was expected of me and I didn't want to look anything other than a doting and concerned husband, but also because I wanted to make sure that she wasn't spouting any more nonsense about what happened that night. She blamed me and, despite her obvious psychotic mental state, I knew that her midwife viewed me with suspicion. That midwife never did like me, so it wasn't really a surprise, but even so it could have been very difficult for me if the police and psychiatric team hadn't readily accepted my version of events and had listened to Hannah's demented ramblings instead. But still, I visited regularly just to make sure no one doubted her insanity and, when I felt it was finally safe, I walked away for good.

I'd thought all of that was behind me, that I had climbed that particular mountain and left Hannah at the bottom, but now I feel like I am stood on a precipice with Hannah's hand hovering on my back, waiting to push me into the abyss. I wish to God I had just killed her back then, when the thought had crossed my mind. At least that would have been clean, over. I think of Amber and a sick feeling settles in my stomach at what seeing Hannah will do to her. I wish now that I had been more open with her about everything. Maybe if I had told her the truth as soon as she was old enough to understand, none of this would be happening now; she wouldn't have felt the need to visit a woman who is genetically nothing to her.

I remember the moment Amber was born, how mixed my feelings had been towards Hannah. I was grateful to her, of course – without her Amber wouldn't have been possible – but, from that moment on, I felt an ever-growing resentment towards her presence in our lives. I knew that Anna would have been a perfect mother and every day I struggled with my feelings of frustration at Hannah's ineptitude. I was frustrated by the way she handled Amber; frustrated by the things she did do; frustrated by the things she didn't do; frustrated that she *wasn't Anna*. Those early months had been an incredibly emotional time for me. I finally had what I had been dreaming of for so long, but Hannah was ruining it, and it had also hit home that I had no real clue as to how I was going to get her out of the picture.

Legally, Hannah was Amber's mother, her "first parent", and technically had more rights than I did, the injustice of which still enrages me when I think about it. It was one of the reasons that I married her – albeit a short, unemotional registry-office affair – to help further anchor my own parental rights. Everyone knows that courts have a tendency to grant custody to mothers in divorce cases, so leaving her was never going to be enough, and I admit that the thought of killing Hannah had crossed my mind as the only clean way out. But in the end it wasn't necessary; I didn't have to find out whether I was capable of that.

The rain is coming down even heavier now and my windscreen wipers are doing a poor job at keeping up with the torrent of water, just as my mind is doing a poor job at suppressing the memory of all that happened next. I don't know what is happening to me lately – so many old, unwanted memories coming back, tainting everything.

Hannah had suffered postnatal depression after Amber was born and, although I knew that many women suffered from this, I cannot tell you how much it annoyed me – how *dare* she be depressed! She had been given everything that had been denied of Anna; she had no right to feel anything other than gratitude. But after a while I realised that something more was happening, that Hannah was becoming increasingly odd in her behaviour. Then, when Amber was about four months old, I heard Hannah talking in the nursery. At first I thought she was talking to Amber until I realised that the hushed tone of her voice was not the gentle, soothing tone she usually used with my little girl. It was an insistent whisper, defensive and forceful, as if she was quietly arguing with someone. Intrigued, I stood by the door to the nursery, out of sight, and listened for a while.

"Why don't you leave us alone?" she hissed into the thin air, as she paced up and down with Amber in her arms.

"Who are you talking to, Hannah?" I asked as I walked into the room, startling her. Her eyes were large and she was blinking rapidly.

"She's here, Jamie," Hannah said in that same loud whisper, her eyes darting around the room. "She's trying to take Amber away from me. She says I'm not a fit mother. Tell her to go away!"

"Who?" I asked, perplexed at her bizarre behaviour.

"*Anna!*" she said, as if it was obvious who she was talking about, and I felt as if I had been punched in the gut at the mention of her name.

"She hides away so no one can see her, but she's here, Jamie, I *hear* her." Hannah sounded crazy, delusional, yet in that moment I wanted more than anything to believe her, believe that my Anna really was present, trying to take back what was rightfully hers. But I knew that was impossible, that what Hannah was experiencing was a result of her own subconscious acknowledging that Amber didn't really belong to her, that she could never be the mother that Amber deserved.

Hannah's behaviour and obsession with Anna got worse over the coming weeks. I did nothing to try and calm her or contradict her – in fact, I enjoyed hearing Anna's name being spoken freely in the house; it felt like she really was around. I did some research and guessed that Hannah was probably suffering from a severe form of postnatal depression and that without help her mental health could spiral. It was perfect. All I needed to do was to make sure her mental state was so bad that she would be deemed unfit to care for Amber. I'd read that sleep deprivation played a big part in the illness, and so I made sure that Hannah got very little sleep. That wasn't too difficult – she refused to sleep much at night anyway, terrified that my dead wife was going to snatch Amber in the night. Despite her best efforts to remain awake, she would sometimes drift off to sleep during the day, her mind and body desperate for some rest, but each time she did this I would find a way to wake her quickly and suddenly so that she would be discombobulated, her mind deprived of its rest.

Sometimes, when I got the chance, I moved or hid things to help nurture her confusion. I even moved Amber, once, from the place where Hannah had put her – she had left her for less than a minute, and when she returned and found her missing she was frantic, convinced Anna had taken her. Even when she found Amber, safe and sound, she would not calm down and I had to slap her to calm her. It was the first and only time that I have ever had to hit a woman, and I am ashamed to say that I gained some pleasure from it. Later that night, after I had gone to bed, I woke to hear her pacing up and down in the kitchen talking to herself, arguing in her now-familiar discordant whisper. As I lay there listening to her mind cracking a fraction more, I thought about what was happening to Hannah and about the slap I had been forced to give her, and I suddenly felt an unusual feeling of guilt. It wasn't what I had wanted, not really; I wanted her gone, but not like that. Hannah deserved more, and for the first time I wondered if I should stop it all and get her the medical help she needed before it was too late; find a way to make it work with her. Eventually I drifted into a dream-filled sleep as my subconscious mind tried to process my guilt.

I was stood in the doorway of the nursery watching as Hannah fed Amber. She was rocking back and forth in the nursing chair, humming gently, and I was smiling at the sight of them both, feeling something warm inside, something akin to pride. I was about to walk over to them when something caught my eye. It was Anna, standing silently in the corner of the room, watching me watching them. She was dripping wet, water pooling at her feet, her blue sarong clinging to her body like wet papier mâché. Her large, beautiful eyes were shining with tears and I recognised the expression on her face – it was the expression she had worn when she felt I had betrayed her with Rachel. Then she turned her head towards Hannah and her tears changed into near-invisible flames, like tiny ethanol fires, and I could feel the heat of her anger and jealousy permeate the room.

When I woke, I knew that Anna had given me a sign, that Hannah needed to go. And when I walked into Amber's nursery that morning and felt a crunch beneath my feet I knew for certain that there was no going back. The floor of the nursery was scattered with raw rice, and when I questioned Hannah about it she looked at me and smiled in the way a person does when they feel they have secured a small victory.

"She'll have to count every single grain before she can come in, Jamie! It will buy me time before she can get to Amber!" The buoyancy of her voice belied the madness of her words. I just looked at her and walked out. It was clear at that point that Hannah's tortured mind was doing a good job of self-destructing without any help from me.

I knew that the longer Hannah went without medical intervention, the more likely it was that she would be difficult to treat and therefore the more likely it was that she would be considered unfit to care for Amber. Everything had been heading in the right direction, until Hannah had an unexpected visit from the midwife. I was livid.

"I was in the area," she said with a disingenuous smile. "So I thought I'd drop in on the off-chance! It's been a while since I've seen Hannah and the little one, as you've cancelled the last few appointments. Is she in?"

I was about to say no but then Amber cried and Hannah appeared in the background. The midwife started to smile at Hannah, but immediately her expression changed to one of shock as she took in Hannah's dishevelled appearance. Without being invited, she simply stepped over the threshold, walking past me, and let herself in. Hannah's dialogue with the midwife was hyper, and she was overly possessive of Amber, reluctant to hand her over. By then Hannah had started to believe that more people were complicit in a kidnap plot, so she trusted no one fully, including me or the midwife.

"How's the breastfeeding going, Hannah?" the midwife asked

at one point, and my heart sank as I remembered the day Amber was born, when this same midwife had helped to guide my baby's tiny mouth onto Hannah's nipple for the first time. I had stood in silence, watching Hannah take a little intake of breath as my baby finally seemed to grasp what she was supposed to do and began to suckle. My mind had been a maelstrom of contradictory thoughts: I knew how important breast milk is to a newborn but, even so, it did not stop me feeling sick at the grotesque sight of my child being forced to suckle someone other than her real mother, and I had to look away to avoid the urge to rip her off Hannah's breast. There was no way I could let that continue.

"We mainly bottle-feed these days." I spoke for Hannah in an attempt to end that line of questioning.

"Hannah?" The midwife ignored me and continued to focus on Hannah, who had become visibly distraught at the mention of breastfeeding.

"It's Anna's fault – she's stealing my milk!" she whispered conspiratorially to the midwife and even I was taken aback. The midwife shot a glance my way, reminiscent of the look she had given me in the delivery room when I'd inadvertently used Anna's name after Amber was born.

"She uses the breast pump on me when I'm sleeping. I can prove it – look, there are the marks!" Hannah had lifted her top, exposing her bare breasts, to show the midwife suction marks that didn't exist, except in her deteriorating mind.

The midwife carried on speaking calmly to Hannah, not refuting any of the outlandish claims she was making, just gently interrogating her. When she had finished, she beckoned me into the hallway, where Hannah couldn't hear us talking.

"How long has she been like this?" she asked me, her tone and expression as accusatory as a jabbing finger.

"I don't know. A couple of days maybe?" I lied, trying to look innocent. "She's just over-tired, that's all – she's not been sleeping very well. That's normal for a new mum, isn't it?"

"What Hannah is displaying is *clearly* far from normal," the midwife said, accenting the word "clearly" for full effect. I knew what she was alluding to – she was insinuating that I was either negligent or stupid not to have noticed something was wrong. I said nothing, rather than say something that I might have regretted. Without saying anything further, the midwife called the doctor, who came out to see Hannah within the hour.

"I suspect she might be suffering from puerperal psychosis, and if that is the case she really needs to be hospitalised for a psychological evaluation and treatment as quickly as possible," the doctor said after he had spent some time alone with Hannah.

Then, upon seeing the look on my face, which he misinterpreted as concern for Hannah, he said, "Try not to worry too much, Mr Attwood. Most women recover with appropriate rest and medication, although it can take some time."

But I *was* worried. Worried that she would go into hospital and they would make her better. I didn't want her to get better; I needed her to be an unfit mother. This was all happening too soon. In the end, Hannah was hospitalised for thirteen weeks, longer than is normal for most patients with puerperal psychosis. Her condition was the worst they'd ever seen, I was told. Whilst in hospital, she was given anti-psychotic medication and cognitive behavioural therapy until eventually her condition stabilised enough for her to be allowed home. I was given a leaflet on puerperal psychosis signs and symptoms, and a business card with contact details for the perinatal mental health team for advice in case I noticed any disturbing changes in her behaviour.

Whilst in hospital, Hannah's medication had helped to suppress the hallucinations and now back home she was thinking more clearly. However, she admitted that her mind still felt "muzzy", as she called it, and I knew that I still had a chance to make this work. The first thing I did was to replace her prescribed tablets with harmless vitamins so that she was not getting her medication. I rigged the baby intercom and started whispering into it and I wrote disturbing messages in the steam of the bathroom mirror whilst she showered. Before long, I found her rocking and talking to herself again, her mind having slipped back off the tightrope of reality.

From there, Hannah swung between being on a high, being low and being paranoid. At one point she believed she had superpowers and could see and hear things that other people couldn't, such as hidden messages on TV or on cereal packets, but when she became convinced Amber's milk had been laced with arsenic and refused to bottle-feed her, I decided to have her hospitalised again, hopeful that it would be permanent, or for the foreseeable future at least. As it happened, she remained in hospital for just eight weeks before being released back home once again. Over the twelve months that followed, the cycle of being admitted into hospital for treatment, returning home and becoming ill again continued several more times, and I started to get really impatient – when were they going to make the decision that she was never going to get well and just keep her in hospital? Surely, they could see she was a danger to Amber?

Back then, Hannah's behaviour was bizarre at best, frightening at worst, but the psychiatric team had remained stubbornly optimistic, believing that Hannah could still respond positively to the right treatment. They tried many different anti-psychotic drugs, mood stabilisers and anti-depressants; the next step they were considering was electroconvulsive therapy (ECT) – electric shock treatment. I'd had enough. I knew by then that Hannah could only be sectioned long term if she was deemed a danger to herself or others. I had argued with them that I was concerned about Amber's welfare, but they simply did not believe she was a danger to Amber. I needed to do something more to convince them; I just didn't know what.

The answer came to me one evening as I was taking a bath. Amber was safe in her cot in the nursery, and as I lay in the hot soapy water, watching the steam rise, I could hear Hannah moving around downstairs. She was going through a "high" phase where she felt elated and excited, invincible. She was noisy and irritating when she was like that, and I needed to shut her out, so I slid beneath the surface of the water, concentrating on the tiny escaping bubbles of air that were rising to the surface. As I lay supine and still, I let myself imagine that the gentle pressure of water on my face was Anna's hand caressing me, that it was her fingers running through my hair, causing it to lift and float from my head. Being under the water had made me feel closer to Anna somehow, knowing that water was the last element to have embraced her before she died, and I felt myself stiffening and aching for her. I remained under the water for as long as possible, until I felt the same terrible burn in my lungs that she must have felt, until the urge to breathe, to live, overcame my desire to stay and be with her forever. And when I rose back out of the water I had the answer.

A loud car horn has just sounded, interrupting my thoughts and making me jump. It takes me a second to realise that I am the reason for the horn – traffic lights have turned green but I am static, holding everyone up. I know it is my fault, but I slam my hand on my own horn in stubborn protest back before I start to drive on. I realise I am feeling angry, and it is not really at the driver beeping his horn at me; it is at the unwanted memory of what I had been forced to do all those years ago. I feel like I want to keep my hand on the horn until the sound invades my head permanently, leaving no room for the trespassing images.

I drive on a short way until I spot a layby to pull in to. I can't drive with all of this going through my head; it's impossible. I park up and switch off the engine, cutting dead both its throaty growl and the love song playing on the radio. The only sound left now is the rain drumming its beat on the roof of the car. With each second it feels as though the rain is getting heavier until it sounds like fists pounding on the roof to get in, to reach me and dig up the memory that I have tried to bury away forever. I cry in shame: trying to forget is clearly not working right now; I am going to have to face the memory to expunge it.

"You're safe, darling," I whisper, my voice echoing the words spoken all those years ago. "Daddy will never hurt you," I say to myself, and as I close my eyes it is not just my mind but my whole body that seems to remember.

I am back there now, in that dreadful, necessary, moment. I can feel Amber's tiny body struggling and flailing as I use Hannah's hand to force my baby under the bath water. It is not easy to hold her there; her instinct and will to survive is making her stronger than I had expected for one so small, and I am also grappling with keeping Hannah under control, keeping her hand on Amber's head. I am whispering in Hannah's ear, telling her that she is responsible, that she is the one trying to drown Amber, that she is a bad mother. It is only for a minute, just long enough for Amber to show signs of being held under the water, not long enough to cause any real lasting harm. As hard as it is for me, I know that the end will justify the means, and I take comfort in the fact that Amber will not remember any of this – for her, it will be as if it never even happened.

My pulse is racing as I remember all of this, and I feel the panic rising in me, just as it did that night when Amber went limp in my arms and for a split, horrifying second, I thought I had gone too far. And then the relief, when she coughed an arc of water and started wailing and I knew that she was going to be OK. Hannah remained on the floor, soaking wet, her arms outstretched towards us, crying.

"You did this!" I screamed at her, and I meant it, before I picked up my phone and dialled 999.

"Police, and ambulance," I said, my voice trembling. "My wife is insane. She's just tried to drown my baby." Then, as I waited for the police to arrive, I told Hannah over and over that *she* was responsible, that *she* had tried to kill Amber, that Anna wanted her baby back, until she became so confused she didn't know what to think.

Amber was taken into hospital for a precautionary measure in case of secondary drowning. I hadn't known about that – if water gets into the lungs it can cause a pulmonary oedema, causing someone to drown hours or even days after they have been removed from the water. I swear, if I had known about it, I would never have risked doing what I did. I spent the entire night, every second of it, by Amber's side talking to her and stroking her head, telling her how much I loved her. I didn't move – not for food, not to use the toilet – until the doctors finally told me she was in the clear, that there was no sign of fluid build-up in the lungs and I could take her home. And when I finally walked through the front door, on my own with my little girl, all the guilt, all the trauma, disappeared, knowing that this was it – from here on in it was just the two of us.

Hannah had been predictably confused in the aftermath of what happened. She reiterated what I had said about it being her fault, and about Anna wanting Amber back, but in her more lucid moments she tried to blame me. I was nervous, but in the end, thanks to her history of psychosis and the physical evidence of strands of Amber's hair tangled in her fingers at the scene, my version of the event was accepted and the court decided that she should be detained under a Section 37 hospital order. This time, Hannah's condition did not respond to medication. Her mind regressed, unable to cope with the magnitude of what she was told, what she believed she had done and she has remained in the secure hospital ever since, locked away with the truth.

The rain appears to be slowing up now, tapping lightly on the roof before making gentle trails, like tears of frustration, down the windscreen. My heartbeat is slowing back down with the gentler rhythm of the rain but I can feel the beginnings of a headache pressing against the back of my eyes. I reach into the dashboard to retrieve the pills that will hopefully stave it off and as I dry-swallow the pills I think about all the precious years that I have had with Amber, years that would not have been possible if I hadn't taken the action that I did all those years ago. Everything I did, and have done since, has been for Amber. So many times I've wanted to tell her about her real mother, to let her know how much more precious she is to me because she is part of her. But the moment never felt right. I missed the opportunity to pre-empt and manage Amber's curiosity and now things feel like they are getting out of control.

Amber is no longer a child. I can't control her in the way I could when she was little and it scares me. I started to notice a change in her after she joined the debating club – she looks at me differently. I see scepticism rather than acceptance in her eyes and her increasingly wilful behaviour of late has confirmed my growing fears. She no longer trusts what I tell her and that is dangerous. Anna died because she didn't trust that I knew what was best for her. After the last miscarriage, Anna insisted on taking a break from trying for a baby, and the biggest mistake I made was allowing her to have her way. I slipped up, I let sympathy rule my instinct, but if she'd listened to me, if she'd done as I'd wished, we wouldn't have been in Sri Lanka and she wouldn't be dead. She would be here with me; *she*, not Hannah, would have been the one who gave birth to Amber and we would be a family, like it was supposed to be. None of this would be happening right now.

My phone rings. The sound is shrill and unnaturally loud in my increasingly fragile, throbbing head and is interfering with my ability to think clearly. I quickly answer the call to stop the noise before I go mad and find it is the hospital telling me that Amber is ready to be picked up. As I hang up, I take a deep breath to compose myself before bringing the car back to life, ready for the short journey back to the hospital. I am apprehensive about what damage seeing Hannah may have done and I know that, whatever has happened today, I am going to have to tell Amber the truth about her real mother, or some semblance of it. She will be shocked, I'm sure of that, but I am determined that I will make Amber trust me again, whatever it takes. I refuse to make the same mistake with Amber that I made with Anna. I won't lose her, I won't let her drift away from me, I would rather be dead. I would rather we were both dead.

CHAPTER 30

Amber

My head has been reeling since meeting Hannah. When Dad picked me up from the hospital, I tearfully bombarded him with questions and when we got home he reluctantly sat me down and told me the truth about my conception and birth, the truth about the person behind the name Anna. Since then, I have been having nightmares that I am drowning. Hardly surprising, really, considering that is how Anna died, and that is how Hannah tried to kill me. But in my nightmare there is something more lurking in the shadows, I always wake up feeling as though I am missing something, that my dream is trying to tell me something.

I still can't really understand why Dad never just told me the truth when I first started asking about my mum. I guess it was too complicated – how do you tell someone that the person on their birth certificate isn't really their mother, that their real mother died years before they were even born? It's enough to spin anyone out, but I would have understood – I'm mature enough, he should have realised that. Having said that, I admit I am a bit confused, though. Who, exactly, should I call my mother? Is it Hannah, the woman who carried me in her womb, felt me move and kick, gave birth to me and was driven insane for her troubles? Or is it Anna, the woman who never even knew that I existed but who I share my genetic make-up with: my hair, my eyes, maybe even my personality? Legally, Hannah is my mother but, genetically, Anna holds all the rights to me. I never got the chance to get to know either of them, and now I find myself with the chance to decide which of them I'm going to call Mum. Christ, what a choice! Am I the most jinxed daughter ever, or what? What is clear, though, is that as far as Dad's concerned there is really only one contender for the post, and that is Anna. I get the feeling that Hannah was only ever a means to an end, and I feel uneasy about that.

When I told my best friend, Amy, about it all, her reaction was to screw up her nose and say, "Ew! That's a bit fucked up, to be honest, Bambi! I always said your dad was weird – didn't I always say that? He's odd!"

Bambi is Amy's nickname for me – partly because it sounds a bit like my name, and partly because of my large eyes. From the moment I first met her when I joined the school debating team, I knew we would be best friends. She doesn't really fit in – she lives on the Oak Tree council estate and gained a scholarship to our school – but this doesn't bother her. She is a force to be reckoned with, and was the first non-adult that I had ever heard swear so much! She is funny and brave and kicks ass and is never afraid to tell it the way she sees it, yet somehow it never feels personal or offensive. She challenges the way I think and I like that; we may not always agree with each other, but we always hear each other out.

Amy's reaction to what I told her wasn't entirely surprising, although for once it did upset me a bit. Amy has never liked my dad, but then Dad disliked her the moment he met her, so the feeling is mutual. He's never really liked any of my friends, actually – he's certainly never made any of them feel particularly welcome – but after he had met Amy he told me straight that he didn't want me being friends with her, that he could tell she was going to be a bad influence. He said she was not good enough for someone like me – he'd never gone so far as to say something like that before and it shocked me.

When I told Amy that he didn't want me to see her, she said, "He's a control freak, Bambi. A control freak and a snob. He doesn't want me to see you because I come from a council estate and because he knows I can see right through him. Are you really going to let him get away with telling you who you should be friends with? You're not five years old anymore."

At first, I got angry with Amy – she didn't even have a proper dad, so what right did she have to judge mine? I told her that my dad loved me, that he was just being overprotective, that's all. He has had to be both a mum and a dad to me – it has always been just him and me and no one else, so he finds it difficult to share me. He worries about me, loves me a bit too much. Wants what's best for me. But deep down I knew she was right, that I was struggling to justify it, that he had no right to tell me who I should be friends with, that I was old enough to make up my own mind. Amy didn't drink or smoke or do drugs. She didn't stay out all night partying. She was an A* scholarship student with dreams of becoming a judge one day. A *judge* – who else do you know with ambitions to become a judge? She is a good friend to have. The best. So, I ignored his request, and carried on being friends with Amy, meeting her in secret, even though it felt wrong.

Amy had made me braver, but I still loved my dad and didn't want to hurt him or disrespect him. Sometimes I think he knew, though, as he would make derogatory little digs that I knew were aimed at Amy at every possibility, although I pretended not to hear them. It was easier to ignore things than confront or be confronted.

Anyway, although Amy's comment had stung a bit when I told her about how I had come to be born, I can't help but think she may be right. The older I'm getting, the more something doesn't feel right, something feels "off". God, I feel like a traitor even thinking that – Dad would be so hurt if he could read my mind right now. Dad loves me, I know that, no question. He has done his best, and his best has been good enough, it really has. I've never felt that I've missed out, not really. He's taken me to theme parks, on holidays, read me stories, played with me, made me laugh. Until recently, he has never got angry with me. As I've got older, he's even tried his best to keep up with teenage fashions and trends so we have things to talk about, and I love him for that even though it can be a bit cringeworthy sometimes!

But the truth is, Amy is the first real long-term friend I've ever had. I rarely had friends over more than once or twice before they made excuses not to come over again. I never understood why, but do remember crying when I was about to turn eight years old and no one wanted to come to my birthday party. Dad said to me, "Friends are transient, Amber – that means they come and go – it's just the way things are. But I'll always be here for you – you don't need them – you've got me and my tickling fingers!" And then he wiggled his fingers at me before grabbing me and tickling me, until I laughed so hard that I had forgotten all about my tears and shattered birthday plans.

The more I have been thinking about it, the more I've realised that Dad has been too overprotective, too possessive of me, to the point where I haven't really been able to sustain friendships in the normal way, and that can't be right, can it? I've never had trouble making friends, but they have nearly always been within the confines of school. I do think he's *tried* to let me have friends as I did get to go to parties and went on sleepovers when I was younger, but Dad always found some reason or other not to let me go back: the parents were too blasé about safety; the children were too noisy, out of control; the house was unsanitary; he could see a bottle of wine on the kitchen counter when he picked me up. It all feels a bit over the top when I think about it objectively.

It is Saturday and Dad is out at the moment. He said he had an appointment in town and would be out for a few hours, so I am in the house alone. Usually I would go to my room, put my earbuds in and listen to music as I get on with some homework, but today I cannot concentrate – there is far too much going through my mind for that. With the house being empty, you would think it would be quiet, but it isn't. Houses are a bit like humans – they make noises that usually go unnoticed in the din and clatter of everyday life: the breathing of a clock ticking away each second, water pipes gurgling and grumbling like a hungry tummy, electrical appliances humming like tinnitus in the background. Right now, I am particularly aware of the windows rattling in their effort to hold back the strengthening wind outside, and another indiscernible sound – a crack from seemingly nowhere – has made me jump. I was told by Janice that Hannah used to hallucinate, believing Anna was in the house trying to steal me, and now I can understand why – the noises are freaking me out a bit, and I shiver. Maybe I will go to my room and put my earbuds in after all.

I walk up the staircase and deliberately miss the step third from the top – the one that I know always creaks in protest. As I walk along the landing towards my room, I pass my father's bedroom. His door is open, and I see the familiar framed photo on his bedside cabinet, set at an angle facing his bed so that he can see it each night. I have seen that photo a thousand times but cannot remember the last time I actually *looked* at it. When I was little, I would run and jump onto Dad's bed each morning and he would pick up the photo and tell me to "kiss Mummy good morning", but once I became too old to be going into Dad's bedroom I never really took any more notice of it. Each time I passed his room, I would see it there, but it was so familiar in its spot it became sort of visibly invisible.

The image in the frame is of Hannah holding me as a baby and I suddenly feel the need to look at it properly, to see the look on her face as she cradled me, to get a feel for what kind of a mother she might have been had she not turned crazy. Dad's bed is beneath his window, which has been left open, and as I walk into his room a gust of wind blows in loudly, lifting the curtains and knocking the photo frame over so that it lands face down on the cabinet with a loud bang. Shit! I seriously nearly wet myself! As I pick up the frame, I can see that the glass has cracked from the force of being knocked over and for some reason I feel guilty, as if I have caused it to happen just by being in the room.

The crack in the glass runs directly between Hannah and baby-me, subtly separating us, which is an irony not lost on me. As I study Hannah's face, I can see that something's not quite right, that the perspective seems wrong, that her head is not quite at the correct angle to the position of her body. It occurs to me that the image has been photoshopped and I realise that I am probably looking at Anna's face on Hannah's body. God, that is weird! It has made me wonder what else I haven't noticed, what else I may have just blithely accepted without question.

As I place the frame back in its place, a squeaking noise behind me causes my head to turn and my heartrate to rise. The noise is coming from the door to Dad's wardrobe, which hasn't been shut properly and is moving subtly with the breeze from the open window, that's all. Seeing the wardrobe reminds me that Dad keeps a box at the back of it. A couple of years ago, Dad asked me to fetch a tie and I remember seeing the box and asking him what it was. "Just old papers and documents, things that I need to go through to see what to keep and what to throw away some day," he said. His explanation was enough to quell my curiosity – who's interested in dusty old paperwork, after all? But now I realise that those papers and documents might be more significant than he was letting on, and so I find myself on my knees now, reaching for that box.

It's still there! It is a heavy-duty cardboard storage box with a lift-off lid and handle holes, and has the tell-tale dog-ear signs of having been handled quite a bit. I feel a little bit sick, although I'm not sure why, as I lift the lid with the care of a bomb disposal expert.

Although it is the middle of the day, the room is gloomy thanks to the ominous, grey clouds outside. I want to get up and switch the light on, but am too caught up with the box in my hands to do that right now. I peer into the box and am immediately disappointed. I don't know why, I don't know what I wanted to see, but on first sight it does look to be full of boring old pieces of paper: old insurance documents, long-since-ended endowment policies, years-old bank statements, curling official brown-letter correspondences. But then it occurs to me that what is there doesn't seem to be enough for the size of the box, that the box is too heavy to be holding just those papers, and I realise that there is a false bottom.

I hesitate – I know this is wrong, that I am snooping – but I'm too invested now, and so I lift out the paperwork and wiggle loose the false bottom. The first thing I see is what looks like a clear plastic evidence bag – the sort you see on crime programmes. Inside I can see a watch and an old leather travel wallet. I lift out the wallet and a strange waft of musty leather mingled with a hint of dried seaweed hits my nostrils. The wallet feels stiff in my hands and there are powdery salt crystals left behind from where salt water has dried on it. I open the wallet to find a wrinkled passport inside, and when I open the front cover of the passport it reveals a smudged and water-damaged photograph with the name Anna Attwood beside it. I spend a minute trying to make out whether I look anything like Anna, my genetic mother, but it is hard to make out her features properly due to the damage.

I place the travel wallet on the floor and reach into the plastic bag for the watch. It is a gold bracelet-watch and there is a tiny amount of water swilling around inside the watch case, making it look as if the face of the watch is moving. The time on the watch is forever stuck on a few minutes past half past nine. I turn the watch over and read an inscription on the back:

Time stops
without you

I suddenly feel an aching knot in my throat as I hold back my tears for Anna, whose life stopped at a few minutes past half past nine, but also for my dad, who could never have known the significance of that inscription when he gave the watch to her. I am about to put the watch down with the wallet but decide to try it on my wrist instead. I can't do it up as the clasp is broken, but it is a perfect fit for my wrist. *We had the same wrist size!* Why am I getting a buzz from that?

The box is not yet empty; there is blue silk material at the bottom that looks as if it is wrapped around something. Carefully I lift this out and unwrap it. The material is actually a sarong, the type you wrap around yourself on the beach, and it is ripped with a rusty-coloured stain on it. The item wrapped in it looks like a scrapbook and when I open it I can see photographs stuck on to the pages. I need light for this, so I get up off my knees to switch on the bedroom light, and as I do so the open window lets in another gust of moaning wind that forces the bedroom door to slam shut, scaring me half to death. I'm so jumpy today. I quickly close the bedroom window before settling down on Dad's bed to take a look at the book.

The photos in the scrapbook appear to be in some kind of chronological order, and in the photos on the first few pages Anna doesn't look much older than me – it could even *be* me, to be honest, we look so much alike. We have the same eyes and the same auburn hair. She is laughing and smiling a lot in those photos, and so is Dad in the ones taken of them both together.

Do you know, I've never considered whether my dad is happy or not before but, seeing these photographs of him and Anna together, I realise that I have never seen him as happy as that, and it makes me sad.

Beside some of the photos, Dad has scribbled words, such as "Beautiful" or "All mine!" or drawn little pictures like love hearts and smiley faces to describe how they make him feel. It is the sort of thing a teenage girl would do – that *I* would do – not something I could ever imagine my solid, dependable, sensible dad doing! I turn several more pages until photos of their wedding day emerge. Anna still doesn't look much older than me, but she does look beautiful. I hope that I will look as beautiful on my own wedding day when it happens – maybe I'll even ask Dad if he still has her dress. The wedding photos are natural rather than staged. Most are snaps of Anna and Dad together, but some show Anna on her own or chatting and laughing with some of the guests and I wonder who those guests are. The only people I recognise are Grandma and Grandpa, Dad's parents, who I rarely get to see as Dad says they are not good people and would interfere in our lives if we let them. He lets them pay for my education, though.

One of the photos shows Dad in the background watching Anna as she chats to another girl of about the same age, and there is something about Dad's expression that I can't put my finger on but I don't like very much. Weirdly, there is a black X through the face of the person that Anna is talking to and a word has been scrawled next to the photo, which I am struggling to read but looks very much like "bitch". It can't be that word, though, surely – my dad has never used language like that, ever. Something tugs at my subconscious, but I ignore it, shake it away, too frightened to see what it wants from me.

The photos now move on to what is clearly the honeymoon, and I relax again as they both look so happy. They both look tanned and happy and in love – nearly every photo shows them scantily clad with their arms or legs draped over each other in a display of mutual, exclusive ownership and it makes me blush to see my dad like this – I have never seen him with a woman in that way before. I know he has dated a few, but he's never brought anyone home to meet me – he's always said they've not been anything serious, and not good enough to bring into my life. As a little girl, I often found myself secretly hoping that one day one of them might be.

After the honeymoon shots, the photos progress and I notice a change in Anna. Starting to get older, yes, but her expression is different, as if she is burdened by something. I recognise the look, as it is how I look when I have a lot on my mind or when something is bothering me. Then, on the next page, there are no photographs, just a couple of newspaper cuttings that relate to a fatal car crash involving a middle-aged couple. I skim-read the article, and the obituary, and realise that they were Anna's parents – my grandparents. I hadn't considered that before, about whether I had other flesh-and-blood family out there somewhere, and now I find out that I do I find that they are also dead. That really sucks! As I'm about to turn to the next page, I spot one of Dad's little drawings near to the obituary cutting, and as I take a closer look I am puzzled to see it is a hand-drawn smiley face.

A sharp scattering of rain suddenly hits the bedroom window like a handful of gravel, briefly taking my attention away. I shiver involuntarily as I return to my task and continue to turn the pages, even though it isn't really cold in the room. There are more photographs now, and in these Anna has an emptiness in her eyes. She looks, I don't know, detached somehow, her smile forced.

I suppose Anna's expression isn't really surprising considering she had lost both of her parents, and I think this must also have been the period that Dad told me about, where they were trying to have a baby, where she was having IVF and miscarriages. I want to tell her that it's OK, that she did it, that I am here! I desperately want to see more photographs of her smiling properly, happy like before, but there are none.

The next few photos are of Anna and Dad on holiday in Sri Lanka and I look at them with a heavy heart, knowing that I am looking at the last images of her before she died. Anna is much thinner in these photos, and this time she and Dad are not draped around each other. In each shot Dad is pulling Anna into him, or he has his arm clamped around her, but you can see that she is not leaning naturally into him, that her head is tilted ever so slightly the other way. The photos end now and the next page is full of more newspaper cuttings – this time about the tsunami, Anna's death and memorial. The space around the cuttings is full of drawings of crying eyes, and angels and broken hearts and the word "why?" written over and over and over, the ink getting blacker and blacker.

I really feel Dad's grief in those images and words, but I also find it a bit disturbing, to be honest. There is a poem on the next page that he has written by hand. I recognise it as Sonnet 43 by Elizabeth Barrett Browning – we covered the poem in English lit last year. It is about eternal love that transcends death, and Dad has highlighted the final line.

I love thee with the breath,
Smiles, tears, of all my life! and, if God choose,
I shall but love thee better after death.

Although I can understand why Dad would relate to this poem after Anna died, a continuing unease grows in me. I am used to analysing the meaning in poems at school, but now I find myself analysing Dad's behaviour. I know he was grieving but, even so, this feels like something more than grief and as I turn to the next page my heart starts to thump in my chest. At the top of the next page, Dad has written HANNAH in capital letters, but there are scribbled lines through both of the Hs, which has turned it into "ANNA". The page contains old photos of a young woman who I guess must be Hannah, and it is striking how alike she and Anna are in those pictures. Some have been taken through the window of a café where it looks as if she was working as a waitress, some are of her just walking in a street or talking to a friend, some going into and out of a building. It is clear, though, that the photos were taken without her knowledge. Shit, was Dad stalking her?

I can feel that my heart rate has risen; there is a dull, steady thumping in my chest as I turn the page once more. The photos have ended once again and now it has become a sort of diary. The first entry starts with:

I don't believe in coincidences. I have been having so many dreams that I am beginning to lose track of what is real and what is not. I feel that it is Anna, her spirit, telling me not to let her go, not to give up hope, and as soon as I saw Hannah I just knew that she was the one. Her likeness to Anna was too great to be a simple coincidence – call it fate, if you like, but not coincidence.

Anna may be dead, but a part of her still lies in the embryo we created. I simply cannot bear the thought that our baby is lying frozen in a test tube, each molecule a part of my precious Anna, waiting to be warmed up and brought back to life. When I saw Hannah, it hit me like a thunderbolt – she's the one! She doesn't know it yet, but she's the one who will make it all possible.

For the first time in a long time, I can feel some hope. Could it be that I will soon have at least a little part of my Anna back with me?

Oh God, reading this it is clear that Dad had been using her. When he told me the truth of how I came to be born, he made it sound as if he cared about Hannah, as if it all evolved naturally, but that was a lie – he contrived the whole thing. I feel sick as I read on and learn how he planned for Hannah to fall in love with him, and how he tricked her into having IVF – into having *me*. Dad was treating Hannah the way farmers treat their breeding cattle and something moves inside of me when I think about this, a feeling of disgust. Disgust in my father, but also disgust in myself, disgust at how I *really* came to be here.

I desperately want to close this scrapbook right now, put it back and pretend it doesn't exist, pretend that I have never seen it, but I can't, it's too late. I know I am going to carry on reading it, but I'm scared of what I will find out, of what else I will learn about Dad that I will wish I didn't know. My hands are shaking uncontrollably as I turn the pages and I find that I was right to be scared, as I am confronted with a dark side of my father's nature, a side he has hidden from me so well. How is that even possible?

I am staring now at pages that are adorned with photos of me as a newborn. Disturbingly, in the images of Hannah holding me, Dad has put a black X through Hannah's face, just as he did to the face of the woman talking to Anna in the wedding photos. I see it now for what it is – an angry, sinister, symbolic gesture – he wants them out of the picture.

As I turn another page, I find printed articles on puerperal psychosis stuck onto the pages, and Dad has underlined or highlighted various passages, and added notes in the columns. As I read the articles and then Dad's notes, a shiver runs through me as it occurs to me that they are things that would make Hannah's psychosis worse.

Deprive of sleep
Limit food intake
Cannabis?
subliminal messages
move things around

Dad was deliberately making her worse? Surely not? Please, God, let me be wrong! But as I read on I know that I'm not wrong, and I am crying as I read his words.

It is surprisingly easy to nurture her illness...

He actually uses the word "nurture", which is ridiculous when you think about it – the word is usually associated with caring and protecting, not harm and abuse. None of what I'm reading sounds like my dad; I don't recognise him in the words and sentences and paragraphs, he sounds like a mad person, someone deranged and crazy. This cannot be happening! It feels like a plot in one of those crappy afternoon movies on the Hallmark Channel, where the good-looking nice guy always turns out to be a complete psychopath. I skim-read through Dad's accounts of Hannah's various admissions into hospital, but even so I can feel the frustration in his words each time she is discharged back home.

I cannot believe how this is all dragging on, why they keep releasing Hannah. They are even talking about electric shock treatment now! When are they going to realise that she is not going to get better, that she is not fit to be anywhere near my little girl? What more do I have to do to convince them?

And then, just as I think it can't get any worse, it does. It is so hard for me to read, not just because my eyes are so full of tears that the words are distorting in front of me, but because of *what* it says. I read it over and over, willing the words to lift off the page and rearrange themselves, for them to land into different sentences, ones that don't reveal that it was him, not Hannah, who held me under the water that day.

As hard as it is for me, I know that the end will justify the means, and I take comfort in the fact that Amber will not remember any of this – for her, it will be as if it never happened. I will be the one to live with the thought of what I have been forced to do.

I cannot believe that he is making it sound as if he had no choice, as if he were forced into it, as if *he* were somehow the victim. And, despite what he thought, what he no doubt still thinks, the truth is I *do* remember that day and as the memory surfaces again now I remember it in a new light.

My head under water; of not being able to breathe; thrashing my arms and legs; the sound of my mum's voice screaming in a faraway land.

"No! No! Please! Let go!"

Of Dad's hand pulling me up by my hair; of Mum tearing at him with her hands; of him slapping her to the ground; of sirens and flashing blue lights...

My heart feels like it stops as I remember the words that Hannah shouted as I left the hospital room, "*No! No! Please! Let go!*" That's what had been poking at my subconscious that day: Hannah had fought to stop Dad. For the past fourteen years Hannah has been locked in a psychiatric ward having been deliberately driven mad and accused of a crime she didn't commit. Just so that Dad could have me all to himself. It's sick.

The wind is howling outside and I feel as though I want to join in with it, to howl and scream and cry. The stress is too much for me and I suddenly feel like something is stuck in my throat, choking me. I need to be sick and I retch as my body attempts to purge itself of all I have just learned, but nothing comes out. Whatever is stuck there is stuck there for good. I think of Amy – I need to speak to Amy – she'll calm me down; she'll know what to do. Shakily, I remove my phone from my pocket and scroll to her name. As I press "call" I continue flipping the pages of the scrapbook, where my eyes scan scores of photographs of me as I grow up. Most are of just me, but some are of me and Dad together and I can see in those photos how much he loves me and my heart hurts. I mean, *really* hurts.

Dad has written amusing anecdotes of things I had said or done alongside some of the photos. In one photo he has drawn cartoon-like additions of rabbit ears and whiskers on me, writing "Daddy's Funny Bunny" next to it; in another he has given me a halo and written "Daddy's Angel". This all feels normal, feels like my real dad – the one who makes me laugh, who cuddles me when I'm upset, who is always there for me. The man who jokingly pleads with me, "Promise me you'll never get married, Amber – you'll never find a boy who loves you like your daddy does!"

This is all so confusing. I am beginning to understand how Hannah must have felt, not knowing what is real and what is not. Is he a loving, kind dad or is he a monster? Is it even possible to be both? Just as I am turning another page, the ringing on my phone stops and Amber's voice sounds out. "Whassup?" she says.

"Amy!" I cry in relief to the sound of her voice, but Amy doesn't appear to hear me.

"Hello? Hello? Are you there?" she says, and then, "*Sucker!* I'm not available right now but please feel free to leave a message…"

I don't listen to the rest of her jokey voicemail greeting, as what I am seeing on the page before me has paralysed me for a split second: photographs of Amy and me together. I was right: Dad has known all along that I have been meeting up with Amy. My eyes are drawn to one photo in particular, which has gained my full attention. It is a close up of Amy and me outside a McDonald's and we are both laughing at something, but what's really shocking, what really freaks me out, is that there is a big black X through Amy's face.

I am so accustomed to the sound of the wind outside and the noises that the house has been making that I don't hear the creak of the third stair from the landing. The door to the bedroom suddenly opens, startling me enough to drop my phone and scream out. I look up to see Dad standing in the doorway.

"What are you doing, Amber?" he calmly asks, as his eyes dart from mine to the scrapbook that I am holding in my hands.

CHAPTER 31

Jamie

I am back early: my appointment in town did not take as long as I had expected. The weather outside is atrocious – it feels as though it has been raining for weeks on end, but the wind has now picked up with it, throwing the rain in every conceivable direction and I am soaked. I call out for Amber as I walk into the house, but she is not responding – she's probably in her bedroom with her earphones in. It is only early afternoon, but the house is dark thanks to the storm clouds that have swallowed up most of the day's natural light. I remove my coat and hang it near a radiator to dry before putting the kettle on. The radiator is making a gurgling sound and I make a mental note that it needs bleeding before making my way up the stairs to Amber's room to see if she would like some lunch. She hasn't been herself since visiting Hannah and I worry that she is not eating properly.

As I near the top of the stairs, I listen out for the familiar creak at the third stair from the top. This has been creaking for a couple of years, and it is something that I would normally have had fixed as soon as I noticed it, but it is actually a handy security feature – it acts as a sort of alarm call to alert me should

Amber try to make her way downstairs in the night. Now, with her recent unpredictable behaviour, I am glad that I did decide to leave it untouched. Amber's behaviour started to deteriorate after joining the debating club and meeting that girl, Amy. She is trash. Her influence on Amber is unhealthy and Amber has secretly defied my direct order not to be friends with her. I can't control who Amber sees in school but she has been hanging around with that girl outside of school and lying to me in order to do it, although she doesn't know that I know. A couple of months ago, I started tracking Amber's movements using an app that I installed on her phone – I needed to know whether my instinct was right, which of course it was. I have followed them a few times now and each time my anxiety levels have risen.

It is so clear to me that Amy is grooming Amber, manipulating her. At first, I followed them to places like the library or the museum – places where Amy must have known that Amber would feel comfortable, where she might not feel she is doing anything wrong. In fact, she did tell me that she was going to those places after school. I guess she convinced herself that she was not really lying to me if she just omitted the fact that she was going with Amy. But before long Amy had somehow convinced my girl to hang around the local shopping centre and, more recently, McDonald's. I'm not stupid; I know that what comes next will involve boys and I cannot let Amy drag Amber down to street level. I can't let that happen. I won't.

I considered confronting Amber, but the truth is that she has changed lately and laying down the law, or even reasoning with her, is no longer enough. Her defiance in contacting the hospital behind my back is further proof of the path she is going down. Of where Amy is leading her. I think back to when Amber was a little girl; she used to adore me, I could do no wrong, but these last few months have been hard. The debating team and Amy have made her headstrong, overconfident even. She no longer just accepts what I say, she challenges me, pushes the boundaries. She reminds me a little of her mother in that way. Anna could be difficult at times, not that I like to dwell on that. I guess she's growing up and it is to be expected, but I'm not ready for it; I want my little girl back.

I am at the top of the landing now, and as I pass my bedroom to head to Amber's room I stop, perplexed. The door to my own room is closed – I never close it completely. I walk towards the door and open it. Amber is sitting on my bed. I have startled her, and she lets out a little scream before she registers that it is only me, her dad, standing here and nothing for her to be afraid of. But then I see what she is holding in her hands and my stomach lurches. Amber's eyes are as wide as saucers.

"What are you doing, Amber?" I try to keep my voice calm, under control, but calm and controlled is the last thing I am feeling right now.

How long has she been sitting there, how much has she seen and read? Strange lights flash in front of my eyes, lightning-strikes of blues and purples and oranges – the precursor to a migraine – and I give my head a small shake to try and rid myself of them. Through my distorted vision, I look down to the floor and see Anna's watch, wallet and blood-stained sarong – the only physical things of hers I have left from that day. Things that were ripped from her by her brutal attacker, things that were washed up on the shore, gathered up and given to me as proof of her passing, and a heat courses through me, a physical reaction to the anger I am feeling at seeing these things cast adrift in this way.

"Daddy?" Amber says in an uncertain tone. She only ever calls me Daddy when she is feeling insecure, needs reassuring. It is my cue, usually, to hug her and tell her everything is going to be OK, but as I take a step towards her she recoils and I realise with horror that I am the cause of her uncertainty. I am more than a little heartbroken; surely she knows that I would never do anything to hurt her?

"How much have you read?" I ask her, inclining my head towards the scrapbook, but I don't need her to answer; the look on her face tells me she has probably read most, if not all, of it.

I realise now, too late, that it was a mistake to write everything down. But after Anna died I didn't have anyone I could talk to – the scrapbook was my friend, if you like, my way of talking things over. It helped me see things more clearly, helped me plan and like a good friend, it kept secrets that nobody else was ever supposed to know.

"Is it true, Daddy?" she asks. "Was it you, not Hannah, who tried to drown me? Did you do things to make Hannah go mad?"

I see her tears running freely down her face and want so much to go to her, to hold her, but I know that it is too soon, that I have to find a way to reassure her first. She is so young. She thinks she is mature, but she is so far away from maturity yet; she couldn't possibly understand. How could she understand what it is like to love someone so unconditionally, so completely, that you would do anything, *anything* to keep them. Part of me feels annoyed that, once again, I am left to explain something that isn't my fault. Hannah wasn't fit to be a mother, she wasn't even her *real* mother. What else was I supposed to do, for God's sake?

My mind flashes back to Anna as I think about the time that she tried to leave me and the overdose I had to take to convince her how serious I was when I said I couldn't live without her. I knew she still loved me; she was just hurt and angry, but I wanted her to know just how it feels to nearly lose the person you love the most in the world. I phoned her as my mind was starting to lose its grip, to tell her goodbye, that I was sorry, that I couldn't live without her.

"*What have you done, Jamie?*" she had practically screamed down the phone. "*What have you done?*" and I could hear a commotion in the background as her parents were trying to find out what was wrong before I blacked out. When I woke, I was in the hospital. Anna's head was resting on the blue cotton blanket covering my legs – she had clearly been with me all night, just as I had known she would be. Later, as I prepared to leave hospital, I heard her speaking in hushed, angry tones to her parents in the corridor.

"For Christ's sake, Anna, can't you see what he's doing?" I heard her father spit out. "He's controlling you!"

"He made a mistake, that's all, and he's *sorry*," Anna replied. "He tried to *kill himself*, Dad! He *loves* me! What more could he do to show me how sorry he is?"

I had known that all I needed to do was find a way to make her see sense. Anna had spent the whole night terrified that I was going to die, and knowing that, if I had, it would have been her fault for trying to leave me. I just need to find a way now, to make Amber see sense.

A dull pain has settled behind my right eye, and I know it will continue to increase with intensity until it becomes almost unbearable and makes me violently sick. This always happens during times of extreme stress and has been brewing ever since Amber visited Hannah. It was the same when her mother was alive: I would suffer every time she didn't behave in the way that she should.

Amber is still looking at me with her hangdog eyes, waiting for a response from me. I realise it is pointless trying to deny what really happened that day, when she has already read about it in my own words. The trouble is, words can be taken out of context; she won't understand that it was all more complicated than it seems. I need to make sure she understands, however long it takes.

"I only held you there for a minute, not a second longer than was needed. Not a millisecond longer. I would never hurt you – you know that, Amber. Daddy loves you, baby," I say as I start to walk towards her.

"So, it's true! You *did* try to drown me!" Amber sobs.

"No! It wasn't like that, Amber. Don't say that! I just needed it to look like Hannah had tried to drown you. You were *my* little girl, not Hannah's. It was the only way I could get rid of her so that it could be just you and me, the way it was supposed to be. And it worked! We've been happy, haven't we? *You've* been happy? It wouldn't have been like that if Hannah had stayed. I did it for *you*, sweetheart. It happened because of you."

But, despite what I am telling her, I can tell by Amber's expression that it is going to take a while before she starts to understand, to see what happened as the pure, loving act it was. A while before it is safe to let her out of this room.

"I can see you are going to need some time to get your head around all of this," I say as I reach over to remove the scrapbook from her hands and pick up her phone, which is lying beside her on the bed. Amber scuttles back on the bed, her back pressing up against the headboard, as if she wants to get as far away from me as possible. I am finding this so difficult, the fact that she doesn't want me near her, doesn't trust me.

"For goodness' sake, I'm not going to hurt you, Amber." I hope the tone of my voice conveys how hurt I feel at how she is behaving.

I lean over her and she hunches in on herself in an attempt to further remove herself from me. What I want to do is kiss the top of her head, to fold her into my arms like I used to when she was little. I want to make it so that she understands instantly and we are back to how we were before. But, instead, I reach over her to turn the key in the window and lock it. As I do so, a large gust of wind causes a bough of the tree outside to whip and scratch at the window and I jump, nearly dropping the key before I have chance to place it safely in my pocket. I turn to the bedside cabinet and hesitate momentarily as I notice a crack in the glass of the photo of Anna and Amber. My migraine cranks up a gear and I feel the first stirrings of nausea.

Ignoring my migraine as best I can, I open the drawer to the bedside cabinet and retrieve the key to the bedroom door that I keep there. As I close the door behind me and lock it, I hear Amber jump up from the bed and the thud-thud-thud of her feet as she runs to it. The door rattles in the frame as she tries in vain to open it.

"Daddy?" I hear her cry. "What are you doing? Let me out!"

"Calm down, Anna," I say to the door between us. I realise my mind is fogging up with the pain and I am confusing this moment with another, very similar one that happened many years ago. "I'll be back in a few hours and we can talk about it then." I try to sound as reassuring as possible. "I'll let you out when I know that you fully understand, when you appreciate that everything I did was for your own benefit. That you bear as much of the responsibility as I do."

I ignore Amber's protests and the sound of her fists pounding on the door – I know that they will stop soon enough – and make my way to the bathroom to throw up violently. The acute pain behind my eye migrates to my whole head with each retch and I have to physically crawl to Amber's room to lie down and close my eyes against the ongoing assault of this migraine. I know it will take much more than a few hours for it to pass, and afterwards I will need to prepare my defence.

I don't expect Amber to thank me for what I have done, but I do expect her to be grateful and respectful. To appreciate all that she has personally gained. I will let her out when she is able to see that she is being selfish, unreasonable. When she can see the truth of how much selfless love I have for her. When she can see that it is inconceivable that she can ever survive without me. Or that I could ever let her.

CHAPTER 32

Amy

It is nearly midnight, but I don't want to go to bed until Mum gets home – she is working a twilight shift. My stepdad is asleep and has left his wallet on the coffee table. To my surprise, there are several fifty-pound notes spilling out of it but I know better than to ask where they came from and, besides, Mum could do with the money – I have seen the red letters piled up on the kitchen counter. I decide to help myself to a couple of the notes – there is a local 24/7 a few streets away that has a PayPoint where I can pay some of the bills and top up the electricity meter. I go to my room to pick up my mobile – it ran out of credit a couple of days ago, so I intend to top that up as well.

I didn't see Amber over the weekend and she wasn't at school today – one of the teachers said her dad had phoned to say she was sick. I feel bad that I haven't been able to text her, and more than a little worried. There is something off about her dad. I remember the day I first met him – Amber had invited me to her house after school and my skin broke out in goosebumps when she introduced me to him. He just stared at me, silent, unsmiling and unblinking, it was fucking weird.

After picking up my phone, I gather up the bills from the kitchen counter and leave the house to make my way to the 24/7. It is pouring down outside, dark and blowing a hoolie, just as it has been for days on end now. I pull the fur-rimmed hood of my old parker down as far over my face as I can whilst still being able to see where I am going, and stuff my hands deep into my pockets. The rain is river-dancing in the pools of light that have been cast onto the pavement by the lamp posts and it doesn't take long before my trainers allow a slow ingress of water to start seeping into my socks. The street is eerily deserted and the lack of noise strangely noticeable – the only discernible sounds are my own footsteps and the rain clattering like ball bearings onto anything in its way.

Just as I think that I am the only person stupid enough to be out walking in this weather, the outline of a man appears up ahead. He is tall and thin, his shoulders and head hunched over in an attempt to protect himself from the driving rain. One arm is wrapped around his middle to keep his inadequate jacket in place, a lit cigarette is dangling through the fingers of his other hand, its smoke battling to make it through the wind and rain. As our paths cross, I am met with the unmistakable whiff of marijuana. The man raises his head slightly to look at me and for the first time I realise how vulnerable I am – it is not a good area for anyone to be walking the streets alone at this time of night, least of all a teenage girl. I keep my head down and quicken my pace, making my way down one street before turning left into another identical version of the one I've just left. All of the streets around here are like that, the only thing marking them out as different are the broken and graffitied street signs as you turn each corner. Walking these streets sometimes feels like one of those bad dreams where you keep finding yourself back where you started, never actually getting anywhere. Eventually I find myself on the street that leads onto the main road and the 24/7.

During the day, the 24/7 looks run-down and depressing, but tonight the light from the window makes it appear warm and inviting. As I open the door, a bell jingles to announce my arrival and a young Asian man behind the counter looks up briefly before returning his attention back to his phone. I am hungry, so first I make my way to the self-serve hot-food counter, where there are a couple of items drying out under the hot lights. I pick out a vegetable pasty and make my way to the till, where I hand over one of the £50 notes and request a top-up voucher for my phone. The Asian man uses what looks like a highlighter pen on the note to check it is real before dealing with my request. Just as he closes the till, his phone pings again and as he starts to reach for it I place the bills I want to pay in front of him. He actually gives a little huff! What a dick! With the bills paid, I put my backpack on and make my way back out into the cold and wet darkness. There is a bus shelter a few yards down the road and this is where I head so that I can sit and eat my pasty and apply the phone credit, sheltered from the wind and heavy rain, if not the cold.

The shelter is deserted as there are no buses at this time of night, and I eagerly reach into my backpack to retrieve the pasty. I feel the residual warmth on my hand through the greasy paper and the smell of vegetables and cheese trickles under my nose. I juggle eating the pasty with applying the credit to my phone, and when I am done I can see that the last person to contact me was Amber, two days ago. She has left a voicemail and so I dial to retrieve it. Immediately it is clear that the phone must have gone off in Amber's pocket as there is no message, only her voice in the background, followed by her dad's. I am about to switch off and send her a text, but there is something about the tone of their voices that makes me decide to listen for a bit. What I hear makes my blood turn to ice.

Fuck!

I leap up from the bench, knocking over my backpack, leaving it to spew out its contents, and start to run through the wind and the rain towards Amber's house. She lives over a mile away from here and I am running into a headwind that has forced back the hood on my coat. The rain is running in rivulets off my now-sodden hair, down the back of my neck to the inside of my coat, but I barely notice it amongst the growing sweat as I run.

Before long, my coat is so wet it has become heavy on my body, making it harder to run and so I unzip and discard it, hardly slowing my pace as I do so. The wind snatches it, playing with it like a kite before it disappears from my sight. I carry on running, head down, trying to make myself as aerodynamic as possible through the force of the wind against me. It is so hard to run that it feels surreal, like a dream where your limbs are so heavy you can't run from danger, except I suspect that I am running towards danger, not from it.

I don't know what the fuck I think I'm going to do when I get there, but I'll figure something out; I have to. My best friend, my only friend in the world, needs me and I will do whatever it takes to help her.

CHAPTER 33

Amy

I am now approaching the turning into Meadow View, the estate where Amber lives, and up ahead I can see a blur of headlights. A car slows down as it approaches me and a middle-aged man winds down his window, rain lashing into the car interior, rain-staining the leather trim and speckling his glasses as he does so.

"You OK, love?" he shouts over the wind, but I don't stop or slow down, even though my lungs are screaming at me to rest. I keep my momentum going. I am so close now I don't have time to acknowledge his kindness or concern, if that's what it really is. You can never tell these days; he could be a bloody serial killer trawling the streets for a victim, for all I know.

I sprint into the estate and only then do I ease up a little to get my bearings. Now that I've slowed down, my breathing feels too fast and too shallow to give me the oxygen my greedy lungs are after, but I jog painfully on regardless, glancing at each house as I pass in the hope that I will recognise which one is Amber's. I have only visited her house once, but it was daylight then and in the shiny darkness I'm unsure as to which one it is.

I come to a house with a weeping willow tree on its front lawn and I immediately recognise it as Amber's house. The strong and flexible branches of the tree are stretching and bending with the grace of a ballerina in the wind. I jog up the driveway, past the willow tree, and come to a halt at the door, taking a moment to compose myself and catch my breath. I am so wet my clothes are clinging to me like a shroud and, now that I am standing still, I realise I'm shaking; whether it is from cold or fear or adrenaline I'm not sure. I'm aware that I still don't have a plan, so I make an instant decision to go with the old saying "*attack is the best form of defence*" and I pound my fist on the door whilst ringing the doorbell at the same time, shouting Amber's name. There are other houses nearby and I figure that this action will disturb enough people to make me visible even at this early hour of the morning, and by being visible I am afforded some form of protection.

I keep on pounding and ringing until a light appears at one of the upstairs windows, followed by several more in other houses along the street, and then I continue pounding until, finally, the front door opens and Amber's dad is standing there in his PJs. He takes a sharp intake of breath when he sees me, wet and bedraggled, on his doorstep. A few people have commented that Amber and I are similar to look at, so I guess I must look equally similar to Anna, his wife who drowned. Maybe he thinks it is her ghost standing here, having risen from her watery grave. I hope I've scared the shit out of him.

"Where is she, you fucking psycho?" I shout, and at the sound of my voice I see the spark of recognition in his eyes. I hope he sees the fire in mine.

"Amy?" He seems stumped, as if he doesn't quite know what to say or how to react and his eyes dart around the estate to check whether anyone is witnessing our exchange. I'm damn sure he will have seen several curtains twitching. Somewhere in the distance I hear the faint sound of sirens: a familiar sound in my neck of the woods, a much rarer sound around here, I suspect.

"Where the fuck is she?" I repeat. I attempt to step inside the house, but he blocks me and as I look up at him angrily, too angry to feel scared, I am momentarily distracted by a strange blue light that is pulsating across his face and onto the wall either side of the door. His attention is somewhere over the top of my head, towards the road, and then a short blast of a police siren pierces through the storm and I realise that the source of the light is coming from a police car that is reversing and stopping in the street at the bottom of the driveway. A tall, heavy-set policeman gets out and I am about to shout out for him to help, but I don't need to; he is already making his way up the drive, head down and holding on to his peaked cap to stop it being blown off his head from the wind.

"We've had a report of a young female running into the estate, appearing to be in distress. Is that you, young lady?" His voice is both authoritative and kind, his brow creased in an expression of concern at my appearance. I am confused for a moment, but then I realise that the report he's talking about must have been filed by the man in the car that slowed down to ask if I was OK. Not a serial killer, then, just a genuinely concerned citizen after all. There are good people out there, it seems.

I can see Amber's dad's eyes widen and I immediately see the similarity between father and daughter. Amber's eyes widen when she's afraid or uncertain. The police officer is looking at me and then back to Amber's dad, waiting for an explanation. Amber's dad is calm but I know his mind is whirring in overdrive as he works out a strategy to get himself out of this situation. I need to be the first one to speak, before he lies his way out of this.

"It's my friend!" I cry. "She's in there! He's locked her up in there!" I fire the words at the officer whilst pointing into the house.

"OK, calm down and take a breath, miss," he says and, as I look into his eyes for acknowledgement of what I have just told him, my heart sinks. I expected him to take charge, take action, save Amber, but instead he is just looking at me as if I am mentally ill. He doesn't believe me. But then why would he? I look crazy and what I am saying sounds crazy. Shit, I'm handling this badly!

Amber's dad has picked up on this and seizes the moment. "It's OK, officer." He adopts a sympathetic expression for the policeman's benefit. "Amy is my daughter's friend. She has psychological issues and has a tendency to overreact. I was about to call her mother to fetch her. She lives on the Oaktree Estate."

He is exploiting the way I appear, making me out to be some kind of a nutcase, using my address as a way to help explain my behaviour, and I can tell from the way the policeman is nodding that he is buying this bullshit.

"Fuck you!" I cry, then I appeal to the officer. "I'm telling the truth. Look. Listen. I have it all recorded." Amber's dad stiffens as he watches me take out my phone from my pocket – he hadn't expected evidence. The phone and my hands are both slick from the rain and as soon as it emerges I drop it, cracking the screen as it lands on the stone doorstep.

"Fuck!" I say as I pick it up and clumsily attempt to retrieve my voicemail, my fingers thick and stiff with the cold. Whether it is from having dropped it or whether it has been water-damaged from the rain seeping into my coat pocket, I don't know, but I am faced with a flickering screen. My phone is unresponsive to my frantic swiping and jabbing.

"Please!" I say, a desperation in my voice that I have never heard in myself before and I am not sure if I am pleading with my phone or with the policeman. Realising the phone is fucked, I look up again at the police officer. "Please, just let me see her. What harm would that do? If I'm wrong, I'll go home. I promise. You're a policeman, for fuck's sake; you are supposed to be helping me!"

I see the policeman hesitate slightly, clearly not sure what is going on, but my appeal to his sense of duty, my direct request for his help, has got to him, I can tell. Amber's dad has seen it too, because he is now filling the doorway deliberately with his frame, a human barrier. He needs to give an explanation that will prevent the police officer doing his duty.

"Amy, I've already told you, Amber is not here – she has gone to spend a few days with her grandparents." He uses a tone of voice that is usually reserved for explaining things to old, senile people who struggle with the facts. The police officer cannot see the look in his eyes as he says this to me; he cannot see the unwavering hatred, because if he could he would also see the lies.

"You fucking liar," I spit at him. "It's school term; why would you send her away during school term time? She's in there somewhere, locked away," I say, jabbing my finger once more towards the inside of the house. "Amy!" I scream out over him, in the vain hope that she will call out back to me. I am terrified of what he may have done to her. The policeman looks as if he has registered my point about it being school term and is about to say something, but, before he has a chance, Amber's dad gives him a feasible explanation for the doubt I have just planted in his mind.

"The truth is, officer, my daughter has been trying to keep her distance from Amy for some time now, but Amy is having a hard time accepting that she no longer wants to be friends with her. Amy has been bombarding her with phone calls and texts and my daughter is afraid. The school are aware – you can obviously contact them in the morning to confirm – but we all thought that, if Amber went away for a few days, then maybe Amy would start to come to terms with the situation. Clearly, it hasn't worked."

It is flabbergasting how quickly and effortlessly he is able to lie, how easy it is for him to manipulate the situation and make me look like a deranged friend from hell.

"No, that's not true. None of that is fucking true. He's lying. Please." I am so angry at myself that for once I don't have the words at my disposal to give a cogent, compelling account of the truth. My words are weak. I am weak. "No! She's in there; you have to look," is all I can manage.

"No, Amy, she is at her grandma's. I understand that you are upset that she doesn't want to talk to you, but this is not the way to behave, is it?" he says slowly but deliberately as if he is talking to an imbecile.

"Prove it, then! Phone her gran now. Go on, you lying piece of shit!"

"Amy, it is 2am. I am not phoning an elderly woman who is not in the best of health, because of some stupid, paranoid, hormonal teenager."

The officer looks at me with a strange mix of sympathy and irritation. I think of what I must look like: a teenager who has run over a mile in a storm with no coat, to pound on the door of her best friend and accuse her dad of keeping her hostage, because I haven't heard from her in a few days. Even I can see how crazy I must appear.

"OK, young lady. I think we need to get you home." The officer reaches out to take my arm, having made a decision on whose side he is taking. But I am not ready to give up.

"Fuck that!" I say, pushing the police officer off me and darting into the small gap beneath Amber's dad's arm and the door frame. I head for the stairs, taking them several treads at a time. Amber's dad and the police officer are in pursuit behind me, but adrenaline and my youth have given me the edge. I reach the landing and scan the doors that lead off of it, until I see one with a name plaque bearing Amber's name and head for it. I sprint towards it and as I push down the door handle I spill onto my knees with unexpected momentum – I hadn't expected it to open, I was certain it would be locked. Amber's dad and the policeman are now behind me as I kneel there, stunned, to see an empty room, neat and tidy with the bed made. No Amber.

"Where is she?" I scream, out of control with confusion and fear and anger. "What have you done to her?"

"I told you, Amy, she is at her grandparents' house." There is a barely concealed smugness in Amber's dad's expression.

The police officer is kneeling beside me now. His voice is calm but he is clearly irritated. "Up you get, Amy." But I don't want to get up, I want him to listen to me, to believe what I'm saying.

"I know you think I'm crazy, but I'm not. I heard it all. On the voicemail. He tried to drown Amber. When she was a baby, tried to drown her and made it look like Hannah did it. Now Hannah is in a mental institution and he has locked Amber up because she knows too much. Look at him, look at the sly bastard! You've got to believe me. Amber is in danger, I know it."

I am painfully aware that I am rambling, that what I'm saying will not make sense without the voicemail. I am only making things worse, reinforcing the idea that I am mentally unstable, but I don't know what else to do and now I am crying, fucking crying, and I don't ever cry. I have never felt so useless.

The policeman puts his arms under my armpits and starts to lift me from my knees. I don't resist this time; there is no point. He takes off his coat and wraps it around me and I realise that I am shivering uncontrollably, despite the fact that, actually, I feel really hot. I allow him to walk me back along the landing towards the stairs and we pass another door on my right. The policeman's hold on me is light and he is not expecting me to reach out and push down the handle of the door, but I do, and this time I am met with resistance. It is locked and the look on the policeman's face tells me he might finally be ready to listen.

To be honest, I expected something more from Amber's dad. Maybe for him to pick up the lamp that was sitting on the console table on the landing and hit the policeman over the head with it. Or push me down the stairs. Something. I don't know; maybe I watch too many crime movies. But he doesn't do any of those things. He does as the policeman asks: he pulls a key from his pocket and unlocks the door. The door creaks open to reveal Amber, still and unmoving, on the double bed. With an actual straight face, he delivers the ultimate cliché.

"It's not what you think, officer. I can explain."

He honestly fucking thinks he can explain this shit away.

PART III

"Ouroboros"
The past, the present and the future

CHAPTER 34

Dawn

I am running along a narrow path. Either side of me are concrete walls, smooth and high and impossible to scale. Every now and then I come across a door in one of the walls, but when I try to open it I can't. There is an old, rusty key in the lock and it won't turn, so I have to leave it and run on. My eyes are trained ahead, scanning for a way out, but the rest of my senses are focussed on what is behind me and I can feel the familiar trickle of sweat that comes with fear. My heart rate rises as I hear the steady, regular beat of a runner's footsteps behind me. I look over my shoulder, maintaining the rhythmic co-ordination of my bent arms, and see a woman gaining ground on me. She is younger than me, has more energy in her pace. She catches up to me and the path widens as she tunes her rhythm into mine, and we run together side by side in companionable silence. She points and up ahead I see a light.

I wake up and out of habit look at my bedside clock, although there is no need. I still wake at 3am every morning, or middle of the night, whichever way you like to look at it, and today is no exception. I lay my head back on my pillow and think about the dream I've just had.

Running is clearly a metaphor: running from the past, running from fear and danger, running from the truth. The other woman in my dream must represent the past catching up with me: Anna or Jeannie, or maybe both. I only borrowed Jeannie's name briefly, just long enough to enter the UK and become Dawn. I had been desperate to avoid detection, to ensure that no paper trace of Anna survived after the tsunami, no trace that could act as a clue or a red flag that Anna was still alive. But, as with all small lies and transgressions, they are seeds that germinate.

Looking back, I was so stupid. I should have just posted that letter to Jeannie's mother twenty years ago, along with one of my own explaining what happened, that she never made it. If I'd done that, then Benedict would not have come looking and mistaken Mary for his own child and I would have had just the one nemesis to fear, just Jamie. When I told Mary the truth, she had listened in silence, and when I had finished she asked just one question. It was an obvious one.

"Why run? Why didn't you just leave Jamie? Or tell someone, get help?"

I know that it sounds like an easy question, but it's not. Within a few years of meeting Jamie, he had managed to isolate me from my friends and had made me financially dependent upon him. Then my parents died and I had nobody to turn to for help. Jamie thrived on that; his behaviour became increasingly unstable and he was threatening in such a subtle way that it was impossible to explain to someone why I was so afraid. I can't prove it, because it is impossible to prove something that hasn't actually happened, but I knew that Jamie would kill me rather than let me go. He was pathologically obsessive, a sociopath. So, when I was faced with the opportunity to fake my death, I took it as my only way out.

But by running from one danger I brought another into my life. Benedict was my own fault, a cause-and-effect scenario – maybe even karma. He had been looking for Jeannie, not me, and I know that I could still have stopped him the evening he turned up at the townhouse. I could have stood in front of him so he could see that I wasn't Jeannie – but I was afraid. I had stolen Jeannie's identity; I had committed a crime. It isn't illegal to disappear or to run, but it is illegal to steal someone's identity, and, worst of all, by helping me use Jeannie's documents to change my identity to Dawn, Philip had been complicit. I had put him at risk. And, underneath all of that, I still feared that Jamie would find me if my true identity was exposed.

The worst thing, though, was that I put Mary at risk. I couldn't even use the DNA test to stop Benedict pursuing Mary, as that would have required me to provide photo identification and no photo identification of me as Dawn exists. There would have been no point in applying for a change of name on Jeannie's passport or driving licence as I couldn't change the photographs on them – it would always be obvious it wasn't me. Although I bear a passing resemblance to Jeannie, the only reason I got away with using her passport to return to the UK was because the photo was water-damaged, her features were unclear. In the aftermath of the disaster, the airport staff were doing cursory checks and, although Jeannie had only been eighteen and I had been twenty-two, I looked younger; I got away with it, but that was a one-off.

In the end, I think I feared Benedict just as much as I feared Jamie. I lived with the hope that Jamie believed I was dead, which meant that Benedict was my greatest threat to being found out. Jeannie's letter left no doubt as to the evil Benedict was capable of and I felt certain that a man like that would be vindictive enough to expose me to Jamie if he ever found out that I wasn't Jeannie. I felt trapped by the consequences of my own actions, consequences that were aggravated in my mind by the fear that crippled me daily. I was afraid of losing Mary, of her being snatched or of me being sent to prison and being separated from my little girl; I was afraid of Philip being treated as a criminal; I was afraid of Jamie finding out I was alive, of what he might do to me, of Mary being left alone. In my mind, these were all very real possibilities and the only option I had was to run.

Mack has always felt that I should stop running and face up to my past, that what I was doing to myself was worse than anything that could happen to me by revealing the truth. I know it has caused a few arguments between him and Marjorie over the years. Marjorie has always wanted to keep me safe and protect me, wrapping me in the proverbial cotton wool. I think she has been as afraid of losing me and Mary as I have been of being found. One good thing to come out of everything, though, is Abbotscliff. Moving here was the best thing that could have happened. We are isolated and self-sufficient enough for me to live some semblance of normality here, most of the time at least. More importantly, it gave Mary a good and happy childhood.

As I lie here now with my thoughts, the sun has just started to open its eyes and I can see the very faint outline of light bleeding through the edges of the curtains. There is a gentle onshore wind which is carrying with it the rhythmic sound of the sea in the distance, a sound as old as time itself. With what happened to me, I know I should fear the sea but I don't – in an uncertain world there is something comforting about the predictability of the cycle of the tides. Besides, I don't think there is room in my head for any more fear than it already holds.

I feel at ease in Abbotscliff, or at least less threatened. A big part of that is because the community here makes me feel safe. There is something about living in a small village where everyone knows you. For some, gossip is a bad thing, but for me it's good. Strangers are noticed and word spreads quickly. It is like having an inbuilt radar. When Mack drove us through the village early that morning fifteen years ago, we assumed that we had gone unnoticed, but we hadn't. Apparently, the whole village had been talking about us. Marjorie had warned me that if I moved to Devon it would not be possible to be invisible in the way I had been in London. In a city nobody looks at you, but in a village like Abbotscliff a newcomer is as visible as a flare. As Mack loaded up the car to leave, she hugged me before putting her hands on my shoulders and moving me at arm's length so that I faced her gaze.

"Darling, remember it is impossible to hide in a village the size of Abbotscliff. Everyone knows everyone – they will have worked out the size of your knickers before you make it through the front door!" she said, doing nothing to allay my fears.

"But that doesn't mean you won't be safe," she concluded. I looked into her eyes as she said this, and I could see truth and reassurance in them.

"The more evasive you are, the more curious they will become," she said. "The best thing you can do is give them a bit of the truth right away. If anyone asks, tell them you are running from an abusive relationship. You don't have to say any more than that, they'll enjoy making the rest up, and that will satisfy their curiosity. Trust me, darling, people look out for each other in Abbotscliff. If they think you need protecting, they will wrap themselves around you tighter than cling film. No one will get to you unless it's through them."

It seemed impossible to me that I could ever give anything of myself away to complete strangers, but I trusted Marjorie, I knew that, of all the people in the world, she wanted Mary and me to be safe more than anyone. So I did what she suggested and told old Mrs Tucker in the village shop that Mary's dad was not a good man and we were in hiding. Marjorie was right: word got round and they were like a stockade.

"Don't you worry, maid, us'll keep an eye out," was pretty much the standard response from everyone we met. And it worked, too – whenever a stranger passed through the village, our phone went into meltdown. It was heartening, but it was also terrifying as each phone call represented a potential threat.

As it happened, no *actual* threat ever reared its head. For the past fifteen years I have heard nothing from Benedict, and, although that should be reassuring, it isn't. It still makes me uneasy, perpetually on edge, but Mary is no longer a child, the stakes are lower, so I am finally trying to deal with those feelings. After Mary found Jeannie's letter and learned the truth, she convinced me to have counselling; it turns out that my daughter can be very persuasive when she wants to be.

Mary has inherited my eyes and has the red hair gene, but she is tall like Jamie, and has his smile. I don't mind that as much as I thought I would – the fact that Mary has inherited some of his physical characteristics. When I met Jamie, his smile was one of the things I loved about him. It had been genuine in those early few months and Mary's smile reminds me of the brief period of happiness that I had with him, when I dared hope for something better, before he twisted and morphed into something else.

Throughout Mary's formative years, I spent hours watching her, searching for any hint of a trace of her father in her behaviour, terrified that nature might prevail over nurture. I even made Mary attend Sunday School at the local church, not that I am religious. I don't believe in the concept of an omnipresent God, but I do believe in the basic teachings of Jesus, whoever he may or may not have been. I don't mean the ramblings of eternal life and God's kingdom, or of hell and damnation – strip that narrative away and you are left with parables about kindness and compassion, about empathy and humanity, about being a good person. Whether Sunday School influenced her or not I don't know, but what I do know is that Mary is a wonderful human being who is intelligent and caring and insightful. Not to mention determined – as soon as I had verbally caved in to her cajoling and agreed to counselling, she arranged it via a domestic abuse charity before I had chance to change my mind. She is wise beyond her twenty years, my daughter, and I could not be prouder of her.

Although I was reluctant to have counselling, I have to admit it has helped me to look at my issues and my actions in a different way and I can feel my mind starting to open up. Mack told me once that I am wasting my life and that is a sin. I know he was thinking of Lucy when he said it, of the life she never had, and he is right, of course – life is a privilege not to be squandered. It makes me feel ashamed, especially when I think of Jeannie, who lent herself to me in death so that I could change my life. I should have done better; I owed her that, and I messed up.

My counsellor tells me not to be too hard on myself. She says that my experiences with Jamie left me in a state of chronic fear. Apparently, chronic fear can actually damage the brain; it blocks the brain's ability to think rationally and as a result I experience something similar to PTSD. I blur the past with the present and have intense and irrational emotional responses to certain triggers that can affect my judgement and decisions; my default response to any threat is to run and hide, rather than to consider other more rational, logical responses. It is one of the reasons I reacted the way I did to Benedict turning up at the townhouse that evening.

Understanding this about myself means I can handle my triggers better. Things like bad dreams or seeing someone who reminds me of Jamie no longer provoke panic attacks that leave me on my knees. I'm still panicked, but I can handle them, rationalise them better. I struggle with silent phone calls, though, as it is harder for my mind to deal with balance-of-probability situations. I know that everyone gets silent calls these days, that they are what Mack describes as robot calls, automated multiple-call technology that abandons the other connections as soon as one person picks up. But there is a part of me knocking on my damaged brain and saying, "But what if it's not that this time? What if this time it is him? What if he's found you?"

I have been lying here thinking for too long and my back is beginning to ache. I decide to get up and go for an early-morning run, leaving everyone else in the house to a few more hours of sleep. I envy how easily they seem to be able to sleep – even when I do manage to drop off, my rest is short, my sleep always pestered by dreams. I get dressed into my running gear, put on the peaked cap that helps partially cover my face, and slip quietly out of the house.

The sun has not long risen and some of the clouds are still gently illuminated in the sky like the faint glow of a child's night light. I run easily across the downward-sloping fields, passing an apathetic audience of sleepy sheep and cattle before reaching the cliffs and coastal path. The coastal path is challenging terrain, rugged and undulating, but there is nowhere on earth that makes me feel more at peace with the world than here. On one side of the path, fields are brought to a stop by a hedge of spiky common gorse speckled with flowers the colour of Inca gold. On warm, sunny days, the gorse smells faintly of coconut, as if it has been rubbed in suntan lotion, and hums gently with the sound of pollinating insects. On the other side, a small margin of dry, yellowing grass and a scattering of pink sea thrifts cling to the edges of the cliff, which crumbles and tumbles down to the rocky ridges of the intertidal shoreline below. Buzzards can often be seen circling the cliffs here and, as I breathe in air that's fresh from its journey across the Atlantic, for a short while I feel as free and unencumbered as those magnificent birds.

I feel a few drops of rain land on me and I look up to assess whether it is likely to be a light scattering or whether I should head back. The clouds above me are peachy-brown now, the colour of muddy water, and despite the years that have passed I still have to squeeze my eyes shut to try and dispel the memory it evokes. It looks like it is only going to be a passing shower and

258

so I decide to continue to push on with my run, at least until I reach the bench that sits where the path widens and looks out over the bay. There is a small brass plaque on the bench that reads:

In memory of Sue, a wonderful wife
  How lucky I was to have something that made saying
goodbye so hard

I have sat here countless times over the years, staring out at a restless sea and wondering about Sue and her husband. It is easy to read the inscription and trust that theirs was a true, reciprocal love. But maybe it wasn't. Maybe his was a suffocating love. Maybe he refused to let her say goodbye and death was a release for her. Maybe, if Sue was to have written the inscription for herself, it would have read:

How unlucky I was to have married someone that made
saying goodbye impossible

I know I am just being cynical, projecting my own disillusionment at life onto Sue and her husband. I just feel so angry at myself sometimes for being such a coward, for allowing fear to steal any chance of finding love. I'm forty-one, Mary is making her own way in the world, Mack and Marjorie are getting older and I am scared that I have a lonely future ahead of me. I want more, but am I capable of it? Perhaps the fact I am even thinking about it now means I am ready to at least try. I don't know. I hope so.

Robert was the closest I have ever come to having a relationship, but despite our kiss under the cherry tree on the night of Mack and Marjorie's wedding, and the promise it augured, it was not meant to be. I ran away before it had a chance to really get started, and, although Robert came to visit a couple of times after I had moved to Abbotscliff, I was too damaged then to be capable of a normal relationship. It is difficult to have a meaningful relationship with someone who second-guesses your motives and is comfortable only in the shadows, and I realised that it would not have been fair on Robert to continue trying, even though he had been willing. Besides, there was no way I could ever return to London, and Robert was not ready for a life of solitary confinement in the countryside, so we had to accept that what we had started at the townhouse was impossible to finish. In the end, we parted as the friends we had started out as, rather than the lovers we had hoped to become.

Robert and I kept in touch, though, and for a while, I think we both wondered whether something in me would heal and we might pick up where we left off. But, as the months turned into a year and then another, it became obvious that all I could manage was friendship. I think a dormant part of me quietly harboured some hope, though, because, when Robert told me that he had met Sarah and they were getting married, I felt a jarring sense of loss even though nothing had really changed between us. A year after they were married, Sarah gave birth to gorgeous twin boys, Isaac and Harry, and they have all visited Abbotscliff each year for a holiday ever since. The boys are eleven now and, although I have always loved their visits, it has been hard for me, watching Robert's life unfold before me and seeing what might have been.

The light rain stopped a few minutes ago but has left me feeling damp and a little cold now that I am sitting still. I get back up from the bench and stretch for a second before making my way back towards Abbotscliff. As I cross the final field towards the house, I can see a light is on in the kitchen. A quick check of my watch tells me it is 6.30am. Marjorie is up earlier than usual, and I know why: she is preparing for our visitor later today. Robert is coming this afternoon, only this time Sarah and the boys won't be joining him. It was Marjorie who insisted he spend some time with us on his own to help him get over his recent break-up with Sarah, and I admit that there is a sense of anticipation in me that I am both afraid of and yearn for at the same time.

More than once over the years I have caught Robert watching me when he thought no one was looking and I am pretty sure he has wondered, as I have done many times, whether things could ever have been different for us. But, whilst Robert has been with Sarah, we have both ignored the undercurrent of unresolved feelings, ensuring they never breached the surface. In the past fifteen years, Robert and I have never once allowed ourselves to be alone together – it has been like an unspoken rule that one of us will make an excuse to leave the room if we find ourselves in that situation. I know it will be inevitable, that we will find ourselves alone together this time, and I feel a flurry of anxious butterflies in my stomach at the thought. I am afraid that it will change things between us, but I am also afraid that it won't. It feels like this visit will be the proverbial line in the sand for us and we will be forced to decide which side we stand on. The thing is, I'm not ready to make that decision; I'm not ready to say I want a relationship but I am not ready to let go of the hope of one, either. And what if we find ourselves on different sides of that line in the sand? What would happen to us then? God, I wish Marjorie hadn't invited him; I need more time to figure things out in my head.

As I walk across the gravel drive, I spot the real reason that Marjorie is up early. The kitchen door opens before I have chance to use the handle. Marjorie is standing back, side on to the door, so that I can see straight into the heart of the kitchen.

"*There* you are, Dawny!" she says with the biggest grin on her face. "Look who's turned up early!"

Robert is sitting at the long kitchen table with a mug of tea in his hands, the steam swirling around in front of him like an exotic dancer. He gives me his mischievous grin, the one he uses when he is being flirty, the one I didn't realise I had missed so much.

"Couldn't sleep," he said. "I was too excited and there was nobody to tell me I had to wait until morning."

I grin back, I instinctively know exactly which side of the line we are both standing on and the butterflies in my stomach flutter happily around inside of me.

CHAPTER 35

Dawn

It has been nearly six months since the day I returned from my early-morning run to find Robert sitting in the kitchen at Abbotscliff. We all had breakfast together that morning and Marjorie didn't stop talking, question after question fired at Robert, the subject of his break-up dominating the conversation, much to my embarrassment.

"So," she asked, "is your separation permanent, or do you think you'll get back together?"

"Marjorie!" I shouted, embarrassed at her lack of a filter, but Robert just laughed.

"Put it this way," he said, "I've filed for divorce." As he said it, his foot brushed against mine. It felt deliberate, and I could feel my heart rate quicken and my face flush. I felt like a teenager.

That afternoon, Robert and I went for a walk down to the beach. It was a walk we'd done many times before, but always in the company of others and nearly always with an excitable Isaac and Harry in tow. During those walks, I had invariably strolled behind Robert, surreptitiously watching him with Sarah and his boys, my eyes darting guiltily away when he turned to glance in my direction. But that afternoon it was just the two of us walking side by side. There was a silence, not awkward as such, more uncertain, as if neither of us really knew how to be alone together. Then, out of nowhere, Robert reached out and held my hand. I looked at him, a little shocked at the unexpected gesture, but he just grinned and we carried on walking as if nothing unusual had just happened.

When we reached the cliffs, we found the familiar zig-zag route down over a sloping edge of the cliff to the beach. It is a natural path carved out over the years by people determined to take a shortcut down to the rocky shoreline below. At the bottom, we sat on a rock and looked out towards the horizon, where the sea met the sky in a contrast of blues, and watched gentle ripples rise and fall on the ocean's back. The part of the beach where we sat is not easily accessible without some effort and so it wasn't surprising to find ourselves alone there that day.

Looking out at the vastness of the ocean, listening to the murmur and lap of the gentle waves, made it easier to talk, somehow, and that's what we did – just talked for hours about how our lives had played out over the last fifteen years; about where we went wrong; about life being too short; about whether we should try again, whether I was finally ready. When Robert and I kissed, it was gentle and lingering, yet full of expectation. It reawakened something in me that I thought I would never feel again and, although I knew I had a way to go, I knew beyond doubt that I was ready to at least try.

That evening, Marjorie had arranged for her and Mack to see a film in town. Mary was at her student accommodation in Cornwall, where she lives now whilst doing her degree. It's been hard letting her go – it is only a couple of hours away but it feels like she is on the other side of the world when she's not here. Both Marjorie and I had tried to persuade her to do a course closer to home, where she could still stay at Abbotscliff, but Mack had been furious with us.

"For Christ's sake, let the lass go and find her own way," he'd said. "I'd have thought you pair, of all people, would know what it is to be held back!"

He was right of course, and, besides, Mary herself was determined to have the "full university experience", as she called it, although she tries to come home for the weekend at least once a month to appease us.

So, with Mack and Marjorie at the cinema and Mary at university, Robert and I were alone together at Abbotscliff that evening. We opened a bottle of wine, which we drank in the kitchen whilst I prepared dinner for us both, and after dinner we migrated to the sitting room with a second bottle. There is an old vinyl record player in the sitting room and Robert made his way to the collection of vinyl records stored beside it. I sat on the sofa, watching him as he thumbed through them with his back to me. He was wearing a black T-shirt and blue jeans and as he thumbed through the collection I could see the muscles of his back moving beneath the fabric of his slim-fit shirt and I ached to reach out and touch him. Robert whipped a record out of the collection and turned to face me, holding out the yellow sleeve of an Etta James single.

"*At Last!*" he said, naming the song's title with a grin. "Seems appropriate!"

He removed the record from its sleeve and placed it on the turntable. There was a gentle scratch as he released the stylus onto the black vinyl and, as it crackled and hissed for a few seconds before the song began, Robert held out his hand for me to join him. I can't describe the feelings that ran through me as Robert held me close, moving slowly to the rhythm of the song as the beautiful jazz voice of Etta James filled the room with lyrics that felt like they had been written for me, for that moment. We made love that night and everything felt right. No thoughts of Jamie or Benedict, no guilt over Jeannie, no fear, just a sense of belonging in the moment, of unencumbered happiness. That night I dreamt only good dreams and for the first time in a long time I did not see the neon glow of 3am.

Robert and I were inseparable for the two weeks that he stayed at Abbotscliff, before work forced him to return to London. He made the journey back to see me every single weekend, sometimes with his boys, sometimes alone. We talked about him coming to live at Abbotscliff, as he had grown to love it here as much as I do, and I could see the heaviness in him each time he had to leave, but he was torn – the thought of being so far away from his boys was an issue. Then, a couple of months ago, he phoned to tell me that Sarah was moving to Scotland with her new boyfriend and taking the boys with her. He was distraught and angry.

"I know she's punishing me," he said, "and there is nothing I can do about it."

He cried and I felt so helpless. I understood, I really did. I was separated from both the man I loved and from my daughter. The time I got to spend with them was never enough, and the thought of either of them moving as far away as Scotland would be enough to send me into a tailspin. After a few tense arguments, Robert and Sarah had mediation, and as a result it was agreed that he would have Harry and Isaac during half-term breaks as well as for three weeks every summer and alternate Christmases. It wasn't nearly enough, but it was something, and Robert had no choice but to come to terms with it. It did mean, though, that there was no longer anything holding Robert back from moving to Abbotscliff, and so four weeks ago he moved here permanently.

So much has changed since the day Mary found that letter. Being forced to face up to the truth and having counselling has been life-changing for me. One thing is certain: Robert and I would not have been possible before. But despite all of this, despite how far I have come, I know I haven't reached the end yet. The hardest part is still ahead and it is Robert who has finally given me the impetus, the courage to finally face it.

It all came to a head after Philip died unexpectedly of a heart attack. We were devastated as Philip was a big part of our idiosyncratic family, and he meant so much to me that I somehow found the courage to travel back to London for his funeral. At the wake, Caitlin approached me. Philip and Caitlin had become close over the years, although more as companions than lovers, and she told me that Philip's biggest regret in life had been in helping me to disappear.

"Philip worried every day that in signing that deed poll, he had unwittingly helped you to fade away, to go through life as a ghost of what you could and should be," Caitlin told me.

"Philip was right, Dawn," Robert had said later. "I love you, but until you fully face up to who you really are there will always be a glass wall stopping us from moving forward. We will never be able to marry."

That stopped me in my tracks.

"Are you asking me to *marry* you?" I asked, incredulous. I'd known things were serious between us, but even so I had not expected that.

Robert grinned that grin, the one that lights up his whole face and makes me weak. "I guess I must be," he said before his face became serious again. "But I can't, can I? Because Dawn doesn't exist, not legally. Dawn is traced back to Jeannie and you are not Jeannie. When my divorce comes through, I want to be able to marry *you*. Properly. Legally. Above board. I don't want someone coming behind us and whipping that away, annulling us. I've waited too long for you."

Although I had not expected the proposal, I can't deny that the hope of marrying Robert one day had crossed my mind – my dreams – more than once. I never thought it would be possible for all the reasons that Robert had mentioned, but also because it was hard to believe that anyone would want to marry someone as damaged as me. But Robert was showing that he loved me, with all my fragility and flaws he was willing to invest in me, accept me and, if necessary, wait for me. I knew that I could face a prison sentence, although Philip had always told me that, because there had been mitigating circumstances, any sentence handed out would most likely be suspended. But I wasn't just worried about me; I worried about the part he had played and what it could mean for him, and, although Philip dismissed that out of hand, I couldn't. Now, with Philip dead and Mary a grown woman making her way in the world, the time was right to do what was right.

So, with Robert's support, I contacted the police, hoping for the best but bracing myself for the worst. I was interviewed at length and after they had taken my statement they let me go and told me they would be in touch. I don't know what I had expected, but it hadn't been that – I'd imagined I would be charged with something there and then, or at the very least have some indication of what was likely to happen to me, but they simply said that they would need to look into the matter further and would be in touch.

That was two weeks ago. I can't help but worry about whether I will end up being prosecuted and given a prison sentence. The thought of being separated from Robert now that I have finally found some happiness fills me with dread. But it seems that I am the only person worried about what is going to happen – everyone else seems to have an unwavering belief that I will not be judged harshly, that I should stop worrying. But worrying has become a habit that is as hard for me to break as a stammer or a tic. To say it has been a tense couple of weeks is an understatement. I know I have been a nightmare to live with and everyone has been tiptoeing around me, having quickly given up on trying to reassure me. I have been behaving badly towards them, snapping at them when all they are trying to do is keep me in a positive frame of mind, but it's just that, having made the decision to come clean, I need it all to be over, to learn my fate, accept my punishment and move on with my life.

Instead of using words to placate me, they have all resorted to gestures. I know they just want to show how much they care and I love them for it. Marjorie has been on a cooking frenzy, rustling up all my favourite foods and treats during the day and getting out all the old and dusty boardgames in the evening to keep me distracted. Mack has made me go for long walks with him where we chat about Mary and Lucy and nature, everything and anything but the subject of me. There are often long periods of silence on our walks, but, even in the throes of silence, comfort radiates from him – there is no one on earth who has the ability to calm me just by being there, like Mack does.

Robert uses humour to bring me round – a look, a grin, a witty quip and I am putty in his hands – and during those times when humour won't cut it he simply holds me and whispers that he loves me. Mary phones me every night, which I know must be a pain for someone of her age. She has started seeing a young man, Luke, who she met on her course and I can hear the same thing in her voice when she talks about him that I hear in my own voice when I talk about Robert. I am happy for Mary, but worried at the same time – she is so young and I don't want her to be held back. Mack tells me not to worry, that Mary is strong, perceptive and independent, that I need to trust her. He says that, if Luke is the right person for her, she won't be held back; she will be stronger for having him in her life. If he is not the right one, she will know and will have the courage and grace to let go. Even so, until I meet this young man, I know I will not rest.

Despite everyone's efforts at distracting me, waiting has been torturous. I am beginning to wonder if what you go through whilst waiting for something bad to happen is worse than what is actually likely to happen. If I think about it, that has been true of the last twenty years of my life – what I went through in my mind was worse than anything that *actually* occurred in the end. I hope this is going to be true of these last two weeks as well, because tomorrow I have an appointment to see Detective Jim Harris; tomorrow I should know what I am going to be charged with.

It is nearly midnight but sleep isn't coming easy for me tonight, my mind a maelstrom of thoughts that I can't rein in. As I lie here, I can hear the wistful call of a male tawny owl, followed by the melodic reply of his mate in the small woodland that borders the back of Abbotscliff. I turn my head to look over at Robert lying next to me, watching him as he sleeps. The curtains are not quite shut and a sliver of moonlight is cast across him in an ethereal glow. I can see his eyelids twitch every now and then with dreams and I wonder if I feature anywhere in his dreams tonight. I suddenly feel the need to touch him, feel connected to him, so I put my hand on his chest and feel it rise and fall gently with each breath that he takes. I close my eyes and find myself breathing in time to his rhythm; I feel myself letting go, drifting slowly into sleep.

***

I am not sure how long I have been asleep but I have been woken rudely by the hawking cries of seagulls on the roof. Everyone thinks that the countryside is quiet and peaceful, but it's not always like that. The seagulls often squawk and land noisily on our roof, oblivious and uncaring as to whether we are sleeping or not. I turn to snuggle into Robert, as I do every morning, but find his side of the bed is empty. I place my hand on the mattress where he should be and it is cool, telling me he has been up for a while. I turn to look at the bedside clock – it is 7am, which means I have a couple of hours before I am expected at the station, and my heart starts to thump in my chest as I think about what today is going to bring.

The bedroom door opens and Robert appears with a steaming mug of coffee in his hand and he smiles at me when he realises that I'm awake. Despite my feelings of dread, I smile back – it is impossible not to respond to Robert's smile; it really is contagious, it makes everything seem alright.

"Morning, princess," he says as he hands me the mug. As well as the smell of fresh coffee, there is a smell of bacon trailing in behind him. "Marjorie's making a full English," he says by way of an explanation. My stomach churns at the thought – there is no way I can face breakfast today; I feel too nauseous.

I lie in bed for a while drinking my coffee before getting up, taking a shower and changing into my carefully selected outfit. I have chosen a dark blue trouser suit with a white silk shirt; I don't know why it is important, but I want to look respectful to show that I am taking what I have done seriously. I make my way down the stairs to the kitchen, where all the people I love most in the world are gathered around the big farmhouse table: Mary, Robert, Marjorie and Mack. They all look up at me as I enter the kitchen and I force back the tears that are gathering behind my eyes. There is a space at the table for me between Robert and Mary and as I take my place, Robert reaches out for my hand under the table and Mary leans in to embrace me.

I think of the saying "All roads lead to Rome" and I wonder if that is true, whether, whatever decision I made all those years ago, these people around this table would still be my family today. I very much doubt it, and that thought gives me strength. Regardless of how I may be judged, my road led to this, and I wouldn't have it any other way.

CHAPTER 36

Dawn

Even in my wildest dreams, I could not have expected what Detective Jim Harris had to tell me that day.

He started by informing me that they had made enquiries regarding Jeannie and had established that Benedict and Jeannie's mum, Charlotte, were both dead and had been for fifteen years. I was stunned. The circumstances surrounding their deaths had been quite extraordinary and had made the news, so Detective Harris had been surprised that I had been totally unaware. But it had happened soon after I'd moved to Abbotscliff, when I was busy hiding and setting up my new life. Neither Mack, Marjorie or I watched any news, or read any papers back then; we rarely do even now.

"The world is all full of doom and gloom," Mack is fond of saying, "we've had more than our fair share of that to want to watch the rest of the world in misery."

Even Philip had been unaware. After Mack and Marjorie's wedding, and much to Marjorie's delight, Philip and Caitlin had started spending some time together and had been on holiday when it had happened. It came as a shock, but did explain why

Benedict had never pursued us, why for fifteen years he was no more than just a terrifying prospect. I couldn't feel bad that Benedict was dead, but I took Charlotte's death hard. I don't think I will ever be able to shake the guilt of not giving her proper closure.

With Jeannie, Benedict and Charlotte all deceased, the CPS had decided it was not in the public's interest to prosecute me. I hadn't benefitted materially from my deception and they decided that my actions had been impulsive and opportunistic rather than planned and calculating. I think they understood that it had been born out of fear and psychological trauma, made worse by witnessing Jeannie's death and in learning of her abuse. But freedom came with a caveat: they wanted my help. What the detectives told me next sent me spinning. They told me that Jamie was being held in custody on some serious charges. He had been charged with causing grievous bodily harm with intent to inflict serious psychological injury – an offence that could potentially carry a life sentence. He was also being charged with further counts of actual bodily harm, administering a drug in order to carry out an indictable offence, and false imprisonment.

They were unable to discuss the specifics of the case as it contained some sensitive information that would not be released to the public even at trial. This meant that, although most of the trial would play out in court, part of it would be carried out in private in the judge's chambers, or "in camera", as they called it, which no one except the judge and jury would be privy to. But they were able to tell me that they believed Jamie had developed an obsession with me after I had "died", that he had targeted his new wife as a replacement for me because she had resembled me. Detective Harris kept it brief but explained that Jamie had coerced his wife into having a child in order to recreate the family he had imagined having with me; he had taken premeditated and deliberate actions to control her and then orchestrated a severe decline in her mental health in order to remove her from his life once she had given him the child he wanted.

I cried when I heard that, repressed memories flooding back. Jamie had been obsessed with me, believing that we were the perfect couple even when it was clear things were not perfect between us. Then he had become obsessed with having a child and, when it looked as if that might not happen naturally, things had started to spiral. Jamie blamed me: it must have been something I was doing wrong, he said. He began controlling what I ate, monitoring my ovulation and controlling when we had sex, even what position was best. I started to dread ovulating. I remembered the day I told him I wasn't feeling great and I really didn't feel like having sex.

"But it's the right time! You're ovulating, for Christ's sake – of course you want to do it!" he said and started kissing my neck and placing his hand underneath my jumper and onto my breast.

"I'm serious, Jamie, I don't want to do it right now."

I pushed his hand down and tried to pull my body away from him, but it was as if I'd said nothing. He continued kissing me, unzipped his jeans and pushed me onto the bed, leaning his weight onto me so I could hardly breathe let alone move.

"We are going to make this baby happen, Anna," he half-whispered into my ear as he manoeuvred his knee between mine to part my legs. "I love you."

It was as if he was so possessed by his vision to make us a family that he lost a grip on reality and was out of control. I had never experienced Jamie like that before. Despite his controlling nature, he had never been physically rough with me. If I had not felt like having sex, he would tease and cajole me into doing it, or at worst sulk until I gave in, but never anything like what was happening then. My pleas and cries were no more than background noise to him; they simply did not register; his expression was determined, resolute. It was confusing and terrifying. Just as he was about to force himself inside me, I pleaded with him once more.

"Please, Jamie, no. Not like this. Not this way."

For some reason, those words reached him and it was like a switch had been flicked. He stopped and climbed off of me, his breath fast and shallow. I was sobbing and Jamie looked at me as if he was seeing me for the first time and started to tremble, the colour draining from his face.

"Shit, Anna. I thought it was what you wanted. I thought you wanted our baby as much as I do."

Then he cried. "I don't deserve you," he said. "I just love you too much sometimes, that's all, Anna, I love you so much that it makes me crazy. All I've ever wanted is for us to be a family, to be happy. Without that, there is no point to anything, I might as well be dead."

The last time I'd seen him that upset was the one time I had tried to leave him, after he had slept with my best friend, Rachel, and he took an overdose before phoning me to tell me what he had done. In that moment, I'd seen his vulnerabilities and become terrified that he might try and kill himself again, rather than being terrified of what he was capable of doing to me.

"It's OK," I remember saying, allowing the subdued part of my brain to overrule the part that could think independently, that could rationalise. That part of my brain was so eroded it was almost impossible to get a foothold. "I just overreacted, that's all. I know it's important. That the timing is important. I'm sorry."

I find it difficult to comprehend now that I actually apologised, but my primary aim in that moment was to make him feel better, to make sure he didn't do anything silly. Jamie took my apology as a green light.

"I knew you'd understand, baby," he said. "That's why I love you so much. We get each other."

Then he dropped down onto me again, kissing my barely responsive lips before parting my legs and guiding himself into me with a groan. I didn't try to stop him; I let him have sex with me, crying silently all the way through it. I hate that I let it happen, but I honestly didn't know what else to do. Afterwards, Jamie acted as if nothing had happened, but the whole incident had upset me so much that I never said no to him again. In the end, I began to feel physically ill at the thought of sex with him, but I just didn't know how to say no. I became depressed and anxious and that is when my panic attacks started. I made an appointment to see a doctor, hoping they might be able to give me some medication and Jamie hit the roof when he found out.

"How do you think it makes *me* look? That I can't even make my own wife happy? Do you not think *I* don't get depressed every time you fail to give me a baby, Anna? It's not all about you, you know!" He waved the prescription he'd found in front of my face.

I started to cry and he immediately apologised. He wrapped his arms around me and kissed the tears on my face before wiping them away with his thumb. He had gone from angry to tender in an instant and it was so confusing.

"You don't need pills. You don't need a doctor, Anna, you've got me. I am here for you. I will always be here for you, baby. It's just the stress getting to both of us. When we have a baby, everything will be perfect – your depression, your panic attacks, it will all stop, just you see. I love you so much, baby. Tell me you love me. Go on, tell me or I'll stop breathing. I'll die, I swear, I'll die if you don't tell me you love me."

I was riding a perpetual psychological rollercoaster and I didn't know how to get off. Soon after that, Jamie booked an appointment at a private fertility clinic. "I've been thinking," he said. "Maybe you should have some fertility tests. There must be a reason why you're not getting pregnant."

"I don't know, Jamie. I'm not sure I'm ready."

He just looked at me unblinking, as if he had been shocked into stillness. His expression was blank except for a tiny yet significant narrowing of his dark eyes. He stood like that, silent for a few moments, before clenching his fists tightly and walking out of the room without uttering a word. I sat alone and shaking as I heard him roar and smash something against the wall. Then I heard him walk up the stairs to our bedroom and slam the door shut. The smashing sound I'd heard had been the vase my parents had given me on our wedding day, and I sobbed as I picked up the broken pieces knowing that in smashing the vase Jamie had really been smashing me. It had been a vicarious act this time, but I couldn't help worrying that next time he wouldn't bother with a vase.

Jamie eventually emerged from our bedroom a few hours later, his face pale and drawn from what I knew was one of his migraines. He walked over to me, and his face fell when I flinched as he reached out to touch me. He looked genuinely hurt.

"I'm sorry about the vase," he said as if it had been no more than an accident. "I'll buy you another one." Then he kissed me on the head. "I don't know what you're doing to me lately, Anna, you're driving me crazy. You have to stop driving me so crazy or I don't know what I'll do."

After that incident I was too scared to contradict Jamie so I agreed to undergo the tests. When the results came back, we were told that there was no obvious reason as to why we couldn't conceive. It was a case of unexplained infertility, the consultant said, which is apparently not that uncommon, but Jamie took it to mean that *my* body was behaving in an unexplained way. I actually think he was right in a way, though. I think it *was* me – that my body was subconsciously rejecting him. I knew that having a baby with Jamie was not what I wanted; I just had no idea how to stop it without making Jamie angry or upset. He had been becoming increasingly more obsessive and unstable; there was something unhinged in him and I was beginning to really start to fear what he was capable of. A baby meant more to him than anything else in the world, and I didn't know what he would do if I denied him the chance, so I found myself swept along the path of IVF when I knew it wasn't right, when it was the last thing I really wanted. And then Jeannie came along and threw me an unexpected lifeline.

When the detectives told me what they could about what Hannah and his daughter had been through, it left me with mixed emotions. I've spent the last twenty years running away from a fear that I couldn't prove or validate, a fear based on instinct. Knowing what Jamie did to them helped salve my conscience in some way, knowing that I had been justified in running, that trying to reason with Jamie would have been useless, that simply leaving him would have been impossible.

"He is a dangerous man, Dawn," Detective Harris had said, as if I would ever need to be told that. "We need you to help us put him behind bars for a long time for what he did. We need you to testify against Jamie, as a witness to how calculating and controlling his behaviour can be."

When I returned to Abbotscliff, the enormity of everything hit me and I felt overwhelmed with emotion. Suddenly, it no longer mattered that my decision to disappear and run had been validated – the guilt I had felt all those years because of that had been replaced by a much bigger guilt. There was no getting away from the butterfly effect that my decision had caused: by disappearing, I had paved the way for another woman and her daughter to replace me and Mary like sacrificial lambs.

"You can't think like that, Dawn," Marjorie said. "You could not have predicted what that man was going to do. What happened to that man's wife and child is *not* your fault; it is *his* fault."

"Hindsight always seems to have the answers that elude the present, lass, but you can't go back and try again; however much you might want to, you can't." It was Mack's soothing voice, always the voice of reason. "But you *can* help his wife and daughter get justice."

"This isn't a coincidence, Mum, the fact that you finally revealed yourself to the police at the same time that Jamie is in custody. It's not coincidence; it is fate giving you a chance to help them. Just like it was fate for Jeannie to give you the chance to escape." Mary likes to believe in the "everything happens for a reason" philosophy but, although part of me felt like it could be used as a cop-out, a way of absolving myself from any responsibility, I could see her point, too. It was a pretty big coincidence.

That night I lay in Robert's arms as he stroked my hair – something he instinctively does when he knows I need soothing – and I asked him what he really thought. "I think of what his daughter has been through," he said, "and what she has been left with. Or rather what she has been left without: a father who will probably be sent to prison for a long time, and a mother in an institution for life. I think that could have been Mary. You did what you did as an instinct to save your own daughter. How can that have been wrong?"

I thought about what he said, what they had all said, and I knew that they were all right in their own way. I can't change the past and, even if I could, I can't say for certain what the end result would have been. The only thing I can control is the present, the here and now, and I have the power to help stop Jamie from ever hurting another person for a very long time.

Thinking that way lifted me for a while, made me feel like I had a purpose, a way of making amends, but the closer it comes to the trial date, the more anxious I feel. Apart from anything else, I know it will mean facing Jamie for the first time in twenty years and it is going to take all of my strength to get through what lies ahead.

CHAPTER 37

Dawn

I am in the crown court, inside a beautiful, yet imposing, wood-panelled room. Nearly all of the room is constructed in the same dark hardwood, except that the wood in the dock, witness box and public gallery is plain and scuffed, in contrast to the shiny panels and ornate carvings that act as a backdrop to the judge's bench. It feels deliberate, as if to exaggerate the polished and intricate superiority of justice versus the flawed individuals facing it.

I look out briefly from the witness stand and force myself to look at Jamie for the first time in twenty years; he is sitting in the dock at the back of the court, his head hung low. There are specks of grey in his chestnut hair and he is diminished, physically smaller than I remember. He looks strained and vulnerable and for a split second I feel an involuntary urge to go to him, to comfort him – a sort of patella reflex of a first-time love that passes as quickly as it is triggered.

It is weird, that despite everything he did to me, everything I know that he has done since, I could not suppress that emotional memory. It might have only been a split second, but for that moment it overwhelmed any sense of rationale. I know that there is something wrong with Jamie, that he is wired wrong, but he was my first love, and that is a powerful emotion. For a teenager, being in love for the first time is like nothing else. It leaves an emotional imprint. It is one of the reasons I found it so hard to leave him when I first knew the relationship was not right – the memory of that love kept lingering long after it was no longer welcome, and then it became too late.

I hear a distant voice on the periphery of my thoughts and realise it is the court usher directing me to take the oath. The Bible hasn't held my conscience to ransom for a long time, so on being sworn in I choose to take the alternative, secular affirmation:

"I do solemnly and sincerely and truly declare and affirm that the evidence I shall give shall be the truth, the whole truth and nothing but the truth."

No God to help me here.

I can barely still my hands, which are holding the piece of paper that I am reading those words from, and I am aware that my voice is shaking just as much as my hands. At the sound of my voice, Jamie raises his head and looks directly at me for the first time since I entered the court, his expression dispassionate as if he is looking at a stranger. But then it is as if he realises for the first time that it really is me standing here and something changes in his eyes, something that looks like hatred; it stimulates a different emotional reflex in me, one I am far more familiar with. My heart rate rises and I can feel the blood retreating in my veins, leaving me cold and shivering, yet my palms sweaty. I want to run, but instead I breathe deeply and engage the meditative techniques I have been learning. My eyes dart to find Robert, who I know is sitting in the public gallery, and when I see him he nods at me reassuringly and I immediately feel calmer. This is the reality of an honest love – it is steadying, calming, reassuring.

Robert came by himself to support me today. I made Mack promise to keep Marjorie away – I know her too well; she is so fired up that I was worried that she may do or say something that would put her in contempt of court. Mary chose not to come as she does not wish to face the man that is her father – she is not ready yet to face the conflict of emotions she knows it is likely to stir in her. I think that one day she might and, although I don't want her anywhere near Jamie, it is her decision and I will be there to support her if and when she decides it is time.

The barrister for the prosecution is rising and I know it will soon be time to tell a room full of strangers everything I have been trying to forget, everything I have been running from for years. My heart is beating so hard, I swear I can hear it echoing around the vast courtroom like a drum roll.

I know that I am not on trial, I am here as a witness, but I can't help but feel like I am about to be morally judged. But then, the truth is I *want* to be judged on some level – I want an authority greater than me to listen and accept that what Jamie did was wrong, that my instinct to run was a reasonable one. I know I won't get a direct acknowledgement as I cannot directly accuse Jamie of an offence. The law that protects people like me from people like him, the law against coercive control, did not come into force until 2015 and so I have to be content with being part of the process of someone else's justice. If what I have to say helps the jury understand what he is capable of, helps convict him, then I hope I might find a way to finally find some peace.

The barrister for the prosecution is Jonathan Evans-Wright. He is a portly man of about fifty with pockmarked cheeks; he is short but ramrod straight. I can't help but notice a light dusting of what looks like dandruff on the shoulders of his black robe and I wonder if it is from his own hair or from the ancient-looking wig on his head. Either way I have to fight the impulse to reach out and brush it off. I first met Jonathan several weeks ago when he invited me to his chambers to go over my witness statement. When he'd introduced himself, I had been surprised by his softly spoken voice. Jonathan's voice is non-threatening; it sets you at ease, allowing you to become more open. You are lulled into thinking he will be gentle in his dealings with you, so you let your guard down, become complacent. But Jonathan is anything but gentle – his soft voice masks an acerbic tongue, a bullying wit. That day, I faced a ferocious interrogation of everything I had said in my prepared witness statement. I was so shocked – I'd agreed to act as his witness, so didn't expect him to cross-examine me, for every word I'd said to be dissected and trampled on and tossed out as meaningless or, worse, as lies. By the end he made me doubt every memory I had and I just wanted to get out of his chambers and never come back. I was crying and on the verge of a panic attack before he stopped and his demeanour changed, becoming gentle again, more worthy of his soft voice.

"I am sorry to have done that to you, Dawn," he said. "But you need to know what you will be up against in that courtroom. The defence will not want the jury to believe what you have to say; they will want to rip you apart, and I need to know that you won't fall apart, that you will be able to handle the questioning."

And so we started again. This time I went over every single memory of every transgression, every word, every feeling, making sure that I had an unwavering belief in my recollection, that, no matter what anyone might try to suggest, the truth never changes.

And now we are in court and Jonathan is standing in front of me. He has started his questioning, using his gentle voice in a gentle way, to help me begin to explain the hold Jamie had over me. He starts by asking me to go back to the very beginning, to when I met Jamie, to why I fell in love with him. I find that hard, especially now that Robert has shown me what real love is, but I know what Jonathan is doing; he is attempting to put the jury on an equal footing with me. Jonathan knows what the jury sees when they look at Jamie sitting in the dock: they see what I used to see before the real Jamie emerged. They see a man blessed with boyish good looks making him appear much younger; they see large, doleful brown eyes, framed with soft lashes, that draw you in and make you want to linger there; they see a face capable of child-like expressions of innocence. They don't see a person to be afraid of, someone capable of manipulation and control.

So, I begin now to tell them how it all started.

I was seventeen, Jamie was twenty-two and seemed so mature physically and emotionally compared to the teenage boys that I knew. He was charming and attentive, and dressed immaculately. He even made jeans and a T-shirt look as though a lot of thought had gone into his appearance. But that was typical of Jamie: everything was meticulously thought-out and planned, even his outfits; every aspect of his life was ordered and orderly.

I was unsure about him at first because he was so much older than me, but he would always surprise me by inexplicably turning up wherever I went, and he would laugh and say it was fate throwing us together. Although he was older, he seemed to be on the same level as me and just seemed to know me, knew what made me tick. He would produce tickets to bands I liked, take me to my favourite places to eat, watch my favourite comedy shows and just talk to me for hours about things that interested me. We seemed to have so much in common, we fitted together so well that I believed him when he said we were soul mates destined to be together. But Jamie was also deep and sensitive and had a vulnerable side that made me feel protective of him. He told me he hadn't begun to live until the moment he met me, how if I ever left him his heart would stop beating. I realise now how clever he was, how he managed to instil in me a sense of responsibility for his happiness and how it also gave him the perfect excuse for the over-possessive, jealous behaviour that was soon to follow.

It all sounds so corny now, but I was so young, I had no experience in life or love, and Jamie made me believe that his version of love was the only version. I hadn't realised then that loving someone is about giving a person freedom to grow and growing with them, not about possessing them. I feel myself getting angry as I remember the friends I once had, the ones that Jamie isolated me from, and the friends in life that I never had the chance to make; how my dreams and ambitions were sidelined; how he made me financially dependent upon him, denying me access to my own inheritance; how he used his fluctuating moods and emotions to confuse me and keep me under control; how he would stand over me when I text or phoned my friends; how he made sure he knew the pin to my phone; how he monitored the mileage on my car.

Jamie developed an obsessive belief that we were the perfect couple, and if I didn't behave in a perfect way, didn't see things in the way he wanted me to, he couldn't handle it. He would seesaw between telling me how much he loved me, how happy I made him, to becoming suspicious of anything I said or did. He would bombard me with endless, draining questions engineered to prove I wasn't being a good, faithful, thoughtful wife, and I had to work so hard at just keeping our relationship on an even keel. Jamie expressed his disappointment in me by being moody and sulky, passive-aggressive or insulting, but after a while he started to change and a different side emerged – one where I could see he struggled to suppress a growing rage, where he would smash things that were precious to me, things that I knew were stopping him from smashing me. This change in him scared me and I tried so hard not to let him down, to be the perfect wife, because, when I was his version of perfect, he was the old Jamie.

But keeping him happy was not easy, it meant ignoring what was right for me. I have to endure the ignominy of telling the courtroom how Jamie controlled our sex life, crying as I remember the day that I thought he was going to rape me and the way I felt coerced into having IVF when we didn't conceive naturally. I feel dirty and ashamed knowing that Robert is listening to this for the first time and try hard not to wonder whether this will change how he feels about me.

I finish by telling the court how I felt so trapped, so scared that he would never let me go, that I believed the only way out was to make him believe I was dead. I am left feeling exposed, my weaknesses laid bare. I know Robert is looking at me, but I can barely bring myself to look back at him, afraid of seeing pity or disgust in his eyes. But, when I finally meet his gaze, I am immediately comforted, because what I see is something different, something that looks like pride.

"I love you," he mouths at me, and the love I feel back for him right then is real and lasting and immeasurable. I want to step down from this box, go to him, slip into that place in his arms where I fit as perfectly as the last piece of a jigsaw, where he will help me to forget, but I can't – I have to face the defence's cross-examination first.

The barrister for the defence is a woman and I have no doubt that this was a deliberate choice. It gives a subliminal message that there is at least one woman who does not believe that Jamie is aberrant. She looks to be in her late thirties or early forties, of medium height and build, with dark hair protruding from the anachronistic horsehair wig that serves to elevate her superiority. When she looks at me, I notice that her pupils look like pinpoints in her blue-grey eyes. When she speaks, her voice is strong and commanding, the polar opposite of Jonathan's voice.

"Did my client ever hit you or actually physically harm you in any way?" is the question she starts with.

"No," I reply honestly. I know it is important to be completely honest, even if I sense she might be setting a trap.

"Did my client ever say, in as many words, that he *intended* to physically harm you in any way?"

"Not in as many words, not directly, but—"

"Just a simple yes or no, please."

"No, but—" I want to say, *need* to say, that it is complicated, not as simple as just a yes or a no.

"You have answered the question – it does not require embellishment, thank you," she says and I feel the burning heat of frustration reach my face. I can tell that her cross-examination is going to be hard, that she is going to try and discredit my version of events, but, thanks to Jonathan's brutal preparation a few weeks ago, at least I am prepared.

She tries to suggest that Jamie wasn't controlling at all, that staying had been my choice and I could have walked away whenever I wanted; it was inconsequential that I had no friends, no family, no money to support me. She argues that there had been no financial manipulation, that his only motive was to protect my inheritance, and points out that I agreed to it – my witnessed signature was on the documents, after all. She addresses the issue of sex by questioning how, if I didn't actually say no, it could in any way be deemed his fault. How could he be considered in any way responsible for something that I never articulated to him? She suggests that what I interpreted as underlying threats to my life were no more than hyperbole on Jamie's part, a way to express the magnitude of the love he felt for me. She brings up the expensive gifts, restaurants and luxury holidays, showing the jury photographs of us smiling on beaches. She conveniently omits that it was all paid for from my own money, my inheritance, and that if you really look you can see my smiles were not real, that I was posing, doing what was expected of me.

It is hard listening to and defending all of this. For years I have blamed myself, even using some of the same distortions of truth that this barrister is using now, as a way of excusing Jamie's behaviour. But not today, not anymore. Throughout all of her questioning I stand resolute, I do not doubt myself, do not waver. A threat of violence is not always obvious, it can be subtle, but when you experience it you are left in no doubt and it doesn't diminish the fear it causes. The truth is the truth and I tell her so.

She finishes by suggesting to the jury that I faked my death and disappeared to punish Jamie for the affair he had. That I had never forgiven him, and that I am here today for revenge. She mentions his suicide attempt and suggests it was not, as I had suggested, to control me but because he loved me so much that he could not bear to live without me. Then she ends her time by facing the jurors and pointing to Jamie.

"Despite what we have heard today," she says, "this is *not* a controlling, manipulative man. This is a man whose only crime was to love his wife too much."

I can see the conflict in the eyes of some of the jurors. I recognise it. Jamie spent years convincing me that everything he did, he did because he loved me, that any problems we had were either caused by me or were all in my head, that I was ungrateful and selfish or too childish to see how lucky I was. But I have done all I can; I have nothing left to offer. I just hope my version of events, the true version, is the one that gets through to them. I feel spent and wait to be told I can leave the witness box, but Jonathan indicates he would like to speak again and is now standing in front of me once more.

"What my learned friend has demonstrated with her questioning today," he says with a nod towards the defence barrister, "is precisely how easy it is to twist and bend a view of events in such a way as to turn insidious motives into harmless ones."

He pauses.

"This is the same technique that my witness endured for years at the hands of the defendant and the fear she suffered as a consequence was not harmless."

Another pause.

"I would ask the jury to consider just one question: is it more probable that a person would fake their own death and live in a self-imposed exile for twenty years – *twenty years* – out of revenge, or out of a *very real fear*?"

As the question hangs unanswered over the courtroom, I am told I may leave the witness box. I have the option to stay and sit in the public gallery for the rest of the trial if I want, but I don't want. I want to get out of there and never look back. I have no idea how this is going to play out, but I have done my bit. I have done my bit and I want to move on with my life with Robert and Mary, Mack and Marjorie. Unencumbered by guilt or fear. Robert rises from the gallery and walks towards me. He puts his arm around me, and as we walk out of the courtroom together he kisses the top of my head gently.

"You did great," he says. "I'm so proud of you."

As we begin to make our way towards the building's exit, I spot two teenage girls sitting on one of the chairs lining the corridor outside of the courtroom. One of them nudges the other with her elbow as she spots me and the other one looks up. Something uneasy stirs in me when I look at her, although I don't know what or why. The teenager stands up and walks towards me. I get the feeling she has been waiting for me. As she gets closer, I immediately know who she is – I can see Jamie in her, although there is also another familiarity about her that I cannot put my finger on. Then my heart flip-flops as it occurs to me that this is Mary's younger half-sister, and, apart from their hair colouring, their resemblance to each other is striking. Maybe there is more of Jamie in Mary than I care to notice.

"Hello. I'm Amber, Jamie's daughter," she says and I am taken aback at how familiar her voice sounds.

I am feeling a little confused as to why she has chosen to approach me, and there is an awkward silence for a second before she continues. "You're Anna? My dad's wife who drowned

289

– well, not drowned but… um…"

"It's OK," I say, finding my voice and nodding gently, "I know it is complicated. Yes, yes, I am Anna, although I call myself Dawn these days."

She looks at me with large eyes that look as though they are holding back tears. "I still love him," she says, "even though I know I shouldn't."

She is barely a year younger than I had been when I met Jamie and when I look at her I see the seventeen-year-old me. With what she has just said, I think I understand why she wants to see me now. I am the only other person who could understand what it is to love Jamie and have no idea of who he really is until it is too late. Instinctively, I reach out and hug her close to me.

"I'm so sorry for everything you have been through, Amber," I say, and there's something about the scent of her that evokes something in me.

"You're my mother," she says out of nowhere, "my biological one."

She blurts the words out as if she can't contain them any longer, and I pull back and look at her, worried that she may be suffering a psychological breakdown – it wouldn't be surprising after everything she's been through. I look directly into her eyes and am about to gently tell her that she is mistaken, that it is not possible, when I finally understand what has been making me uneasy: it's her eyes, the colour of amber. They are Mary's eyes. They are my eyes. Amber looks so much like Mary because they both look like *me*.

My head starts to spin as I try to make sense of the impossible, something I instinctively know is the truth but also know cannot be. And then it hits me, the only explanation.

The one remaining embryo.

Just when I thought my world was beginning to rebalance, it capsizes all over again. I can feel myself start to black out as a cloak of darkness attempts to cover what my mind can't cope with. Robert catches me as I fall.

"Mum!" is the last thing I hear.

CHAPTER 38

Dawn

The mug of coffee in my hand has an aphorism on it that says *Every day is a fresh start.* It has certainly felt that way since the trial, such a lot has happened over the last year. Amber coming into our lives has been the biggest change and one that is continually evolving. There has been so much for all of us to try and take in, not least of all for Amber, who is taking things with us slow and steady.

After the shock of finding out that Amber was my biological daughter, I began to understand why certain parts of the trial had to be held in private. My identity as the biological mother of Amber was integral to the case, but legally I had no right to know. I had been declared presumed dead, so Jamie had every right to use our remaining embryo, and as Hannah actually gave birth to Amber, in the eyes of the law she is, and always will be, Amber's legal mother. I, by contrast, am nothing; my genes count for nothing.

There was no way that the facts of Amber's conception and birth could have been presented in public at the trial in such a way that it did not identify me, and therefore compromise Amber and Hannah's human rights. If Amber had not approached me that day outside the courtroom, I would never have known. If I am honest, I had forgotten about the last remaining embryo. I hadn't once considered that it might be used by Jamie and I wonder now if I would have done things differently had I known that it was a possibility. I can't help feeling that by abandoning the embryo I somehow abandoned Amber. She is a part of me; she carries my DNA. She is in this world because of me, yet I had simply dismissed her potential to exist.

Until the day I came face to face with Amber, I believed that only a man could casually release their DNA and walk away unfettered by the potential consequences. But that is exactly what *I* did. I must be unique, must be the only *woman* in the world to have experienced what it feels like to be blindsided by the revelation of a child they never knew existed. I know that it is the same for Jamie, too – until last year he had no idea that Mary existed. I deliberately denied him that, and, even though I know I had a good reason to, having experienced feelings of such loss over my missing years with Amber, I can't help pondering the morality of my decision. Jamie has written to Mary, a letter full of scorn and anger towards me and an outpouring of love for her. He says he wants to meet her but Mary hasn't replied to him. I haven't actively influenced her decision but I cannot pretend I am not relieved.

Jamie was found guilty of all charges against him and was sentenced to a minimum of sixteen years in prison. It hit Amber hard; he is still her father and she loves him, despite what he has done. I understand that – he has manipulated her mind – but, whilst he remains connected to Amber, he will always remain a danger as far as I am concerned. Prior to sentencing, Jamie had to undergo a psychological evaluation that revealed that he has borderline personality disorder. In particular, the way Jamie experiences love, his reaction to losing it, isn't normal and he will do whatever is necessary to keep hold of it. He writes to Amber every week, long rambling letters telling her how sorry he is, how much he loves and misses her. He talks about what they will do together when he gets out of prison, seemingly oblivious to the fact that Amber will be a grown woman by then, with a life, and possibly a family, of her own.

It is clear from those letters that Jamie cannot contemplate a life without Amber in it, just like he couldn't contemplate a life without me. I think the reason he reacted the way he did with Amber is because he could not cope psychologically or emotionally with her growing up. He sensed he was losing his control over her and he panicked. It is ironic, really, because in many ways he did a great job in bringing her up. As a parent, we are only ever loaned our children – our job is to help them to grow into strong, independent individuals capable of making their own way in the world, and in many ways that is exactly what he did. Amber is kind and intelligent and well-balanced, but, instead of sitting back and enjoying watching his daughter flourish, Jamie wanted to keep her as his little girl forever. In his mind, she had no right to exist outside of that narrative. The thought of what lengths he might have gone to had Amy not intervened still gives me the occasional nightmare.

As a result of Jamie's prison sentence, his parents were granted guardianship of Amber. I wanted more than anything for Amber to come and live with me at Abbotscliff, but understandably Amber wasn't ready for that. In the end she decided not to live with her grandparents either; she decided that she would become a boarder at her school whilst undertaking her A levels. I still find it incredible that, despite all she went through, she passed her GCSEs with flying colours. Although it hurts, I do understand her decision; despite our shared DNA, I was a stranger to Amber, and she had only seen her grandparents a handful of times, so regardless of who she lived with she would have had to leave her school and her friends behind. Her school is the one constant in her life, the only familiar thing she has left, and she is holding on to it.

Amber does visit us, though. She has been to Abbotscliff several times during this past year and always brings her friend, Amy, with her for moral support. They are incredibly close, and I get the feeling that there may be something more than just friendship brewing between them. We all love Amy almost as much as we love Amber – she is a breath of fresh air and makes Mack and Marjorie hoot with laughter at her witty observations and bad language. At the moment, Amber seems to be more comfortable around Marjorie and Mack than she is around me – they have found a place in her life as surrogate grandparents, but I think she is finding it more difficult to establish where I fit in. I felt love for her instantly – as far as I am concerned, she is my daughter – but it is more complicated for her. She has two mothers and I think, on some level, she feels it is a betrayal to Hannah to feel anything too much for me. She carries around a guilt that doesn't belong to her, a trait I'm ashamed to say she seems to have inherited from me.

Every time she visits, I just want to be close to her. I want to reach out and touch her beautiful face, to chat as I brush her long hair, to snuggle on the couch with her and watch a comedy: things I've always done with Mary. But, even though she calls me Mum, she has always kept a subtle physical distance. It breaks my heart that I cannot share all the love I feel, but with each visit I feel her letting me in a little bit more, so I remain hopeful.

Amber's relationship with Mary is a different thing altogether. Their bond was immediate and Amber adores her "older twin sister", as she laughingly calls her, acknowledging the unusual circumstances of their conception. They message and talk with each other regularly and I know that Mary gives her good, sound, sisterly advice. I can't help but think of Robert's sons, Isaac and Harry, how lovely it has been watching them grow up together, and I grieve for the childhood years that my two girls have lost with each other. *My two girls* – I don't think

I will ever tire of being able to say that, even if it is only in my head until Amber is fully on board with me.

Amber has a strong sense of responsibility towards Hannah and I know she visits her regularly. I understand that sense of responsibility because I share it. The law allowed me to reclaim what is left of my inheritance once I resurfaced, and I am using it to move Hannah to a better facility where she will receive better care. It feels the least I can do for her; I owe her so much. I know Hannah will never be fully well, but we are hoping that maybe one day she will improve enough to be able to visit Abbotscliff along with Amber.

Over the years, our menagerie of animals has grown and we are a proper smallholding these days. I think there is a real sense of purpose here, which makes it special and healing. Each day there is something that needs doing: animals need to be fed and tended, stables need to be mucked out, fences and pens need mending, the vegetable garden needs digging and weeding. It reminds you that, no matter what goes on in the world, life still goes on and we all have a part to play in it. At the beginning of the year, we decided to open our doors to helping other victims of domestic abuse, and for the last seven months we have been working alongside Ouroboros, a domestic violence charity that provides refuge to abused women. Ouroboros is an ancient symbol depicting a serpent eating its own tail and is a symbol used by many different cultures around the world. The tail is thought to represent the past and symbolises the eternal circle of life. The charity interprets it as a symbol of accepting your past and of moving on – allowing the past to be consumed by the present, rather than the allowing the present to be consumed by the past, which is what I let happen for far too long.

The charity refers women to us, and those women are free to come and spend time with us in an environment where they can learn new skills and feel safe doing so. They can help in the vegetable garden; they can help Marjorie make lunch or jams and preserves with the produce we grow; they can learn about animal husbandry and beekeeping; they can do crafts; or they can just sit quietly and take in the views and fresh air. Many of them enjoy taking the dogs out for a walk as they have learned that dogs are the best listeners – they don't interrupt, don't judge and don't offer unwanted opinions. Mack has recently started to run small workshops from one of our barns teaching basic home and car maintenance. He doesn't realise it but he is teaching them so much more than just how to be independent; he is teaching them to trust men again. At the moment the charity only serves women, but they are exploring ways to help the growing number of men that are finding the courage to speak out about their own similar experiences of domestic abuse. It is tricky to serve both, as the women we currently help are often wary of the presence of men, but I am sure they will come up with a solution that can provide help to all those that need it.

I am studying psychology at the Open University, but also going to college once a week to do a counselling course. I know it will be a few years before I am qualified, but my aim is to provide a free counselling service for survivors of domestic abuse, which I intend to call Genesis Flood Counselling. It feels so good to be using my brain and finding a way to give something back to society, a way to help others. Interestingly, Amber has chosen psychology as one of her A level subjects, which has given us a common topic to bond over. She is toying with the idea of becoming a criminal psychologist, which I think is her way of trying to understand her father better. Amy wants to be a barrister – a judge, eventually – and Jonathan has graciously arranged for both of them to do some work experience within the criminal justice system during the summer holidays. They are both so excited about that.

Mary is well on her way to pursuing her dream of becoming a marine conservationist, which I know is going to take her all over the world. I am excited for her but also bereft at the thought of her being so far away where I cannot protect her. Letting go is hard, but I of all people know I have no right to try and hold on to her too tightly. I never did get to meet her boyfriend, Luke, as it fizzled out before it had a chance to get going. Apparently, he turned out to be a "creep" – she didn't elaborate and I didn't ask. Mack was right, as always.

I take a sip from my mug and grimace: the coffee has gone cold. I've obviously been lying here reflecting for too long. I look wistfully at the empty space in the bed beside me, the space where Robert should be, and a knot forms in my stomach as I think about why he is not here beside me today. As if reading my thoughts, there is a knock at my bedroom door and, without waiting for a response, Mary bounds in wearing her dressing gown and her red hair in rollers.

"Come on, Mum, you don't want to be late to your own wedding!" she says, handing me one of the two glasses of Buck's Fizz she is holding.

I take the proffered champagne glass, placing it down on my bedside cabinet without taking a sip. I pat the space on the bed beside me, indicating for Mary to come and join me, which she does.

"Heather's waiting downstairs to do your hair," she says, taking a large gulp from her glass. "She's so good – you should see what she has done to Amber's hair!"

Heather is one of the first women referred to us by the charity and has become a good friend. She is a trained hairdresser, and during her time with Ouroboros she would cut and style the hair of the other women in the refuge. Since leaving the refuge, she has continued to work as a volunteer, coming in once a month as a resident hairdresser. It always amazes me how powerful such a small gesture can be – what she does helps to humanise these women; it gives them confidence, makes them feel like they are worth something.

As if Amber has heard Mary mention her name, she suddenly pokes her head around the bedroom door before walking in.

She takes my breath away. Her long hair has been pinned up on one side and glossy chestnut waves are tumbling down the other side. She is wearing make-up, which I have never seen on her before, and it has accentuated her amber-coloured eyes. She is so pretty – apart from the colour of her hair, she really is the spit of Mary. Mary automatically moves to the edge of the bed, creating a space between herself and me for Amber to join us. I know she has done that deliberately, placed Amber next to me, and I love her for it. Without thinking, I automatically place my arm around Amber and then freeze, wondering what her reaction will be. I feel her tense slightly, and then her body relaxes and she allows herself to lean into me. I relax, too; it feels so good.

Mary places her arm around Amber and as she puts her arm behind Amber's back her hand touches my arm and I feel her squeeze it gently in a show of solidarity. For the first time all three of us are physically connected to each other. I really think that this is the best day of my life, having both my beautiful girls sitting here with me on the morning of my wedding to Robert.

Amber looks at the Buck's Fizz in Mary's hand. "Where's mine?" she says and I laugh as I reach over and hand her the one that I placed on my bedside cabinet. She is only sixteen, but this is a special occasion for so many reasons; I am not going to deny her this. Marjorie's voice calls out to me from the bottom of the stairs.

"Get a wiggle on, Dawny!" she says. "The photographer will be here soon!"

I'd forgotten about the photographer, and for a moment my mind pictures Philip, who had taken the photos at Marjorie and Mack's wedding all those years ago. I choke back tears; I miss him so much, but it shows just how far I have come, allowing an outsider into my home to photograph me. That would not have been possible even a year ago and I know Philip would approve, that he would be proud of me. I don't want to move from this spot on the bed, I want to get married right here like this, but the girls get up and break the spell anyway, so I take a quick shower before making my way down the stairs into the kitchen, where Heather is waiting for me.

"Take a pew, My Lady," she says.

Amy is sitting on an adjacent chair. Heather has styled her dark brown hair into a low and loose bun, and Mary is poised over her with an eyeshadow brush, ready to apply some make-up to her face.

"I fucking hate that stuff!" Amy says. "Don't use too much and make me look like a drag queen!"

Mary laughs and Amy goes still and quiet as Mary transforms her from a pretty fresh-faced teenager into a beautiful young woman. When she hands Amy a little hand mirror to see the results, Amy raises her eyebrows in a show of approval.

"Not bad," she says turning her head one way and then the next before peering in closer and pursing her lips together. "I'd quite fancy me if I saw me in the street."

"You look beautiful, darling," I tell her as I sit in the vacant chair, and as Heather combs my hair I close my eyes and enjoy the feeling.

In a few short hours, Robert and I will finally be married. I think of the night under the cherry tree, all those years ago at the townhouse, where our love was first sparked, before I allowed my past to consume any hope of a future with Robert. It makes me think of the symbol of Ouroboros and I realise that I am in the middle of a perfect example right now – I have come full circle; I have accepted my past, consumed its many lessons, and am finally moving on.

EPILOGUE

Kegalle, Sri Lanka – present day

A woman sits on the front porch of her house, watching her two youngest children playing in the yard. They are twins, a boy and a girl of about ten years old, and are of Asian ethnicity, although both their hair and skin are lighter than average.

Before long, their play turns into a disagreement and a young man walks towards them, admonishing them for arguing. He is tall and broad, around twenty years old, his shirt undone to reveal a toned and bronzed torso. He is a Caucasian man, extraordinarily handsome with brown hair that is flecked with rose-gold and copper-green eyes that shift colour with the movement of the light. The children look up and stop their fighting immediately, running from their brother towards their mother and into her arms.

The woman embraces her children, whispering something to them before getting up and walking back inside the house, holding tightly on to their hands. She calls out to her eldest son, telling him to join them for some lunch. As she disappears inside the house, the back of her head shines like molten lava as the hot Indonesian sun reflects onto her red hair.

As the young man starts to make his way towards the house, a small lizard scuttles across the hot concrete in front of him. In an automatic reflex, he steps onto its tail, preventing it from running for cover. He bends down and picks the lizard up by its tail, dangling it in front of him, watching it furiously twist and turn in a fight to free itself. After a few seconds, the young man places the lizard into the palm of his hand, closes his fingers around its body and squeezes; gently at first, watching its reaction, then harder. The young man's eyes darken as he watches the life being crushed slowly from the defenceless creature. When the lizard is dead, he opens his hand and allows it to drop to the floor with a gentle thud, before stepping on the tiny body as he makes his way back towards the house for his lunch.

Jeannie watches Christian, her son, from the window of the kitchen and an old fear winds its way around her heart as she wonders, not for the first time, whether the decision she made all those years ago – the decision to keep Benedict's baby – had been the right one after all.

Acknowledgements

I would like to thank my hubby, Nigel, for the cups of tea, glasses of wine and endless encouragement provided during the writing of this book. I couldn't have done this without your love and support: "Love ya Honey".

To my sister and best friend, Tracy, whose belief in me never falters. Thank you sista!

To Debz Hobbs-Wyatt whose editorial advice on form and structure was invaluable.

A special shout out to my eager readers whose feedback on the first draft really helped to kick this book into shape.

And finally, to my brother, Lee: thank you for making it safely home to us, all those years ago.